westland ltd
THE BESTSELLER SHE WROTE

Ravi Subramanian, an alumnus of IIM Bengaluru, has spent two decades working his way up the ladder of power in the amazingly exciting and adrenaline-pumping world of global banks in India. Four of Ravi's seven bestselling titles have been award winners. *If God Was a Banker*, won the Golden Quill Readers' Choice Award. He won the Economist Crossword Book Award in 2012 for *The Incredible Banker*, The Crossword Book Award in 2013 for *The Bankster* and more recently in 2014 for his thriller *Bankerupt*. For Ravi, *The Bestseller She Wrote*, marks the beginning of a new chapter in his writing. A significant departure from his usual fare, this is Ravi's first book on romantic intrigue.

He lives in Mumbai with his wife, Dharini, and daughter, Anusha. To know more about Ravi visit www.ravisubramanian.in or email him at info@ravisubramanian.in. To connect with him, log on to Facebook at www.facebook.com/authorravisubramanian or tweet to @subramanianravi. You can also stay in touch with him by downloading the Ravi Subramanian App on iOS or Android.

Also by Ravi Subramanian

If God Was a Banker
I Bought the Monk's Ferrari
Devil in Pinstripes
The Incredible Banker
The Bankster
Bankerupt
God is a Gamer

The Bestseller She Wrote

RAVI SUBRAMANIAN

westland ltd
61, II Floor, Silverline Building, Alapakkam Main Road, Maduravoyal, Chennai 600095
93, I Floor, Sham Lal Road, Daryaganj, New Delhi 110002

First published by westland ltd 2015

Copyright © Ravi Subramanian 2015

All rights reserved

10 9 8 7 6 5 4 3 2 1

ISBN: 978-93-85152-38-2

Typeset in Electra LT Regular by SÜRYA, New Delhi

Printed at Manipal Technologies Ltd, Manipal

The author asserts his moral right to be identified as the author of this work.

This book is sold subject to the condition that it shall not by way of trade or otherwise, be lent, resold, hired out, circulated, and no reproduction in any form, in whole or in part (except for brief quotations in critical articles or reviews) may be made without written permission of the publishers.

This book is dedicated to all my readers.
Especially those who glimpsed their reflections in its pages.

1

THE CHATTER IN the packed auditorium at the prestigious Indian Institute of Management, Bengaluru, had reached its crescendo, when a member of the organising committee walked up on stage and addressed the audience.

'He has arrived, everyone. He's talking to the Diro right now . . . should be here in three to four minutes.'

Almost immediately the conversations died down. The noise level dropped and everyone, including the two hundred students and faculty in the room, trained their eyes at the door.

'Why him?' someone in the front row whispered to the person seated next to him. The front row was reserved for the faculty members. The neighbour shrugged his shoulders. 'Possibly because he brings in both perspectives—corporate experience and creative excellence . . .'

'Don't think so,' the first gentleman responded with disdain. 'I am sure it has something to do with the placement season. Pampering these corporate types always helps.' His neighbour nodded and almost immediately stood up as did most of the people in the auditorium.

He had just walked in.

A tuxedoed emcee strode onto the stage and announced, 'Ladies and gentlemen, it gives me great pleasure to present to you Shri Aditya Kapoor, Director—Branch Banking at National Bank, and an alumnus of our own institute,' he paused for effect and then proudly added, 'the Indian Institute of Management, Bengaluru!' The firm and effective baritone, blaring out from the public address system was completely drowned in the thunderous applause that followed.

A beaming Aditya Kapoor stepped on to the stage and stood there, taking in the ovation. He felt on top of the world. He was special and it showed on his face. 'Thank you, thank you,' he mumbled with his hands folded even as he bowed down a couple of times in humility, acknowledging the crowd.

This time the emcee's voice rose a notch before.

'Ladies and gentlemen, I am sure it is because of his achievements and not because he is a banker. Friends, even though Aditya Kapoor needs no introduction, he deserves it. Let me at least make an attempt. Not only is Aditya a banking professional par excellence, he is also India's numero uno writer. With four books to his credit, all of them topping the fiction charts, he is *the* most successful new generation Indian author. In a country where 95 per cent of books published sell less than 5000 units, his books have sold over four million copies. Two of his bestsellers have already been made into films. And that's not all; unlike the rest of his breed, Aditya Kapoor has managed to achieve the unusual feat of keeping the masses and critics equally enthused. Today he is going to talk to us about pursuing our dreams; about his journey from a boring banker to a bestselling author. Ladies and gentlemen, presenting to you, the Paperback King of India, Aditya Kapoor. India's most successful author . . . ever!'

The whole auditorium resonated with applause. Aditya Kapoor, who had been standing in one corner of the stage, walked up to the podium. Holding the stem of the mic, he pulled it closer to his mouth. The emcee who had been using the microphone earlier was a good ten inches shorter than Aditya's six-foot-something frame. He cleared his throat, an act which he had rehearsed a number of times in the past and spoke into the microphone: 'Good Evening.'

His deep baritone could make many a woman go weak in the knees. 'It feels good to be back after fifteen years,' Aditya carried on. There was an awed silence in the auditorium. 'Isn't it surprising that IIM Bengaluru has never invited me to talk about my professional exploits, something for which this institute trained me, prepared me? Instead, you have given me the honour and privilege of speaking to all of you about what I have achieved by pursuing my passion, my dreams.'

He paused and looked around the room. 'I am here to speak not about what I have achieved, but about what I have enjoyed. Someone once said, "Find what makes you happy and go for it with all your heart. It will be hard, but I promise it will be worth it." The fact that I am standing here in front of all of you, talking about my exploits, only goes to show that it is, in fact,' and he again paused and looked around the room, '. . . that it is, in fact, truly worth every single minute that I spent pursuing my dream.'

Aditya continued, 'When I began writing in 2008, it was for my own self. I became a writer, not only to tell a story but to broaden my own perspective. I don't know whether readers took away any message from my books or not, but for me, writing was a process which left me intellectually enhanced. It transformed my personality completely.'

There was another round of applause.

A confident orator, Aditya went on to talk about his books, the writing process and getting published. The audience listened to him in rapt attention as he talked about his experiences and how he was able to differentiate himself in a crowded marketplace.

'Every author puts in a fair bit of effort when he or she writes a book. But not everyone markets it well. Remember the easiest part about writing a book is . . . writing the book. The hard work starts once the book is written. The task of marketing the book and bringing the product to the reader is . . .'

'Product? Rubbish!' someone in the gathering exclaimed. The voice was loud enough for at least a few in the room to have heard it. Aditya heard it too. Stopping for just a brief moment, he glanced around before moving on. He had been in such situations before. The person who had made that remark was in the minority and could be ignored.

'Marketing the book and bringing the product to the reader is a very critical task in the entire product life cycle. If you don't get the product into the buyers' consideration subset, how will he or she buy it? Isn't that what they teach you in your two years at management school? In my case, the book is the product and the readers are our consumers.'

'Balls!' This time the voice was louder. It sounded out like a whipcrack. 'It's a book for god's sake, not a product.'

Aditya stopped as heads turned. The sound had come from the right hand corner of the auditorium. If anyone had missed it the first time, they were sure to have heard it now.

From where the sound had emanated, stood two young girls. One of them looked quite embarrassed, which was enough for Aditya to confirm that it was the other one who had spoken.

'Sorry?' he questioned, upset at being rudely interrupted. 'What was that?' The girl had been a bit too loud. Maybe she didn't realise it, but now, for him, it was a matter of his fragile male pride.

Neither of the girls responded to Aditya's question. After what seemed like thirty seconds of uncomfortable silence, the girl who had made the comment stood up. All eyes were on her, including those of the outraged academics sitting in the front row.

'Pardon me, Mr Kapoor, but a book is not a product,' she spoke up. Despite her ostensible apology for her impropriety, she didn't need any coaxing to stand up and speak. 'A book is an expression of an author's creativity. Do not demean it by calling it a "product". We respect you as a good writer, as a successful professional and as a senior from our campus, but that does not mean that anything goes.'

A few whispers went up in the auditorium, gradually escalating into chatter.

'Young lady,' Aditya began, the quiver in his voice quite apparent. Camouflaging his thoughts had never been his strength. His face had gone red with anger. He was not going to be shown up by a young kid.

'You are correct, but only partly. A book is not a product when an author is writing it. At that moment it is a dream. It is the purpose of existence for the author. But the moment you put a price tag on it and place it on a shelf in a bookstore, it becomes a product.'

He looked at the others in the audience and after an intentional pause, added, 'Otherwise why even bother to sell it? Give it away for free.'

He was angry, but he had learnt that in this day and age of social media, being rude and arrogant to the audience, especially in public, was a recipe for disaster. Someone might just record it and upload it on Facebook for everyone to see, putting him at risk of brand erosion.

'Sure,' the girl said, 'but there has got to be a difference between peddling a bar of soap and selling a book. A book is a lot more personal, a lot more involving. A book is not a movie. It may be entertainment, yes, but not cheap entertainment. The romance of a book is lost by the in-your-face promotion that you guys do. In any case, most of the new Indian authors write rubbish. In the name of romance, trash sells. And on top of it, you guys call a book a product! It reveals a mindset of mediocrity. Push any book, however mediocre, through an aggressive sales campaign and you have a bestseller.' She was worked up now and sounded irritated.

Aditya forced a smile. Blood was still flooding his cheeks, rendering them pink. 'Mediocre? Young lady . . .' he said, catching on to the last point and conveniently ignoring the rest. He looked around the room. Everyone was waiting for his response. 'I am sure you haven't read my books?'

Seeming a bit embarrassed, the girl nodded in agreement.

'Read them,' Aditya spoke with forced humility, 'and then call them mediocre if you want to. Half the people, who have an opinion on current Indian authors, haven't even read them.'

He raised his right hand and pointed directly at her. 'And as far as marketing my books is concerned—it's simple. If I spend a year writing a book, I will leave no stone unturned in making sure that everyone knows about it, and buys it. I don't mind my books adorning bookshelves as long as the bookshelves we are referring to are not in bookshops, but in people's homes.'

The girl just looked at him without saying a word. Her friend sitting next to her held her hand and pulled her down. 'Sit down,' she whispered.

'If after reading my book, you hate it, please write to me. I can't refund your time, but to make up for it, I will gift you ten books of your choice. Think of it as kind of a money-back guarantee.' He attempted a smile.

'And just to complete the discussion on promotion of books by authors, all I have to say is that after giving it their everything, an author cannot just sit back and hope that the world will appreciate his or her effort and automatically flock to stores to buy the book. So it has to be brought to the customer, quite like a product, with full focus and energy. If you still don't agree, I am happy to engage with you offline.'

He smiled triumphantly at the audience, looked at the girl again and asked, 'Deal?'

The girl smiled, and gave him a thumbs up. He reciprocated the gesture. Truce was called. However, the interjection had a terminal impact on his speech.

He stopped his lecture soon thereafter and they broke into a Q&A.

2

IT IS OFTEN said that what is more depressing and miserable than being an author is being married to one. An author often leads a lonely life. Books, research, computers and hours of typing away in isolation, can often drive a wedge between an author and his or her immediate family. Being an author's partner is not for everybody. It needs someone with resolve and patience, someone like Maya, who held Aditya's family together.

He loved her, for she was different. He had met her when they were in their first term at IIM, but they had not started dating till they were well into their second year. He was smart, extremely intelligent and arrogant—quite a contrast to his other classmates from semi-urban India who were fairly subdued and nerdy. He had worked on his attitude to shake off his small-town complex and compete with the bullies from the metros.

She was equally bullheaded and tenacious. This had kept them away from each other, initially. When they did start going around, many in the batch wondered what it was that glued them together. Even Aditya and Maya didn't quite know.

Soon the carefree days of college were over. Maya got placed with a Switzerland-based bank. Aditya too joined a European bank. After a year, in 2000, they got married. Maya, soon after, was transferred to Hong Kong and Aditya followed suit. For a few years both of them worked hard in Hong Kong, chasing their professional dreams. Maya's career was on the ascendency, at a pace faster than Aditya's. Everything was running smoothly for them.

And then three incidents changed the course of their lives.

Aditya lost his job in 2008—collateral damage because of the global financial market meltdown. His first book, on the life of an engineering college student, released the same month. The book became a runaway hit. Both these incidents coincided with the birth of their son, Aryan.

Lack of help to manage and take care of the newborn, and unwillingness of either of their parents to shift to Hong Kong to help them out added to Aditya's frustrations with the job loss. This was coupled with his inability to promote his book. They decided to relocate to Mumbai. Maya, despite her scorching corporate career, had always wanted to do something more meaningful in life. She too felt the move would give her the opportunities she desired.

She gave up her job to focus on family. She stayed at home for a year, before taking up an assignment with the Dhirubhai Ambani International School (DAIS). Apart from teaching twelfth graders, she also managed the group's social initiatives; most of them directed at improving literacy levels of the urban poor in Mumbai, particularly the slums of

Dharavi. Maya's involvement in the project as a Lead changed her approach to poor children. Educating them became a mission in her life; a passion. She was the wife of a rock star author. Yet rather than bask in his reflected glory, she chose to chart her own course.

*

Maya was home that night when Aditya called her after the lecture at IIM Bengaluru. He had just checked into Hotel Vivanta by Taj on MG Road.

'Hey baby,' Aditya began.

'Where have you been, Adi? No call, no SMS.'

'Just checked in. I was with people throughout the day; couldn't call.'

'Comfortable room?'

'Hmm . . . it is nice. Nothing beats the Taj. What say?'

'I would say, nothing beats home. And when you are away from home . . . honestly, I don't care.' She laughed into the phone. Aditya laughed too. He loved to hear her laugh.

'When did you get back?' Aditya asked.

'Early. I came in by 4.30. I had a conference call with the global sponsors of the project in Dharavi Ward 3 at 6.00. So I wanted to prepare for that.'

'Oh yes, yes, I completely forgot about that.'

'Both Aryan and I have stopped expecting you to remember anything but your books,' Maya faked anger. 'I wonder how Tim manages to get you to do his work.' Tim Xavier was Aditya's boss at National Bank.

'Tell me, how did it go?' Aditya asked.

'It was good. They might contribute a million and a half for the project,' Maya revealed happily.

'That's nice. Mrs Ambani will be thrilled. Not that a million and a half means a lot to her, but the project is getting global sponsorship and recognition.'

'True. Had dinner?'

'Hmm. What's Aryan doing?'

'Fast asleep. Your son was missing you. He was tired today. Wanted you to put your leg on top of his and hug him when he went to bed.'

'Aww. Why was he tired?'

'Cricket practice, that too in the sun.'

'Cricket practice is never fun in the shade. Let him grow up into a rough and tough man.'

'Hmm . . . How was your lecture? And the crowd? Did people turn up?'

'Oh! You should have been there to see. The auditorium was full. Every seat was taken. People were squatting in the aisle. Everyone was completely floored with my *gyan*.'

'That doesn't sound like anything new.'

Aditya laughed. 'Oh, but you know, there was this idiotic bitch who . . .'

'Language, Mr Writer,' Maya interrupted him.

'Yeah yeah, fine, Mother Teresa. There was this woman who was trying to rubbish what I was saying. She was being very condescending about Indian authors and book promotions. I took her head on and completely bullied her into submission,' Aditya said and launched into an account of the entire discussion, albeit with loads of exaggeration.

'My super intelligent baby,' Maya teased him.

He laughed. The conversation continued for a few minutes, after which he bid her goodbye and switched on the television in the room. Finally when sleep did force him to shut his eyes, he didn't bother to switch the lights off. In a hotel room, he always slept with the lights on and the television playing some meaningless channel.

Some habits just stay for life and this was one of them.

3

SHREYA HAD JUST changed into her nightclothes and snuggled into bed, a copy of John Green's *The Fault in Our Stars* in hand. Hardly had she got herself comfortable and started reading the book when someone knocked on the door of her hostel room.

'You there?'

'Yeah! What is it?' she yelled from her bed.

A couple of knocks followed.

'Open the door, will you?'

'Why the hell can't you let me read in peace?' said an irritated Shreya as she stomped towards the door.

The half hour before she went to sleep was unwind time for her. Unwind time as in trouble-me-at-your-own-risk unwind time. Nothing matched curling up in bed with a book. For Shreya, an ardent reader, a guy roaming in the aisles of a bookstore carrying a few books in hand was a bigger turn-on than someone lifting weights in a gym. A man needs to be judged by his reading quotient, she would often say.

'Nerdy and well read are two completely different personality traits,' Shreya would often argue. 'Nerdy guys are socially inept, well mostly anyway, whereas well read guys are intelligent, confident and great to talk to.'

Aditya Kapoor had impressed her initially. He had the magnetic appeal of a successful professional. The conversation in the auditorium had turned into a confrontation, and that was not something that she would have ideally liked, but Aditya was being too arrogant. He had asked for it.

Shreya's love for reading went back a long way. Her parents had never got along. Constantly at each other's throats, screaming and shouting at each other all the time, they never really worried about the impact it had on their daughter, who was still growing up. Every evening, the moment her mother came back from work, Shreya would retire to her room, book in hand. Books helped take her mind off the trauma in her real life. Her parents separated when she was ten years old and her mother went to live with a successful business tycoon.

'Relationships with the right people always pay in life,' her mother had said while explaining the change to Shreya. At times it pays even more than what you get from all that you learn at school. This was not said but implied and Shreya was quick to catch on.

'What happened to you today? The director is very upset with you,' Sunaina, started off the moment she walked in through the door. Sunaina's hostel room was adjacent to Shreya's and she was her closest friend on campus. She was taller than Shreya, leaner and dusky. Curly hair which she usually tied in a high pony, giving it a nest-like appearance, made her neck look attractive. Born to a Muslim father and a Malayalee-Hindu mother, Sunaina had spent a large part of her childhood in Dubai.

'Upset with me? Impossible,' Shreya replied.

'Well, you showered so much love and affection on Aditya Kapoor that you didn't leave the Diro with much of a choice, did you?' Sunaina continued, ignoring Shreya's cold look. 'He thought, and rightly so, that your tone and objections were unwarranted. Aditya Kapoor must have felt extremely insulted. After all he was our guest. And what did you say? Balls! Right!' Sunaina rolled her eyes.

'Rubbish,' Shreya dismissed it with a flourish of her hand.

'Yeah, that too. "Rubbish". That's what you said the first time around.' Sunaina was quick to pounce on her.

'Come on, Sunaina. You know I didn't mean it the way it eventually turned out,' Shreya said. She wanted to sound indifferent, but was clearly a bit rattled. Almost immediately she looked at Sunaina. 'Did the Diro say something to you?' she asked sheepishly.

'Not to me. But to the student council at the discussion, after the event.'

'Storytelling is an art and Aditya was trivialising it. That got me worked up. He upset me. I upset him. So we are quits now. The Diro should stay out of this,' Shreya exhaled. She turned to the other side, rolled over, dug her face into the book and said, 'Now if you are done, I want to read. Have you seen how cute John Green is? I am beginning to get a crush on him.'

Sunaina smiled. 'You are impossible, Shreya. Anyway, I just wanted to let you know that the Diro was telling these guys that he will speak to you tomorrow. Be prepared for it.'

'I am scared . . . ooooh!' Shreya rolled her eyes and made a face.

Sunaina was not amused. 'This bravado is counterproductive, Shreya,' she warned with a straight face. 'Remember you are in line for the Chairman's gold medal. After Melwin left the course midway, you are the only one in the race. Why do you want to tick off the Diro at this stage?'

Shreya had to admit that there was merit in what Sunaina was saying. Melwin, the only other student who was running neck to neck with her till the end of the first year had left the course abruptly, midway and gone back to his home town. The institute had graciously granted him leave for a year and so he was now out of the reckoning. In such a scenario taking a risk would be stupid.

Shreya now had a nervous look in her eyes. 'What should I do?'

Sunaina just shrugged her shoulders. 'Make up a story that will satisfy the Diro.'

'Shut up. I can't fake it.'

'Then deal with it,' said Sunaina as she walked out of the room. 'I am sleepy. I am off.'

'Wait!' Shreya yelled. 'Wait wait wait wait wait,' she continued and ran out of her room. 'Hey! Wait.' She stopped Sunaina, just as she was about to enter her own room. Sunaina turned in mock irritation. With one hand on her hip and the other on the doorframe she looked at Shreya. 'Whaaaat?'

'What if I read his book tonight?'

'Tonight?'

'Yup.' Shreya jumped a bit, rubbing her hands in glee.

'Where is the book for you to read?'

'Here,' she held up her iPad. 'I will buy the e-book right away and read it.'

Sunaina was confused. 'How will reading the book help?'

'You will see,' Shreya smirked.

4

THAT NIGHT SHREYA stayed awake and read Aditya Kapoor's fourth book—a 250-page novel—from end to end, without a break. When she kept the iPad on the side and looked out of the window, she could see light. It was 5.45 in the morning. A few early risers were out on their morning jog.

She walked to her table, opened her laptop and logged into her mail. She started typing.

A few kilometres away, Aditya had just woken up. He was checking his office mail on his BlackBerry when his iPhone beeped. A mail had just come in on his personal id.

Dear Mr Kapoor,

After our interesting but not so welcome conversation last evening during your lecture, I picked up your book to read. I am writing to you immediately after reading the 254th page. I got your email id from the author bio in the book.

While I consider myself to be a voracious reader, I have never ever finished a book in one night. This is the first time. The book just did not leave me with a choice. It is simply UNPUTDOWNABLE. I am cursing myself for not having read your books earlier. You have brought me back to reading Indian authors. As long as people like you write, reading will never go out of style.

I have become a fan. I will order all your books and read them. You have just got on to my "authors to watch out for" list.
You rock.
Best wishes,
Shreya Kaushik
(The one who asked you the question last evening).

Aditya smiled to himself. So he had a convert. The day couldn't have started better. He started to type a response—an arrogant dismissive message—but something within him protested. He deleted everything he had written and began afresh.

Dear Ms Kaushik,

Thanks for your lovely mail. You cannot imagine how thrilled I am to see that you liked the book. It means a lot to me, especially given the fact that you were completely anti-Indian authors.

Thanks for promising to read my other books too. I nervously await your feedback.

While on the subject, back in my hotel room, I was thinking of our brief conversation from last evening. I think you are partly correct, to the extent that treating a book like a product can be demeaning to books and the trade. While selling a book aggressively is the need of the hour, I suspect you may be right. Books are a bit more private and personal and that needs to be respected. I will keep that in mind whenever I write or promote my next book.

Keep in touch.
Cheers,
Aditya.

The moment Shreya saw the mail from Aditya she clenched her fist and let out a muted scream. 'Yesssss!'

*

As expected, the Director called for her that afternoon.

'Sir, I realised that my conduct yesterday was inappropriate and hence I stayed up all of last night and read Mr Kapoor's book. I even wrote to him. This is his response.' Shreya handed a copy of Aditya's mail to the Director. In the message trail was her mail to Aditya. 'You know I will never let you down,' she added, finishing off with a seductive, 'sir.'

The Director read the mail and smiled. 'Good,' he said. 'Not only is it important to realise one's mistake, but also to make amends. I'm happy that you did what you did, Shreya. We cannot have our prospective gold medallist losing out in life on account of indiscretions. I'm proud of you, Shreya.'

*

In the evening, on the way to their classes, Sunaina asked Shreya, 'Why did you have to stay awake the whole night? You could have written to him without reading the book. There is no way he could have known.'

'I don't lie. You know that.'

'Yeah right!'

'Shut up, you bitch,' Shreya hit her playfully. 'Actually the book didn't let me sleep. I just couldn't put it down. There are moments in life when something comes and blows your mind. This was one such moment. I read the entire book and after finishing it, I cried. Buckets. Such a moving story it was. I couldn't hold myself back. The best I have read thus far by any Indian writer. Forget Indian writers, this is the best I have read in a while.'

'Hmm . . . And it does help that the guy has the looks of a rock star. No?'

'He is cool. Real cool. But watch . . .'

'Watch what?'

'One day I will write a book which will beat his books hollow. A book far better than anything he has written.' Shreya looked at the sky. 'I will be all over the place. Bookstores, launches, events, media, readers . . . everyone will love me.'

'Oh . . . oh . . . oh . . . Stop, stop, *desi* John Green! Stop dreaming. It's not easy to write. Even if you write rubbish, it takes time, effort and skill. Do you realise that?'

'One day, Sunaina, I am telling you . . . one day. I will be a world-famous author. You will be proud of me.'

'Even if you don't become one, I will still be proud of you,' Sunaina retorted as they entered their classroom.

Their final job placements were to begin in a couple of months.

5

THE KAPOOR RESIDENCE was in a chaotic state that morning. Aditya was getting ready to go to work. Maya was running around fixing Aryan's tiffin box. The maid had not arrived.

The doorbell rang at the most inappropriate time.

'I will get it,' yelled Aditya as he rushed to the door. He knew that Maya got extremely hassled if anything disturbed her morning schedule. The maid not turning up had already messed up her morning. She was going to be late and she hated that. Fearing a backlash, Aditya was trying to keep her calm and at the same time, stay out of her firing line. The driver was at the door. Aditya handed the car keys to him and got back to helping Maya.

On a normal day he would drop Aryan at school. Occasionally, even Maya would join him and he would drop her on his way to work. Today, given that Maya was a bit hassled, he decided to drop her. Whenever he did that, the driver followed in Maya's car.

After dropping off Aryan, they were heading towards Maya's school, which was a mile away.

Maya looked at him and smiled. 'Thank you,' she said.

'For what?'

'The morning.'

Aditya raised his eyebrows. He had a naughty grin on his face.

'I don't say anything doesn't mean I don't notice,' Maya smiled.

'Aaah . . . that's an interesting confession,' Aditya teased her. 'You must try not to get so stressed, Maya.'

'It's just the morning. I don't want you guys to get late because of me and I want you to take food from home. Stress is inevitable.'

'Once in a while we can manage by eating outside.'

'That's what I don't want you to do. Stressful work, sedentary lifestyle, inadequate sleep, zero exercise . . . All my pleading and prodding for you to work out falls on deaf ears,' she complained.

Aditya looked at her and flexed his left bicep. 'Naturally gifted with a great body,' he joked.

'Be serious, Aditya. I don't want to add outside food to the list of problems that you have. That's why I am so insistent that you take home food. Remember, you are not getting any younger. You are the one in the rat race. It adds to your stress levels,' she argued.

'What to do, Maya? I am forty; reaching the midway mark of my corporate life. Another twenty years and we will be gone, wiped from people's memories. What have we achieved? What will we leave behind?'

'What's wrong with you, Aditya?' Maya cried. 'You have such a great career; from Junior Executive to Director— Branch Banking, in fifteen years. Not just that, you also have a successful alternate writing career. And to top it all, we have Aryan, a nice little family. People would kill to be in your place. Do you even realise that?'

Invariably in such situations, Aditya would just smile and the discussion would end. He knew that Maya was a contented soul, happy with what she had. But he was different. He wanted everything from life, not only for himself, but also for Maya and Aryan.

They reached Maya's school. As she was getting out of the car, she looked at Aditya and said, 'I forgot to tell you yesterday. The school trip to NASA is on.'

'Oh. But I thought that's still some time away.'

'Yes, but I have to tell them if I am taking a vacation around it. I can't just dump them. There will be 60 kids with us. Someone has to herd them and bring them back.' Maya was hopeful that they would be able to take a vacation around the same time.

'Okay, baby. We will close it out this week,' he said before waving at her and driving off to work. He had a National Bank Annual event to attend that night.

6

SELDOM DOES ONE see bankers letting their hair down. But the occasion that evening was clearly special. It was the year-end event, where winners were identified and teams were rewarded. It was a complex combination of team performance; voting by heads of select support functions like Operations, HR, Compliance, etc; and the judgement of the segment heads that was used to pick the winners. For National Bank, this was the biggest awards night of the year, which saw almost 100 per cent attendance. To be a winner here meant getting noticed by the entire top brass of the bank, propelling one's career to the stratosphere.

Aditya was the cynosure of everyone's eyes. His deft moves, his jigs, his expressions left everyone spellbound. When he got off the dance floor, his partner, a wealth manager from his Bandra team looked at him with eyes dripping with admiration, and said, 'Never knew that you could dance like that, sir.'

'Well, I am stuck behind the desk the whole day, you see,' Aditya smiled. 'Maybe you didn't realise, I have legs underneath,' he started laughing. The wealth manager beat a hasty retreat.

'Poor girl,' Sanjay Narang, the head of Human Resources, commented when Aditya walked up to him. 'You were mean to her.'

'Nonsense!' Aditya tapped Sanjay on his back. 'Flirting with your super boss is just not on.'

'Says who?'

'Being in HR, you can't ask that question,' Aditya responded.

Sanjay smiled. 'At least this one day, don't judge us. Allow us to let our hair down. We in HR are human too, aren't we?' he said. 'After all, when all the girls fall for you, we don't complain.'

'Human? You guys are dogs,' said Aditya. 'At least you are, for sure.' He laughed even as he hugged Sanjay and led him towards the bar.

Sanjay and Aditya were classmates at IIM Bengaluru. Best of friends on campus, they had stayed that way ever since. Despite going through some trying times, the friendship had survived. Sanjay's first marriage to another batchmate of theirs had ended in divorce. He was secretly dating the product manager of National Bank's Premier Banking Proposition, Diana Moses. Aditya was one of the few who was in on the secret. And he was not happy about it.

Diana and Aditya, both reported to Tim, the head of Retail Banking. Aditya always felt that Diana went to Tim, behind his back and often undercut him, because she aspired to Aditya's job. Sanjay had often tried to convince him that this was not the case. All his attempts at making Aditya understand that even if his presumption were to be true, professional aspirations could not form the basis for disliking someone, had been in vain. The good thing was, both of them had been mature enough to ensure that Diana's relationship with Sanjay did not in any way impact their friendship.

'And now, it's the time of the evening that everyone has been waiting for,' the emcee took over. Both Aditya and Sanjay turned towards the stage.

'The National Bank Annual Awards!' she exclaimed loudly into the mic. The proceedings began. A few individual awards were announced before moving on to the team awards.

'Coming to Retail Bank Team Awards, the second runner-up for the Best Team in Retail Bank goes to . . .'

Everyone waited. A few yelled out their team names.

'Goes to . . .' the emcee continued, '. . . Personal Loan sales team! Put your hands together for the Personal Loan sales team!' The entire team led by their head went up on stage and collected their trophy.

'And now for the runner-up . . . Who do you think will walk away with the runner-up trophy for retail banking this year?' she said as a cacophony erupted from the crowd.

Aditya was standing there with Sanjay and a few others. He was quiet. 'The runner-up trophy goes to . . . the Branch Banking team!' The people standing around Aditya went wild. They threw their hands up and jumped around in joy.

Sanjay was silent. He was looking at Aditya who quietly turned around and started walking towards the bar. The Branch Banking team and the four regional heads went up and took the award from the CEO. They waited on stage for some time for Aditya to join them.

Aditya reached the bar. 'A whisky, please,' he ordered.

'What happened?' Sanjay had caught up with him.

'Losers,' Aditya said.

'Losers?' Sanjay expressed surprise. 'Come on. They have won the second prize. It's your team. You should have been up on stage with them.' He shook his head in disapproval.

Aditya looked straight at him. 'As far as I am concerned, they lost the winner's trophy, Sanjay. To me that's what matters. Whether I write a book or lead a team. I need to be . . .' He picked up his glass of single malt and sniffed the heavenly fragrance before he sipped at it. 'I need to be like this.' He held up his glass of single malt. 'Like this peg of Laphroaig. The best. My team needs to be the best, Sanjay. Nothing else is acceptable.'

'Slow down, Aditya, slow down,' Sanjay said as he patted him on his back. 'Learn from Maya. Enjoy life,' he said and held his glass up to Aditya. 'Cheers.' Aditya didn't respond.

'And now, finally we have the winner of the award for the Best Team in Retail Banking,' the emcee could be heard in the background. 'And the winner is . . . the Premier Banking Product team for the excellent work they did in the relaunch of the high-end Premier Banking Proposition!' she yelled in high pitch. The entire Premier Banking team hooted in glee. Diana walked up to the stage. 'And let me also add that they have won this award, by beating the second best team by just one vote. It was a tough fight, a very tough fight. Ladies and gentlemen, let's hear it for the Premier Banking team,' the emcee's voice screeched over the PA system.

Aditya hurriedly gulped down the whisky and looked at

Sanjay, with anger in his eyes. 'So,' he said, his voice dangerously low.

'So? So what?' Sanjay asked him.

'So this is what it had to come to. Right. You made sure the HR vote went to your girlfriend. To the Premier Banking team despite knowing that we deserved it more.' He raised his voice just that little bit. He was not happy. It didn't matter to him that his team came ahead of twelve other teams to win the runner-up position. What mattered was that they lagged behind one.

'Is that what you think, Aditya? After so many years . . .'

'Well, years of friendship don't matter, Sanjay. When you had to demonstrate your loyalties, you chose the woman instead. You decided to think not with your brain but with something dangling three feet below your brain . . .'

'Don't talk rubbish, Aditya,' Sanjay interrupted his tirade. 'I have never done anything that would impact our relationship. Never ever; you get me? There have been enough reasons in the past. Yet I have always been fair.'

'Oh come on,' Aditya screamed. A few people had gathered around. 'You always wanted that woman to go ahead of me. Always! And when you got a chance, you played your card. How could you be so weak, Sanjay? That's not the way you were on campus. That's not the way you were all these years. You kept your mind in control and ensured that your head ruled. But now? I never expected you to do this. Never.' Aditya banged down his glass and walked out in a huff.

'What happened?' Diana walked up to Sanjay, just in time to see Aditya walk away.

'Congratulations, Diana.' Sanjay hugged her as formally as he could.

'Thanks, but what just happened?' Diana repeated her question. 'Nothing. Come. Let's go.' Sanjay held her hand and started leading her away from the bar. Diana looked around.

'Kapoor sir was extremely upset that his team didn't win the award, so he screamed at Sanjay sir,' one of her team members who was around the bar when the argument happened, blurted out.

Diana looked at Sanjay. 'Me?' she asked. 'Was it because of me?'

'What else could it be?'

'What was it this time?'

'He felt that I ensured HR cast its vote in your favour, and that single HR vote took the award away from him.'

'Did you tell him the true story?'

'What's the big deal, Diana? He would never have believed me.'

'You should have told him the truth, that HR withdrew from the voting, because my team was in the running. And true to the spirit of the awards, there was no partiality whatsoever. He can be upset that he lost, but he has no reason to be upset with you.'

'You know him. He will come back once he recovers his senses. This is not the first time he has fought with me about you.'

'Then why is your face looking like a roasted brinjal?' Diana asked.

'Because this is the first time he did it in public. All our fights have been in private, away from everyone,' Sanjay said, angrily. 'He could've exercised some restraint, if not for the sake of our friendship, at least for the fact that I helped him resurrect his career by getting him this job.'

Diana patted him on his back to calm him down. The two of them, left the party venue and drove back home. On the way back, Sanjay's phone beeped. He looked at Diana. She smiled at him. On the screen was a notification. <Aditya. iMessage> Sanjay opened his inbox and read the message.

<Sorry. Was quite a few pegs down. I think my behaviour was inappropriate. We had agreed not to bring Diana into our relationship. I am sorry I broke the code.>

Diana smiled when she saw the message. Sanjay was sternly looking ahead at the road.

'Let it go. He is apologising,' Diana said. Sanjay lifted her right hand to his lips, kissed it and smiled back at her.

The next day, both Sanjay and a slightly shame-faced Aditya, hugged and put the issue to rest.

7

'Hello?' Aditya picked up the intercom on the first ring.

'Free on the 8th of February?' Sanjay asked.

'I don't know what I am going to do tomorrow and you are asking me about 8th February, Sanjay?'

'Well, we are kicking off our campus placements at IIM Bengaluru, on the 8th. I was wondering if you would like to be a part of the interview panel.'

'What will I do there? Campus interviews are fucking boring.'

'Can you imagine my plight? I have to go to ten colleges this year.'

'You are paid to do that, Sanjay. I am not,' Aditya said cheekily. 'Give me a day, I will get back to you,' he muttered and hung up. For him, it was a zero value-add activity. He was in the finishing stages of his next book. That demanded time. And he didn't want to waste his days travelling on some non-productive work. That's when he remembered the invitation.

He went back to his inbox and searched for a mail from Vani Mahesh, who ran a quaint little library in Bengaluru — EasyLib. Patronised by the large corporate executive crowd in Bengaluru, EasyLib was a preferred destination for book events in town.

Vani Mahesh had requested him to visit her library. She wanted him to do a reading session and promised to make the visit worth his time by doing a classy event, which would get adequate media coverage. And that was a carrot he found difficult to refuse.

He picked up the intercom and dialled Sanjay.

'You wouldn't mind if I did a book reading event on the 7th, would you?'

'Why are you even asking me?'

'In the interest of full disclosure my friend. I don't want anyone coming back to me later on this.'

'Not at all. Be my guest. If I do get into Bengaluru on the 7th, I would love to attend it.'

'And we can go on a drinking binge after the event, like old times. Life was so much fun on campus, wasn't it? You, me, Maya, Shefali and all the others . . . the drinking binges, the late nights. Best two years of my life,' Aditya reminisced.

'Yes, it was a great time. Let's plan something,' Sanjay hurriedly agreed. Any discussion about Shefali, his ex-wife, irked him.

8

SHREYA WAS IN her hostel room preparing for the placement interviews, which were to begin the next day. She had a packed schedule over the coming few days. Citibank, Hindustan Unilever and BCG—three interviews on day-zero of the placements. And then there was National Bank and ITC, the day after. Landing a job, early in the placement cycle was about pride. After all she was the most likely recipient of the Chairman's gold medal.

'Coffee,' Sunaina called out. She was returning from the hostel's night canteen, with the coffee that Shreya had asked her to grab for her. Sunaina made herself comfortable on the couch in Shreya's room and they began to revise all the possible interview questions. Shreya had lost count of the number of times they had done that. The questions were standard fare.

What is your ambition?
Where do you see yourself five years from now?
What are your strengths and weaknesses?
Why do you want to join our company?

After a point, Shreya got fed up with the entire preparation. 'If they ask me why I want to join them, I'll say, it's because you pay the most, damn it! It's sexy to see my name next to the logo on the company visiting card. Isn't that why you are also there, you idiot . . . How nice it would be if we could say this.' Shreya frowned.

'Ha ha! Say this to your friend. He will be there day after I think.'

'Who?'

'The one who you have a history of messing up with,' Sunaina chuckled. Seeing Shreya's blank look, she volunteered, 'Aditya Kapoor. Who else?'

'Really? When? Where? For what?' Shreya was surprised. She suddenly got up from her chair. 'How do you know?' she demanded.

'Relax, relax. Aditya Kapoor is in town tomorrow for a book event. There is an event poster down in the mess. If he is in Bengaluru a day before the campus placements, isn't it logical to assume that he will be here too?'

'Fair assessment.'

'Correct. But it worries me. It reduces the placement options for you. If he interviews you, you stand no chance. Authors never forget anything,' Sunaina cautioned Shreya.

Shreya sat upright on the couch. 'You are forgetting that I made up with him. So the probability of him remembering me for the right reasons are extremely high.'

'You TRIED to make up with him,' Sunaina corrected. 'We will know soon if he also let go and made up with you.'

Shreya rolled her eyes and went back to the paper with the interview questions.

'Well,' she said, looking up from the sheet in her hand, 'it is not without reason that I've made up with him.'

9

Aditya was busy packing for his Bengaluru trip.

'Suit, check. Three shirts, check. Two ties, check. Undergarments, check. Socks, check. Shaving kit, will be packed tomorrow morning after my shower. iPhone charger, check.'

Maya observed him from the corner of her eyes as he strode up to the mirror and looked at himself. He patted his belly, proud that even at this age he had washboard abs. He pulled his cheeks down and examined his eyes. They looked perfect. The eyebrows were groomed well. He then ran his fingers through his hair and stopped. Ruffling them, he let go of all but a single strand. Then he repeated the action, this time holding on to another strand of hair. This went on for a few minutes. The growing concentration of white hair on his head was beginning to worry him.

Maya watched him for some time and then asked, 'Is everything okay?'

'Why?'

'Your increasing obsession with your looks worries me.'

'I am an author, baby. I have to look good,' Aditya said. 'Don't you think so?'

Maya nodded, 'Yes, you have to. And you do.'

'This white hair . . . Have you seen it?' He held a strand up for her to see. Scissors in hand, he cut it off and threw it down on the floor. Maya glared at him.

'Oops! Sorry,' he said.

'It is okay. You look good,' Maya said reassuringly. 'Salt and pepper is in.' When Aditya didn't seem convinced, she added, 'A mature look works for a writer.'

Aditya smiled. Maya always made him feel good—about himself, about everything. He hugged her.

'Haven't seen you so excited about travelling in a long, long time. Is it the placement interviews?'

'No, babes. It's the book event tomorrow. Watch out for me in the Bengaluru newspapers later this week.'

Maya smiled. She knew how much Aditya loved all the attention that sections of the media showered on him. For Aditya writing was not about money. Yes, the money he made from his books rivalled his salary. It is said that in the world of publishing, you don't make money unless you are a bestselling author and Aditya was a bestselling author by a mile. 15 per cent of his publisher's turnover could be attributed to Aditya's books alone. Such was the scale of his success. Yet, he was not in it for money. He was in it for the fame. People in India normally don't mob authors when they see them in public. But Aditya was different. He was besieged wherever he went.

He was more like a film star than an author, and he loved it.

10

THE EVENT STARTED at 6.30 pm, half an hour behind schedule. There were over sixty people in the room, packed like sardines in a jar. Vani Mahesh introduced Aditya Kapoor to the readers and referred to him as *mannina maga*—son of the soil—referring to the fact that he had been born in the city. Never mind the fact that the only real connection Aditya had with Bengaluru was the two years that he spent there during his post graduation. Otherwise most of his life prior to his MBA had been spent in the industrial town of Ludhiana.

After a brief intro, Vani let him take over. Aditya's monologue, which lasted for over 45 minutes, was well received. A few photographers present at the venue were happily clicking away. The media-savvy Aditya tried to give them the best angles and adequate opportunity to capture a good picture of him, while he was speaking.

Soon the Q&A began and the routine questions were brought out.

How many times were you rejected before you got your first book published?

How important is marketing for you?

Has your profile as a banker helped you in your career as an author?

Banking or writing?

Will you ever give up banking to pursue a career in writing?

They never deviated from these questions, did they?

Finally when Vani got up and announced that they only had time left for one last question, a number of hands went up.

The last question over, it was time for the customary book signing and photographs. Aditya patiently signed the books and posed for selfies. In the end, there were six people left in the room. Aditya, Vani Mahesh, the press photographer, two employees of EasyLib and a reader. The reader, who was waiting for the crowd to disperse, walked up to him and gave him a copy to sign.

Aditya looked at her and smiled. The reader was the one who had asked him the last question. 'That was a smart question,' he said, coolly, even as he took the book from her, signed it with a flourish and returned it. Instinctively she opened it and looked at the message that Aditya had written for her, and smiled.

'Dear Shreya, I will never forget 22nd November . . . Aditya Kapoor.'

'You remembered my name?'

'Not many people hold the distinction of embarrassing me in a public forum,' he smiled.

'And the date too!' she exclaimed. 'Wow! How on earth do you remember the date?'

'I seldom forget dates, young lady.' He was not boasting. Be it birthdays, names of family members of colleagues, important days in their lives, he remembered everything. It was a skill he possessed that helped him give a personal touch to his interaction with people, which often made his team members feel special.

'Very impressive,' Shreya said and hastily added an apology. 'I am so sorry. Really, I am sorry. It was just an impulsive reaction that day. I didn't intend to sound so belligerent.'

Aditya smiled and patted her arm. 'Just kidding. You have a knack for asking intelligent questions. Don't change.'

'So sorry to interrupt the conversation,' Vani butted in, 'but before the photographer packs up, we wanted to take some pics with you, Aditya. The press photographers are also waiting.'

'Yes, of course,' Aditya said, ever willing to pose for the media. The entire team of EasyLib posed for pictures. 'This will go up on Facebook tonight,' Vani announced proudly.

'Come, Shreya, join us,' Aditya called out to her. Shreya happily joined in and posed for some pictures. She even took some selfies with Aditya. After thanking him, she apologised once again and took her leave.

Aditya's eyes followed her all the way through till she turned into the corridor at the far end and exited the hall.

11

TWENTY MINUTES AND a *masala dosa* later, Aditya left EasyLib. His car had just moved 50 metres ahead when he saw Shreya standing on the left, waiting. He instructed the driver to stop and got off the car.

'Waiting for someone?'

Shreya smiled and nodded her head. 'Autorickshaw,' she said. 'It's always difficult to get an autorickshaw to go to the IIM-B campus at this time of the night.'

'No problem. I can drop you. I'm going there myself. Staying at the Executive Block tonight,' he told her. 'Let's go.'

After some hesitation, Shreya got into his car. She seemed nervous.

'Is it okay if I get into the back seat, or do you want me to sit in the front?' Aditya asked in jest. Shreya smiled, but didn't respond. She was too overawed. Her heart was beating fast. She was sure that her pulse rate had doubled. Over the last few months she had read and re-read all his books. And here he was, a couple of feet from her, breathing the same air. Wait till she told all her friends. She would be mobbed with questions. When she had declared her intent back in the hostel room that she was going to meet Aditya, there were many who wanted to accompany her. But no one had the courage to leave their placement interviews and come. She had prioritised him over her interviews despite Sunaina's vehement objections.

'How are the placements going?' Aditya started the conversation, snapping her back into reality.

'Today was the first day, sir.'

'Aditya please, not sir. "Sir" makes me feel too old,' Aditya smiled.

'Three companies had their placement interviews today,' Shreya continued.

'And how many got placed?'

'Not sure, sir.'

'How come? Not keeping track?'

'I will get to know, sir . . .' Shreya stopped mid-sentence and laughed as Aditya play-acted anger. 'Okay, okay. Aditya it is. The interviews are currently on. My phone battery died,' she said pointing to her phone. 'So I can't even call and enquire about the fate of my friends.'

'You didn't attend the interviews?' Aditya looked at her as if she was from some other planet. 'Why?'

'Because it clashed with your session,' Shreya shrugged.

'Wha . . . aat?' Aditya was stunned. 'You've got to be kidding me!' His eyes nearly popped out in disbelief. He couldn't believe what he was hearing. Missing the first day of placement interviews was unheard of in management institutes.

Shreya looked at him, amused. He looked so fresh, even

after a long day. 'I wanted to come to your event,' she said at last.

'You left your day-zero companies just to come for my event?' Aditya had still not come to terms with it.

'Yup,' she said. 'Feeling sorry for me?' She was grinning.

'I am flattered. But it is extremely stupid of you to have done that. You are smart enough to get into any day-zero company. You can't be playing with your career like this.'

Shreya kept smiling. 'Life is all about choices you make, isn't it? I made one. Why regret it?' She turned her gaze towards the horrendous traffic that snailed on the roads of Bengaluru.

Aditya observed her closely. Her hair beautifully cascaded down her shoulders, comfortably resting on her upper back. Dark brown, they were the colour that sand is just before sunset turns to night.

Today, sitting in the back seat of his car, he couldn't help noticing how attractive she looked. Regulation denim that fitted her well, a maroon top with earrings to match; her dress sense was simple yet elegant. She looked like someone who took good care of herself. Her toned arms, slim figure and upright posture had him unwittingly thinking of what was under that maroon top. Aditya quickly checked himself.

'You came to my event. I thank you for that,' he declared. His right hand went up to his chest and he bowed his head in an expression of gratitude. 'But what made you miss your placement interviews? It has got to be more than just ME.'

'No really, it was you!' Shreya blurted and then hastened to clarify. 'That night when I read your book, it wouldn't let me sleep. The way you described the emotional turmoil the killer in the book goes through, made me cry. It felt as if I was living the lives of the characters through your book. That's the level of association it created. And when you killed your key character, I sobbed. I have never cried on reading a book before. You are the best storyteller in contemporary India. I felt that I had to see you. It was more important than anything else.'

Aditya was confused. He had always held that authors do not have fans. They have readers. But this girl was turning that logic on its head. She was behaving like a smitten fan. She was also probably his prettiest fan. Aditya felt a gush of luck and happiness.

'You know, Aditya, someone once said, books make sense of life. The only problem is that the lives they make sense of are other people's lives, never your own . . .'

'Julian Barnes.'

'Excuse me?' Shreya made a face.

'Julian Barnes said that.'

'Oh is that so? The point is, when I read your book, it made me feel that I was the protagonist as well as the antagonist. I was not reading the story. I was living it. And that feeling has never come to me while reading Indian authors—at least the few that I have read.' She gave him a thumbs up. When her hand returned to rest on the back seat of the car, it accidentally brushed against his palm. It sent a shiver down his spine. On an impulse he pulled his hand back and immediately felt stupid when he realised that she noticed his action.

'And what was that about the . . . spouse of the author?' he hesitated. At the EasyLib session, Shreya had asked him whether the spouse of the writer had a wretched life, because of the purported solitary life that writers lead. 'Are you . . . Is your boyfriend a writer . . . as in . . . are you in a relationship . . . with . . .'

'Haha!' Shreya burst out laughing. It sounded like music to Aditya's ears. 'Oh no, not at all. I don't even have a boyfriend. For the last one year, all that I have focused on is the Chairman's gold medal. I wanted to prove to the world that people with a small-town background can achieve big too.'

'Aaah . . .' Aditya nodded his head as if Shreya had made an all important disclosure. He felt relieved at the fact that Shreya didn't have a boyfriend. However he quickly realised that he was making it too obvious and in a bid to cover up, said, 'Small town?'

'Raipur. I was brought up in Raipur. My father worked with the government of Madhya Pradesh in the Anti-Maoist cell.'

'So did you manage to get the Chairman's gold medal?'

Shreya smiled. 'I have done my best. Hopefully it should come my way. There are three of us in contention, but my academic credentials are far ahead for any of them to match,' she replied.

'That's wonderful. Congratulations,' he paused. 'Then why did you ask me about the wretched life of an author's spouse?'

'I want to become an author. So, I asked if it is really true that an author's spouse leads a wretched life.'

'Haha! No, it's not that bad. It's more the romance of saying such things that attracts people towards making such statements. In a public forum we have to say things which we may not necessarily agree with, just to sound cool. In reality, my wife doesn't seem to be leading a wretched life at all. Yes, she doesn't enjoy the limelight, but then, that's okay. I think whoever said that must be going through a terrible marriage at the time,' he laughed.

Shreya laughed too. His heart skipped a beat. She looked even more attractive when she laughed.

Strange feelings were going through Aditya's mind. This was not the first time he was sitting next to an attractive looking reader who was so taken by him. But it was the first time that he was finding it difficult to keep his head straight. Shreya, meanwhile, seemed to have gotten over her initial nervousness and now looked extremely comfortable; far more comfortable than Aditya felt.

'What kind of books do you read?' Aditya asked. 'Thrillers?'

'No, I don't read thrillers. I find them to be too casual. I haven't read one in years,' she smiled, 'except yours.'

'Really?' he asked, feeling a strange thrill himself.

'Yes, I prefer the ones that show rather than tell,' Shreya continued. 'I am a bit high-brow in my literary preferences. I'm not the kind who'll quote Shakespeare, mind you, but I do like Murakami. I don't know too many other Indians who love Mario Vargas Llosa as much as I do.'

Despite all his bravado, Aditya was a poor reader. He knew that if the conversation veered towards Murakami and Llosa, he would struggle. He had tried to show off his superficial knowledge by commenting on a statement made by Julian Barnes. Sanjay, a voracious reader himself, had mentioned it to him once, and Aditya had latched on to that quote. It was an impressive statement to quote in his lectures, and he had simply committed it to memory.

'Nice, nice,' he managed to say.

'Have you read their work?' She smiled as if she knew his answer.

He looked at her sheepishly. 'Why do you ask?' he questioned. He was quite amazed at her ability to read the other person's mind.

'Just ...' she giggled. Aditya's cheeks went pink with embarrassment.

'You know, it doesn't matter. Many great authors don't find time to read. They just have time to research and write. What matters is that you have written four massive ... massive ... bestsellers and you are the boss at a large organisation. That's impressive enough!'

Despite her appreciation, Aditya felt a bit inadequate. He had nothing to prove to her, yet he felt incompetent.

'You seem to read a lot. A book a night?'

'Well, not exactly. If a book grips me, then a day and a half, or else I drop it like a hot potato.'

'Do readers like you also dislike books?' He made a sad attempt at sarcasm.

'Of course. I don't enjoy reading erotica. EL James' *Fifty Shades of Grey* ... didn't like it at all. Started reading it only because of peer pressure, but then couldn't go on.'

Aditya didn't have the courage to ask her why she didn't

like the most erotic book in recent times. That was the only book he had read recently, that too on his Kindle because it lent him privacy.

The driver honked. Aditya realised that thankfully they were at the gates of IIM Bengaluru. He didn't want to carry on the conversation any further. The car came to a halt and they alighted.

'Thanks, Aditya. It was wonderful meeting you. And thanks for the drive back.'

'It was a pleasure. And I should be thanking you for the wonderful conversation.'

'Will you help me write my first book, Aditya?' Shreya asked without any warning.

'For sure,' was all he could mumble before she turned and walked away from him.

As she walked towards her hostel, Aditya stood there admiring her. She looked like an angel. He was floored by her intellect. She was clear in her thoughts and had an opinion on everything. She was one of the most well read readers that he had interacted with. He thanked his stars that Sanjay was only coming the next day, otherwise he would have been out with him and would not have been able to drop Shreya back to the hostel.

As he stood there, Aditya felt like an idiot who had all the chance in the world, yet did not ask her for her phone number. He did not even ask her what she wanted to write about. He didn't even wish her good luck for her placement interviews the next day. That was the least he could have done. Aditya cursed himself.

12

It was the second day of the placement season. The atmosphere in and around the designated interview zone was tense. Students were running from one room to another attending job interviews. National Bank was one of the six companies recruiting that day. Of the forty-five students that it had shortlisted, six had already been placed the previous day and had been taken out of the placement process.

'What's our target, Sanjay?' Aditya asked when they entered the interview room. Apart from Aditya and Sanjay there were two other corporate bankers. The four of them had split themselves into two interview panels.

'Seven. If we find those many good hirable candidates,' Sanjay looked at the pile of papers in front of him and said. 'Let the pain begin. This fucking campus interview process makes life so miserable for me. First you hire them, then train them and then deal with their attitude. Wonder why people even hire management trainees,' he complained. Sanjay was irritated that he had to spend the entire day interviewing smart-ass students and listening to their gastric outbursts.

'So this is the list of candidates?' Aditya asked and snatched the résumés from Sanjay and started going through them. He was hunting for one particular CV. It was the fourteenth in the pile. He picked up the top twenty CVs and kept the others back in the envelope and handed it to his colleagues in the second panel. 'There you go,' he said.

As they started interviewing the candidates, they found nothing substantial to separate the good ones from the bad. It was boiling down to a draw of lots.

The fourteenth candidate walked in.

'Good morning, sir. Good morning, sir,' she repeated twice, looking at the two men in front of her on the panel.

'Good morning, Shreya. Please take your seat,' Sanjay took the lead.

'Thank you.'

As she sat down gracefully Aditya couldn't help but notice how stunning she looked. He felt as if he were in a trance. Shreya was wearing a black and white dress, vertical white stripes on the sides and black in the centre. She had tied her hair up in a simple pony. Light pastel lipstick to go with the miniscule make-up and just the right dose of perfume. Chanel No. 5; Aditya knew the fragrance. Maya used the same perfume.

'So, Shreya,' Sanjay began the interview, 'tell us about yourself.'

Shreya gave a brief introduction, concise and to the point. She was confident, and extremely articulate.

'What do you want to do after your MBA?'

'I want to make a difference to the world. I want to be remembered as someone who did something worthwhile. I want to do my bit to help the poor in the world—work towards improving the living conditions of households below poverty line. Rehabilitate slums. Ensure kids living in slums are not deprived of their right to be educated,' Shreya said with conviction.

'And you expect to be able to do all that in your role at National Bank?' Sanjay queried.

'And more. At some point in time, I would love to do a stint in the Corporate Social Responsibility division of National Bank, or for that matter any other organisation that I join. That apart, only if I have a good career and if I fight the demons within myself will I be able to help others. It is always difficult for a struggler to make a difference. How I am going to make a difference, at a personal level, different from the organisation that I join, I'm not too sure. I will figure that out. I have a few options in mind,' Shreya stated.

'Like?'

'I want to become an author. Write meaningful and socially relevant books and leave a mark on the world. Hopefully I will be able to do that.'

'Then why do you want a job?' Sanjay was a bit surprised at her response. Her confidence was beginning to irritate him.

'Writing is an expression of creativity, sir. I want to be independent—a woman who writes her own destiny. I don't think that is possible without the confidence that a successful career will give you.' All along Aditya was nodding his head. 'And I am not sure if one can bank on writing for survival. In India at least, I have heard that one cannot make a living off writing alone,' Shreya finished.

Sanjay asked her some questions about her strengths and weaknesses and a few other pointed questions about life at IIM-B and ended the interview.

'Are we taking her?' Aditya asked the moment she exited the room. 'I think we should.'

'Just because you are on the panel, she thinks she can play to your instincts and get the job. I didn't like the way she had tuned her answers to your engine. She played to your instincts as an author. I am striking her from the list,' Sanjay declared.

'I think she was being honest. She came across as confident and credible. Have you considered that maybe, just maybe, she was telling you the truth? It could well be possible that she really wants to become an author.'

'Then why should we waste time on her?'

'She gave you an answer for that too.'

'Cock and bull story.'

'Have you seen her grades? Besides, she is the top contender for the Chairman's gold medal.'

Sanjay looked at him, surprised. 'And how on earth do you know that, Mr Aditya Kapoor?'

Aditya realised his faux pas. Nowhere in her biodata was it mentioned that she was contending for the Chairman's gold medal. She had casually brought it up during their conversation while driving to the IIM-B campus. 'Well, with grades like this you are bound to be a topper,' he managed. 'Anyway, forget all that, I liked her.'

'Hmm . . .' Sanjay nodded, 'I liked her too. She looked good. Cute and sexy.'

'And, Sanjay, what's life without a few cute management trainees around?' Aditya joked.

'Now I know why I am in HR while you are terrific in business roles. You spot an opportunity better than me, and . . .'

'And what?'

'You guys move faster and are better at closing transactions than us HR types. History bears evidence to this, doesn't it, Aditya?' Sanjay's eyes looked away, towards the door and moved all around the room and finally came back and rested on Aditya. 'Don't you think so?' he asked again. There was a strange look in his eyes.

Aditya was not listening. He had turned selectively deaf. 'Do it for me, Sanjay. I came all the way to Bengaluru for you, didn't I?' he pleaded.

'Asshole,' Sanjay smiled. 'Fine but only on the condition that I reserve the right to keep her in HR.'

Aditya was jubilant. 'As if I have a say in it!'

Shreya was hired as a management trainee, slated to join National Bank in May.

Just as they drove out of the campus that evening, Aditya wondered why he was so keen to have Shreya join National Bank. Was it just a surge of hormones at the sight of a cute young girl or was it a desire to reciprocate the belief in him that she had demonstrated by turning up for his book event the night before?

He didn't have any answers.

13

LATE THAT EVENING, Aditya was on his laptop busy plotting his next thriller, when Maya called out, 'Adi, did you see the TOI in Bengaluru? Your EasyLib event has been featured there.'

How could he have not? For a long time now, he had a Google alert on his name which would send him the link to any mention of his name on the internet. The journalist had waxed eloquent about Aditya and also carried a picture taken at the event.

Aditya had however missed mentioning it to Maya. She liked reading press coverage about him and would have got upset had she known that Aditya didn't tell her. So he feigned ignorance.

'Oh is it?' He walked up to her. 'Show me.'

Maya turned the laptop screen towards him, 'Here, see,' she said. 'Sanjay has tagged you on the post. It's on your Facebook.'

'Hmm . . . yes,' Aditya agreed.

'Nice pic too,' Maya commented. 'Who are the others?'

'Folks from the Library I think,' Aditya said. 'Good people. They always do a good job of such events.'

He felt a touch guilty about the fact that he was lying to Maya that all of them were folks from EasyLib, especially when there was no reason to.

He did not tell her that Shreya, who was also in the photo, was an outsider.

14

'CAN YOU COME to my room, Aditya? We need to talk,' Tim's voice came over the intercom.

Aditya was worried. *We need to talk*—when a wife or boss utters these words, it can only mean trouble. He ran up the two floors separating him from his boss's office and was outside the room in a jiffy.

After letting him in, Tim shut the door and sat on the sofa opposite Aditya. 'How is the book doing?' he asked casually.

'It's doing well, Tim. It's gone into its twenty-seventh reprint. Sales numbers look encouraging. Let's see how long it sustains.'

'Thanks, Aditya. I was actually referring to the Liability book—the deposit and investment book. About your writing, I keep getting updates in the newspaper and of course on Facebook.'

'Oops,' Aditya said sheepishly. 'I am sorry, Tim. Yes, the Liability book is doing fine. I am putting together a presentation for you. Will complete and send it to you by evening or latest by tomorrow.'

'Hold on to that, Aditya.' Tim got up and walked to his

table. He fiddled with his laptop. Aditya could figure out that he was just prepping himself. He turned, faced Aditya and with a serious expression on his face, said, 'I have some news for you, sonny.'

Suddenly insecurity gripped Aditya. Was Tim unhappy with him about something? He had never hit it off with Tim, but things were not too bad between the two either. 'Is something wrong?'

'You are aware of the compliance and money laundering related problems the bank got into with the US government, right?'

Aditya nodded. He knew that a senate permanent subcommittee had pulled up National Bank in the US. They had been held guilty of exposing the US financial system and its stability to significant risk due to poor compliance and controls of existing anti-money laundering regulations. Along with HSBC and SCB, National Bank had been severely indicted in a report that came out three months ago.

On account of the indictment, National Bank had given the US government certain assurances on the controlled manner in which they would run their wealth management businesses across the world.

'If we follow all that we have committed to the US government in terms of enhanced controls and consumer diligence, it will render the wealth management business unviable. Unprofitable. We won't be able to fight competition in India,' Aditya protested.

'That's true and that is why the regional office has decided that rather than build this business, we will shrink the wealth management book significantly. Stop selling wealth management services and offer it as a shelf product. Give it to people who ask for it. Don't market it. Disincentivise customers from using us for wealth management. Have few people on the shop floor, just servicing those few customers who insist on staying with us.'

'But why? We have such a beautifully controlled portfolio. Best in class,' Aditya argued. 'Other banks would kill to have these customers. This is a knee jerk reaction, Tim.'

'I know. But the organisation wants to play it safe. It's a diktat from Singapore. In fact it is a global diktat.'

'So what will we tell our customers? And our employees?'

'That's why I called you. We need to put together a note on how many people we need, to keep the wealth management business on a ventilator. More importantly how many we need to let go.'

Aditya was stunned. 'We will sack people for no fault of theirs? We are shutting down a cash cow!' he cried.

'Relax, Aditya. Sometimes we must not fret over things that are not in our control. Global diktats have to be adhered to, not argued against. Go write a few more books in the time that you will get for yourself.'

'That was unnecessary, Tim, completely unnecessary,' Aditya barked. He had taken extreme precaution to make sure that no one ever pointed a finger at him and accused him of his writing affecting his work. He was very touchy if anyone were to even subtly hint at that.

'Okay, okay. Calm down. I was kidding.'

'Kidding. Really, Tim?' Aditya was upset at Tim's tone yet decided not to dwell on it. 'In any case, we have four hundred people working in wealth management. My guess is that we will not need more than hundred. Of the four hundred that we have, over seventy-five have been hired in the last three months. What face do we have to go back to them and tell them that they don't have a job?'

'I can understand,' Tim said though he didn't look apologetic at all.

How can someone be so cold, thought Aditya. 'But,' Tim continued, 'it is what it is. We will keep a straight face and tell them that they are no longer needed.'

'What about me?'

'What about you?'

'Do I have a job? You won't need a person of my seniority to run the business anymore.'

'Of course we need you. Who will manage the branches, the sales efforts through the branches, and customer service? You do a lot more than wealth management,' Tim tried to reassure Aditya.

*

By the time he left Tim's cabin, Aditya was worried. In one stroke three hundred families were about to be deprived of their livelihood. Three hundred families, whose only crime was that they did what the organisation wanted them to do. What got him even more worked up was that the overall job market was bleak. Many banks had stopped hiring.

He had to do something to protect his people.

He went to the cafeteria. Wanting to be alone, he picked up his cup of coffee from the vending machine and walked to a distant corner. Leaning against the glass wall, he stared out into the open. He could see traffic on the road. 'It's a dog-eat-dog world out there,' he mumbled to himself. Everyone was only bothered about protecting their own job and winning brownie points. The three hundred people about to be sacked were nobody's responsibility. They were at the bottom of the pyramid and didn't matter.

'Thinking about the plot for your next book?' A sweet voice interrupted his flow of thoughts.

He had heard that voice earlier.

15

'Shreya! What a pleasant surprise!'

Aditya smiled and extended his hand. She walked up to him and was about to give him a hug. He deftly stepped back in a manner to make it look like a normal movement and not an offensive one. In public he had, thus far, been extremely careful about others' perception of him.

He could smell the same heady Chanel No. 5 on her. God! Wasn't she beautiful? He found it difficult to take his gaze off her. Her glowing skin made her look like an angel. Her long and wavy hair was smooth and silky as molten chocolate. Her deep bluish-green eyes attracted him like iron to magnet. For a moment he wondered how on earth an Indian girl could have eyes like that. He wanted to ask her, but held himself back.

'How are you, sir?' she asked, and then cheekily bit her tongue, 'Oops . . . Aditya.'

'Good, good,' he smiled. 'What brings you here today?'

'You don't seem too happy to see me.' Tilting her head to one side, she made a show of displeasure.

'Not at all,' he spluttered into his coffee. 'Not at all. In fact you just managed to cheer me up,' Aditya confessed.

'So you are happy to see me, right?'

He smiled. And then as if he just remembered something he asked, 'But you guys were not expected till the beginning of next month. That's when the MT programme begins, isn't it?'

'I had nothing to do. I am a very restless soul. I can't sit at home and I have no friends with whom I can go on a holiday. I wrote to Sanjay sir asking if I can join early and he agreed. I formally joined today.'

'Wonderful. Welcome on board. So happy to see you here. By the way, what happened to the Chairman's gold medal?'

'Could it have gone to anyone else?' she asked, the sparkle in her eyes telling a story.

'Oh wow! I knew you would get it. I hope you have a wonderful career with National Bank.'

Shreya smiled. 'Thank you. To work with someone like you is a dream come true. Sanjay sir told me that he will be speaking to you and place me in your team till the other management trainees join.'

'You're going to work with me?'

'Yes,' Shreya began and then realising her faux pas, she hurriedly added, 'But I guess I jumped the gun. He said he will talk to you about it.'

Aditya was super thrilled. The three hundred people getting sacked were forgotten for the time being. While he wanted to be upset with Sanjay for not having told him, he just couldn't be. The favour was bigger than the complaint.

'So, how is your writing coming along? Are your writing

dreams intact or have you sacrificed them at the altar of your career?'

'Not at all,' she said nonchalantly. 'I expect the dream to take flight. Now that I am with you, I want to spread my wings and fly. Will you help me?'

'Surely. In these uncertain days, it helps to have an alternate line of revenue,' Aditya said, his mind forced back into the reality of the three hundred people he would soon have to sack.

'Uncertain . . . why uncertain?'

'It's okay. Let it be,' he said. 'This is not a discussion to have on your first day here. Let me quickly chat with Sanjay on what's the plan for you. We can then decide on our course of action,' he said casually as they were walking down the steps. They reached the HR floor. Sanjay, who was in his room, saw them coming and peeked out of his room.

'I called you,' he yelled from across the corridor, 'but you were with Tim.'

'Thank you,' Aditya said as he walked up and shook hands with Sanjay. 'Can we step into your room?' He turned towards Shreya and nodded his head. 'Wait for me on the first floor. I'll be there in ten minutes.'

Once they were inside the room, he waited till the door shut firmly and asked Sanjay, 'Why couldn't you have told me earlier, you prick?'

'I wanted to surprise you. You wanted her desperately. The management trainee induction doesn't start till next month. I thought it might be a good idea to let her float with you till then.'

'Thank you for that.'

'See. I do take care of people's motivation.'

'Doesn't Tim have to be told?'

'A mail has gone out to him five minutes back. He knows. It's all at HR cost. So dude, you will be having fun at HR's expense.'

'Shut up. I am a nice married man.'

'Nice?' Sanjay rolled his eyes. 'At least that's what she thinks, I guess,' he smiled. 'If not her, that's what Maya thinks.' The smile grew wider. 'Wonder what she saw in you. I would have surely been a better option for her,' Sanjay sighed deeply. 'Woman too make mistakes, Aditya.'

'You are impossible, Sanjay.' Aditya rolled his eyes and walked out of the room. Just as he was walking out, his eyes fell on a set of books arranged neatly behind Sanjay. He couldn't recall having read any of them. Next to them was a copy of their IIM student journal—*iimpressions*. It had a write-up on every student along with a candid picture. It took him back in time. He flipped through it before putting it down. His hand hit the bookend which moved from its spot. Hurriedly he set it right and looked at Sanjay. 'These are nice,' he commented, admiring the carved wooden bookends on either side of the books.

'Diana gifted me those. So I had to put them to good use,' Sanjay shrugged.

'Aaaah . . .' Aditya nodded as he admired them.

Amongst the many books stacked was James Patterson's *Private* series. It was in the news because Ashwin Sanghi, one of India's leading writers was co-writing a book with

James Patterson in the same series. Aditya knew about it because being India's leading thriller writer, it would be embarrassing for him to sound ignorant if any journalist asked him about it.

'James Patterson's latest. Nice!' he said as he picked up one of them. 'Can I borrow this from you?'

'Keep that book down if you don't want your hands chopped off,' Sanjay thundered.

Aditya smiled and turned towards him.

'You know how possessive I am about my books,' Sanjay replied as he took the book from Aditya's hands and placed it back from where it had been picked up. When he turned back to face Aditya, he saw him furiously flipping through *iimpressions*. On opening the page that he wanted to, Aditya started reading out from it:

'The deceptively serious looking self-proclaimed fitness freak,
would struggle through jogging, gym and ten hours of sleep.
After crunching all available novels in a sleepless night,
He would awake sleeping wing-mates and give gratuitous advice.
His room gave you the feel of an old bookstore,
You would be hit instantly with a sense of vellichor.
Books are his solace, books are his zone,
Never lending them to others, for that he is known.
In the first year, romance took his life by storm,
But his lady turned him down before too long.
"Let's be friends" ahh the cliched curse,
He was left at the water tank, with a broken heart to nurse.
He was an HR genius from day one, for he understood
hierarchy and rank

Everyone agrees, that for Sanjay, there is glory in store
He'll make us proud, he is an achiever to the core.

'Still the same. Eh! Not changed one bit,' Aditya said, shaking his head as he read through the passage describing Sanjay in the yearbook. Sanjay had always been like this. Never one to share his books, Sanjay took great care of them. Aditya had known him for fifteen years now, but had never even once seen him lend his books to anyone. Not even to someone as close as Aditya. He was beyond possessive when it came to his books.

'But this reminds me,' Aditya stopped. 'Something I have never had the courage to ask you.' Sanjay looked up at him wondering what was coming next.

'Why did you choose a location as unimaginative as the place underneath the water tank to propose to her? Couldn't think of a more romantic spot?'

Sanjay's face went red. He was embarrassed and struggled to hide it. He managed a smile. 'Fuck you, bastard,' he exclaimed. 'Be happy with what you have. Don't ridicule someone who didn't get what he wanted.' He sat down on his chair. 'Asshole.'

16

ADITYA ENTERED HIS cabin to find Shreya waiting for him.

'When will you be giving us your next book, Aditya?' she asked.

'Well,' Aditya replied, 'I'm almost done with it.'

'Almost?'

'Yes, almost. I'm not getting enough time to finish it. I was hoping to complete it on my US trip.'

'Oh wow! You are going to the US? When?'

'In a couple of weeks. I wanted to go for a month. But now it seems like I won't be able to go at all.'

'Why?'

'We are shutting a business,' Aditya let slip. The moment he said it he wished he hadn't. But it was too late. 'Please don't talk about it. At least for a few days.'

'Oh! Is that why you were so dry when I met you?'

'Shutting a business is always painful. I hate it when people lose jobs for no fault of theirs.'

'So you can't go?' Shreya tried to change the topic.

'No. The transition has to be managed here. If I go, my people will be pushed around. I don't want that to happen. I want to save as many jobs as possible.'

'How lucky they are to have you as their boss.'

Aditya looked pleased. Any bit of praise coming from her elated him.

'I don't mean to sound opportunistic, but do you think it will make for good reading? Writing about this?'

Aditya didn't understand what she was trying to say. 'As in?' he asked her.

'A story about a guy who loses his job,' Shreya said. Before Aditya could respond, his phone started ringing. He picked it up as Shreya left the room.

'Hi Maya, we have a small problem,' he started off and then went on to tell her about the scaling down of the wealth management business and how his presence here was necessary.

'So NASA is out?' she asked.

'I will have to skip it,' he said, sounding sad. 'If I go, these people will be tossed around. They have worked for me. I need to protect their interests and help them find jobs in other units within the bank.'

*

That night when they were in bed, she cuddled up to Aditya and said, 'Don't worry. We will miss you but we will not hate you for not coming.' She hugged him tight. 'On the contrary, had you come leaving those people to suffer, we would have hated you for it.'

This is what Aditya loved about her. She never put him under any pressure.

'I am not worried about you, Maya. I know you would

never ask me to leave them and come. I am worried about Aryan. He will surely be disappointed.'

'Leave that to me. I will manage him,' Maya assured him.

He smiled, kissed her on the forehead and switched off the light. Maya always made sure that he had fewer problems to handle at home.

A few miles away, curled up in bed, Shreya was re-reading one of Aditya's earlier books. Over the last few months, she had read it so many times that she knew most of the lines by heart. She couldn't help but admire the subtle subtext in his prose. As she turned the pages, she wondered if Aditya meant what he said—'If instead of malls we built libraries, the future generations would be a lot smarter.'

In the dead of the night, Aditya's sleep was disturbed by the beep of his phone. Turning towards the side table, he picked it up and looked at it. It was a message.

<Just read your book again. Simply breathtaking. Loved the malls vs library argument.>

Aditya looked at it momentarily, smiled and kept the phone down. He turned towards Maya, hugged her and went back to sleep.

Beep! the message tone sounded on his phone.

This time Maya woke up. 'Who is it?' she asked him.

'A reader.'

'Reader? A fan? At this hour?'

'How do they care?' he mumbled with a sleepy drawl and turned towards her. Before turning however he quietly put his phone on silent.

Sleep had deserted Aditya. His mind was far, far away. What had made Shreya, a mere management trainee, message him so late at night?

But did he really mind her sending him those messages? Aditya knew the answer.

17

Aditya was always the first to reach office. The next day was no different and at 8.30 am, he stepped out of the lift and walked towards his cabin. The rest of his team would normally come in by 9.15 am, giving him time to clear out the pending work and plan out his entire day.

Surprisingly, the light at the far end of the hall was on. He walked towards the corner.

'Shreya?' he exclaimed the moment he saw her. 'How come so early?'

'Sanjay sir wanted me to sort out some data for him.'

'On your second day at work?' It was obvious that he didn't believe what she said.

'Some donkey work,' she smiled. Her teeth were perfect. There was something irritatingly cute about her.

He just nodded and turned away. It took an effort to look away from her. He started walking towards his room.

'Aditya sir,' she called out after him.

'Again "sir"?'

She didn't reply but just extended her right hand towards him. It held two sheets of paper. He took it from her. 'What is it?' he said as he looked at her.

'A love letter,' she said and burst out laughing at her own joke.

'You could have professed it verbally and saved yourself the trouble of typing this out,' he retorted, even as he took the paper from her hand and looked at it.

He started reading it with full concentration. As he turned the page, Shreya muttered, 'I wrote it down last night.'

He laboured to raise his eyelashes and look at her. 'Last night? I thought you were reading my book last night.'

'I was. After I finished your book, I penned this.'

He looked at her a bit aghast. 'You wrote all of this last night?'

'Hmm . . . You only told me about it yesterday evening. It couldn't have been before that, right?'

His phone rang. 'Damn,' he muttered as he pulled it out of his pocket. It was Maya.

'Yes, Maya,' he said even as he indicated to Shreya that she could stay, while he was on the call. 'Hmm . . . okay. I will have to call you back. Hmm . . . No, not today evening. I'll be home late. I told you that . . . hmm . . . Tell them we will come some other day. Love you. Bye.' He disconnected the call.

'Come on in,' he said to Shreya and led her back to his room.

Once inside, he started reading what she had given him. Shreya quietly sat down on the chair in front of him. Her eyes betrayed the anticipation of a child.

Aditya didn't speak a word. He read the entire document from end to end. His eyes didn't move from the paper for even a fleeting second. His intercom rang in between. He didn't pick it up, just flicked it to silent mode without even looking at the telephone instrument.

'What prompted you to write this?' he asked when he was done.

'I told you. Our discussion about the shutting down of a business and sacking of people got me thinking. I felt that it would be a good idea to write about the life of someone who gets sacked for no fault of his. And after I finished your book yesterday, I again thought about it. An idea for a plotline crossed my mind and I just wrote it down. I didn't think too much. Just, whatever thoughts came to my head, I penned them down.'

'How long did it take you?'

'Four hours.'

Aditya was stunned. 'You texted me at 1.30. Four hours after that would mean 5.30 am. You were already here at 8.30 when I came in. Did you sleep at all?'

'Sleep is a waste of time, Aditya. I came in here at 7 and was refining this to get it in presentable shape. I didn't want my first submission to you to be horrible,' she said. There wasn't an iota of evidence on her face to show that she hadn't slept the whole night. 'If you like it, you can use it for your next book.'

'Plotting of a story overnight . . . Wow! Now I know what makes you special,' Aditya said. He was genuinely impressed at her ability to conceive a story and pen it down in such a short time. Shreya secretly blushed at his compliment.

Aditya paused to think for just about a second and

continued, 'Great start. If this is the first plotline that you have written, it shows enormous potential. There are a few gaps, but then even after months of effort, authors leave gaps in their plots. In four hours, you can't be expected to plug everything.'

'Can this be converted into a book?' she asked excitedly.

Aditya thought for some time. 'Yes, for sure, but it needs one change in the plotline if it has to work for the Indian market.'

'This won't work?' The let-down was evident in her voice.

'Don't be disappointed,' he said even as he placed his hand on top of hers on the table. It was a subconscious move. She didn't move her hand away. He realised what he had done and hurriedly pulled it back.

'I am sorry.'

'It's okay.'

She decided to ease the awkwardness by bringing the conversation back to her plot. 'Tell me why it wouldn't make a good story in India.'

'Because you have romanticised the loss of a job. There is nothing romantic about a job loss. Losing one's job is tragic. In the plot you have turned the guy into a hero. You have shown how he fights his way out of a job loss and turns an adversity in his favour.'

'But isn't that what one is supposed to do?'

'Sweetheart,' he began to explain with a drag. She loved the way he called her sweetheart, though she tried not to show it. But the blood rushed to her cheeks, which was something she couldn't hide.

He continued, 'That's not the way it works when you write a book. Rags to riches works for non-fiction books and true stories—at times even for films. But for fiction, in India specifically, tragedy rules. Reading about someone else's woes and crying bucketfuls is a national pastime. Unrelated people dying for no fault of theirs, tears, sob stories . . . These are all formulae for success. And after writing about all this, if you give the story a twist and a happy ending, you will end up a winner. It's about the journey. As long as the journey is tragic and the ending happy, you will end up with a bestseller.'

'Tragic journey . . . happy ending,' she rolled her eyes. 'Is that possible?'

'That's where creativity comes in,' Aditya spoke patronizingly, a pro explaining the rules to a rookie.

'Got it,' she said. Shreya was not sure if she completely understood what Aditya was saying, but was confident that she would figure it out.

'Let me tell you one last thing which comes to mind. You are better than most of the people whose work I have seen. The clarity of thought that reflects in this synopsis is amazingly brilliant. You have it in you to make it big.'

'Really? You think I will be able to become a big author, an author like you?'

'Hehe . . . I am not a benchmark. I have a long way to go.'

'But for me you are a role model. I want to learn from you. Will you help me, Aditya?'

'Of course I will. Whatever I can do, I will do. You have it in you to make it big. And to top it all you are extremely good-looking,' Aditya said, making Shreya blush again. 'You start with an advantage. Glamorous, sexy authors tend to sell more. You will be the darling of the media. A pretty author gets away with a lot.'

'Now I know you are pulling my leg. Let me disappear from here before you make more fun of me,' she said and left the room.

Aditya stood there holding the synopsis in his hand, wondering what had come over him.

He opened his laptop. Time to get back to work.

18

ADITYA WAS UP till late that night. He had a deadline to meet and was awfully behind schedule. He had no option but to sit up till late and finish the book.

His phone beeped from the other room.

Maya was sleeping. He tiptoed into the room and picked up the phone. The screen announced that it was an SMS from Shreya. Maya saw him sneaking out and mumbled, 'What happened?'

'Nothing, some stupid SMS,' he walked out of the room, back to his story. He flicked the SMS open on his screen.

<Hey, have you read *The Luminaries* by Eleanor Catton? Want to read it, but it is huge. 1000 pages.>

Since when had he become an expert on recommending books? He was just a writer who had no time to read. Family, work and writing took away all his time.

<Not sure.>

<Oh. ;) I forgot that you hardly read. I tried the reviews on the net. But they are too mixed. Unable to decide.>

<:) Read the new James Patterson.>

<Naah. No thrillers for me. I like literary fiction. You know that.>

\<But you read my books.\>

\<The only notable exception, Mr Aditya Kapoor.\>

He responded with a smiley and went back to his writing. Within a couple of minutes she SMS'd again.

\<Busy?\>

\<No. Tell me.\>

\<Was feeling bored.\>

\<Get a life. Get some friends. Move out of the PG. Better that way.\>

\<Sunaina, my bff, is coming to Mumbai next week. Hopefully we'll have some fun once she comes. Have told you about her, right?\>

Aditya knew that Sunaina was her hostel buddy and soulmate. \<Yes you have.\>

\<Hope I am not disturbing you.\>

\<No, not at all. Was just giving the finishing touches to my manuscript.\>

Aditya was enjoying the thrill of their exchange. Middle age had set in faster than he would have liked. Maya and he had long stopped giving this sort of attention to each other. Those leisurely morning cups of coffee and eating lunch out had been replaced by fretting over Aryan. This left little time for overt display of romance. Aditya lied about not being busy, because he didn't want this attention to stop. Books could wait.

\<Wow. 5th book. Right?\>

\<Yup.\>

\<Would love to read.\>

\<Sure. Let me complete it first.\>

\<Can I be the first one to read it?\>

Aditya didn't respond. He had walked to the refrigerator to get himself a glass of water. It was a warm night.

\<After your wife, of course.\> Shreya's next SMS read.

\<Sure. I will be giving it to her to read in a few days' time. Will give it to you too at the same time.\>

\<Really? Thanks, Aditya. You are adorable.\>

They went on chatting for a long time that night, for over an hour. Only when Aryan woke up and groaned for his dad did Aditya realise what the time was and called it a night.

Maya woke up sensing him slither into the quilt. 'You need to take care of your health, Adi. You need at least seven hours of sleep.'

Aditya felt a touch guilty. He loved her, and Aryan too. But he was beginning to enjoy his tryst with Shreya, a bit too much.

19

WHEN TIM CALLED for a follow-up meeting on the shut down of the wealth management business, he was joined by his boss; the CEO of National Bank, Sanjay; a representative of group HR, and the heads of the other businesses of the bank. The agenda was to come out with a working plan and timelines for communicating the redundancy of the 300 employees to the bank in general and the impacted employees in particular. National Bank had, of late, been in the news for adopting a flip-flop business strategy on various business lines.

Aditya had his favourites within the wealth management team, those whose jobs he wanted to protect. He derived enormous comfort from the fact that Sanjay was there and would be able to pull some strings to make sure that people he wanted to ring-fence would be largely insulated. It was upon his recommendation that Tim had invited the heads of other businesses too, for he wanted to impress upon them to hire as many people from the wealth management team as possible. Sanjay was driving the meeting and the discussion.

Beep. It was Aditya's phone. Hurriedly he put it on silent and glanced at the screen. It was Maya. <Mixed up the

snack boxes. You will not like what's in your box. Eat something in the cafeteria. Healthy ... not junk.> Typical Maya. It is not that he would have thrown a fit if the box didn't have what he liked.

The meeting went on. They debated and agreed on the number of wealth managers to be moved out—297 of them. The CEO instructed the other businesses to hire as many people as possible from the wealth management team so that they could save people from getting sacked. 'We can train them for different roles. So go ahead and hire them to fill the vacancies in your respective teams. We need to take care of our people,' he reiterated. 'With immediate effect all recruitment from outside, at the Manager and Deputy Manager levels, are frozen.' Sanjay smiled. This is what he had wanted the CEO to say, and the CEO had effectively delivered the message.

Aditya's mobile vibrated in his pocket. He pulled it out and looked at it. It was a message. He swiped it open.

<Where are you?>

He smiled. <Someone missing me?> he typed back into his smartphone and pressed the send button.

<Hehe ... Your room is open, but you are not there, so asked.>

<I'm on the 4th floor, in a meeting.>

<Meeting? What meeting? You never mentioned it.>

<Same old wealth managers shit. Got fixed last night. Will tell you when I see you.>

He had just pressed the send button when his phone vibrated again. Another message.

<Aditya, can you please focus? It is your business we are discussing.> Tim had sent him an SMS from across the table. Extremely embarrassed, Aditya kept the phone down. It vibrated a few times post that, but Aditya stoically refused to look at it.

By the time the meeting ended everyone agreed that the entire staff retrenchment exercise would be completed within the next ninety days.

At 6 pm Aditya packed up his bags and was ready to leave. He looked around for Shreya. When he couldn't find her, he sent her a message. She came hurriedly towards his cabin within a couple of minutes.

'I was leaving, so was looking for you,' Aditya said.

'Leaving early today?' Suddenly she remembered her discussion with him earlier that day. 'Oh you have that Bollywood party, right?'

Aditya pretended to frown, even as he murmured, 'I hate these Bollywood parties. They suck.'

'But isn't this one for you?'

Aditya nodded. Viacom, one of the largest film production houses, was throwing a party to celebrate the commissioning of a film based on Aditya's third book.

'You obviously have to look dapper and sound excited,' Shreya added.

'Haha! Yes. I don't have a choice. Professional hazard,' he commented and picked up his bag. Before leaving the room, he asked her, 'Wanna come?'

'Me? Would have loved to but Sunaina is coming.'

'So?'

'She is transiting through Mumbai. I'm to meet her at the airport. She will get upset if I don't,' she sighed.

'Oh!' Aditya nodded.

'Had I not committed to meet her, I would have come with you.' Shreya was feeling quite disappointed at having to turn him down; she loved these parties. 'I will come when you have a proper book event . . . Like the EasyLib one. I am a sucker for those. But . . .'

'But what . . .?'

'Don't get me wrong . . . but you are going for a Bollywood party dressed like that?' she pointed towards his suit and said.

He looked confused.

'Isn't it too formal . . . ish? Don't you need to look slightly cool for these Bollywood parties?'

'Haha! It is fine. If they don't like me they can throw me out,' he laughed.

She laughed too.

They had been walking and had now reached his car. 'Cool. See you tomorrow,' Aditya said. He waved at her and drove off. Once he reached JW Marriott, the venue for the party, he went straight to the washroom and looked at himself in the mirror. Why did Shreya say that he didn't look cool enough?

*

Maya was awake when he reached home that night. She was correcting some answer scripts.

'How was the party?'

'Awful. You know how much I hate these filmy do's,' he

lied, to show solidarity with Maya who herself felt stifled at these parties. 'You should have come. I wouldn't have felt as bored.'

'I am very happy with my world, Aditya. You know how much I hate these air kissing and backside groping parties,' she winked at him.

He smiled and sheepishly asked her, 'How do I look in this suit?'

'Awesome, Mr Kapoor. I would have married you, had you come in front of me in this suit.'

'Well the question to be answered then is whether you would have married me because of this suit, or despite it,' said Aditya. He patted her head and walked to the bedroom to freshen up and change. On the way, he remembered something and stopped.

'Oh by the way, Siddharth Malhotra from Midas Touch Entertainment was there. He approached me to be a judge for a reality show on TV, a dance show.'

'Ewwww . . .' Maya exclaimed.

'Hahahaha!' Aditya guffawed. 'I knew this is how you'd react.'

'Are you mad? Don't be so blinded by the arclights that you make a fool of yourself. You have a huge stature in this industry. Maintain some mystique around yourself. And a reality show? Where is the synergy?' she went back to her papers. She looked up through her reading glasses and added, 'I hope you didn't say yes!'

'I want to do it. It will give me a foothold in this industry. There is so much to do, film, scripts, screenplay. And more books of course. Unless I get the fame and adulation, no one will give me respect in this space.'

'Remember this success comes at a price. The price you pay for this is your self-esteem. Are you ready for that, Aditya?'

'Hmm . . .' was all Aditya could say as he walked into the bathroom. He and Maya were on different planets as far as his film escapades were concerned.

A message was waiting for him on his phone, when he walked out of the shower.

<How was it?>

<Great. Good crowd. Viacom managed to get some big stars to come. Priyanka Chopra was there. Arjun Rampal too . . . You should have come.>

<Hmm . . . So you missed me.>

<LOL>

<LOL is not an answer. A yes or a no would be better.>

<It would have been even more fun with you around.>

<:) Yes. I know. Later I thought I should have come. But by then it was too late.>

<You should have called. I would have come back for you.>

<It's okay. And by the way, you looked cool. I was just pulling your leg when I said what I said.>

<Hahaha! Thank god you told me. Wouldn't have slept had you not clarified.>

< Have you completed your manuscript?>

<Not yet. A week more . . . maybe two . . . Will send it to you once done.>

<Thanks, Aditya.>

<Sleep well. Be good.>

<Of course I will be. ;) I am not a bad girl.>

20

THE NEXT FEW days at work were extremely stressful for Aditya. The impending retrenchment was constantly playing on his mind. The only solace for him was his life outside office. His books helped him escape the agony at work and get into a world where he was the king. And as long as he was at work Shreya provided a welcome distraction. Just talking to her and being in her company calmed him down.

Over the past few years, he had considered quitting his job many a time to get into writing full time. The intensity and frequency of those thoughts had gone up. But he couldn't gather enough courage. He was worried that the day he started to rely on his writing to make ends meet, the fun would go out of it. It would become just another job for him.

That day he was on a restructuring call with the regional head of HR in Singapore. The India team was being represented on the video conference call by Aditya, Sanjay and one of Sanjay's deputies. It had become a bit of a routine ever since they decided to shut down a business. Aditya was anchoring the call, when he saw Shreya pace up and down the aisle outside his room. He tried to catch her eye, but she refused to look up. She looked disturbed. Aditya couldn't leave the room. It would have been too obvious had he got off the call to talk to her. He picked up the phone to SMS her but then kept it down instantly. Sanjay looked at Aditya's worried expression, then looked out of his cabin and made a face.

The call was a long one. By the time they ended the video conference, Shreya had left. Aditya stepped out of the room and looked around. He couldn't see her. He stepped back into his cabin. Sanjay was still there, hanging around and waiting for him.

'The person you are looking for is there,' he pointed to Aditya's iPhone lying on the desk.

'What?'

'There,' he again pointed to Aditya's phone. 'See that.'

Aditya walked up to his table and picked up his phone. There were seven SMSs from one person—Shreya.

Aditya picked it up and swiped through screens to get to his inbox.

<Will you take time?>
<I need to go.>
<Can I go?>
<Is it okay if I go?>
<I can't sit here any longer.>
<I can't bear to sit here any longer. Can I go?>

And finally the last message: <I am going.>

He was worried. Had he said anything which had upset her? Had someone else noticed their closeness? He started sweating as he assumed the worst.

'Whatever you are reading, I presume it doesn't bode

well, eh?' Sanjay spoke after a long time. Aditya looked at him blankly.

'Aditya, you are old enough to decide what you want to do. But why do I get the feeling that you are not headed in the right direction?'

'What, what do you think is going on, Sanjay?' Aditya looked straight back at him.

'Nobody is blind here, Aditya. We hired her on an impulse. You know that. I placed her in your team because she joined a month early. Do whatever you want to do, but for fuck's sake, please be discreet.'

'Save some healthy flirting, there is nothing going on,' Aditya said through gritted teeth.

'Whatever! All I can say is play it carefully, dude. If it comes to my attention formally then there will be a problem. So watch it.'

'What's going on here isn't even a fraction of what is going on between Diana and you,' Aditya smiled and patted him on his shoulder.

Sanjay was flabbergasted. He hadn't expected him to bring her into this discussion. Except for a one off occasion, Aditya had largely stayed away from treading down this path.

'I am not having fun, Aditya,' Sanjay retorted. 'I am single. And we are giving it a shot by trying to see if we can develop it into something long term. Both of us have suffered in our previous marriages. This is the first time I am with the person I love.' There was an angry look on his face. Unlike you, I have always had poor luck in relationships. So, both Diana and I are playing it safe. There is no comparison between what you are doing and our relationship.'

'You are thinking too much, Sanjay.'

'Paid to do that, my friend,' Sanjay said as he got up. 'Poor Maya. Wonder why she trusts you so blindly. I don't know what she saw in you,' he said as he exited the room, shaking his head in disgust.

21

THE MOMENT SANJAY left the room, Aditya dialled Shreya. Her phone was switched off. He walked to her desk. It was clean. Not a shred of paper on the table. He casually checked with people around. No one seemed to know anything.

Creases appeared on his forehead as he walked back. He had seen the build up of tears in her eyes and that had him worried.

He fidgeted around in office till five in the evening. He called her at least seventy-five times but her phone remained switched off. He toyed with the idea of sending someone to her house to see if everything was fine, but then decided otherwise.

Finally he decided that he had had enough and picked his bag and walked out. There were a few actionables which had arisen out of the conference call that morning, which were still pending. He decided to come back later for them.

Aditya drove out of the bank. He had Shreya's address; she had given it to him. He knew the building so it was easy for him to get there. He parked his car in the lane and walked straight up to her apartment.

Standing at the door, he composed himself, straightened his jacket and rang the bell.

He could hear some muffled footsteps coming from inside the apartment. He waited patiently for a couple of seconds. He could hear the door unlatch. And then it opened.

He stood spellbound.

In front of him was Shreya looking extremely sensuous. Someone had once told him, that every woman, at a particular age, looks good. He disagreed today. Shreya would look good at every age, and that too, irrespective of what she was wearing. She looked fabulously attractive even in her house clothes. He sized her up in a glance. In that fleeting moment he noticed that she had not worn a bra under her flimsy t-shirt. Her shorts ended a foot above her knee giving him ample sight of her silky thighs. A male mind can process so much information in nanoseconds when it comes to a woman's body that no supercomputer can match it.

Almost immediately he felt guilty, for Shreya was in a horrible state. Her nose was red, probably because she had been crying. Her eye make-up had smudged and dark circles had formed around her eyes. Her hair was unkempt. She looked as if she had woken up from a nightmare. Emotionally she was a wreck.

'Shreya!' Aditya exclaimed. 'What have you done to yourself?'

Shreya ignored his question. 'Aditya, you should not have come here. I stay with extremely conservative people. They might not approve of me meeting someone in this state in their house,' she stuttered. It was a bad attempt at getting him to leave and Aditya knew that.

'Don't worry. I will go away, but before that tell me what

happened.' Without giving Shreya a chance to react he walked into the living room and sat down on the sofa. 'And why is your phone switched off?' he demanded.

Shreya came and sat down next to him. She was still snivelling and the tissue in her hand had almost completely gone to pieces. There was a tissue box in front of them, on the centre-table. Aditya picked it up and extended it towards her. As she pulled out a tissue he looked at her legs. The glowing skin on her velvety legs, made her look like a goddess. For a moment he chided himself for being able to compartmentalise Shreya into two distinct boxes—the box of physical appeal, which he admired and that of emotional distress which he was trying to fix.

He waited for her to wipe the remnants of the tears from her eyes and then asked her again:

'What happened?'

She looked away from him, tears building up yet again, 'Nothing.'

'Before the dam in your eyes breaks and we go through one more round of tissue paper, can you tell me what happened?'

Shreya snivelled a few more times. Her cheekbones tightened and her eyelashes fluttered in a laboured manner— the way they do when you are trying to hold back tears that come rushing into your eyes. 'I am ashamed of myself, Aditya. I am a failure. I can never do anything good in life.'

'Says who?'

'Look at you, Aditya. India's number one author ... A big success. Everything you touch turns to gold. You have everything going for you. And me?' she sniffed through her tears, 'Me . . . nothing.'

'Fuck the preamble. Tell me what it is. And why are you doing this to yourself?' Aditya delicately placed his hand on top of hers and pressed it comfortingly.

She quietly got up from the sofa and walked towards a room at the far end of the hall. Aditya couldn't help noticing her swaying hips through the flimsy fabric of her satin shorts. He sighed and looked the other way, to distract himself. Within a minute he saw her emerge and walk back towards him, a paper in hand. He could see the silhouette of Shreya's body through the apology of a t-shirt that she was wearing. The narrow frame of her body, with her breasts projecting beyond the silhouette looked enticing.

Aditya took the paper from her. 'What is it?'

'Read.'

It was an email.

22

'*Dear Ms Kaushik,*

Thanks for submitting your manuscript to us for publishing . . .

Aditya looked up at her, surprised. 'Manuscript?' he muttered before going back to the letter.

'*. . . We are grateful that you considered us for publishing your book. However, we regret to inform you that the manuscript does not fit into the kind of books that we would like to publish. Hence we will be unable to take this up for publication.*

Please note that this is in no way a reflection of your skills or . . .

Aditya stopped reading because by then Shreya's sobs had filled the room. He looked up to see her crying uncontrollably, her body shaking.

'I am a failure, I am a failure,' she kept repeating even as tears trickled down her cheeks.

Aditya kept the letter on the table and turned towards her. 'You never told me about it,' he said in a low voice.

'I was . . . was . . . like . . . like . . . scared to tell you,' she covered her face with her hands. 'I was worried what you would think of me,' she continued sobbing.

She appeared to be hurtling towards a nervous breakdown, mumbling all the while. 'Nothing that I do turns out to be good. One thing I wanted to do in life and even that I can't do properly. You will also start hating me now. Why does this happen to me? It always does, it always does.' She started howling even louder.

A worried Aditya slid towards her on the sofa. When he was within arm's length, he reached out and hugged her. 'Calm down, calm down. It's okay,' he consoled her. He held her head against his shoulder, trying to pacify her.

'It's okay. Rejections are common in this trade.' It was an uncomfortable posture for him. He could feel the softness of her breasts pressing against his chest. It was turning him on. He was worried. He couldn't be seen getting turned on especially at a time when she was going through trauma. He abruptly released his hold. She didn't show any signs of moving away. He let her be for some time, forcibly trying to bring some other thoughts to his mind, to distract himself. After a couple of minutes, when he felt that she had calmed down, he pulled himself away.

'Look, Shreya,' he began, 'it's no big deal.'

'It is, Aditya. For me it is,' she screamed. It took him by surprise. 'You can afford to say it's no big deal. I cannot,' she howled. 'I have given it my sweat and blood. Who is that fucking editor sitting in a godforsaken publishing house to take a call on my book and on me? I bet they can't write a line for nuts.'

'That is not what I meant, Shreya.'

'Then what did you mean?' she cried. 'Don't demean my

effort. What's the difference between you and the goddamn publisher?'

Aditya kept calm. 'You know, Shreya, it is not about you or your writing. In publishing no one knows what will do well and what will not. Sometimes the best-written books fail and the miserable ones do well. It's also a matter of luck. The editors just go by their instinct. Unfortunately your manuscript may have landed up on the table of an editor who does not appreciate your style of writing. That's it. It doesn't in any way mean that you are bad. I always advise new authors to reach out to a publisher through an agent or through someone they know. There is no point sending the manuscript directly. Those that are sent directly go into a slush pile,' he finished.

'Slush pile?' Shreya asked.

'Yes. That's what the publishers call a pile of unsolicited manuscripts. Do you really think they have time to read thousands of manuscripts that land at their doorsteps? The easiest thing is to flip through it. See if there is anything worthwhile as per their limited vision. If not, they just dump it. A lottery gives you a better chance at success than getting a book published. I haven't seen anyone cry over not winning a lottery. Then why cry over a book contract? I just wish you had told me about this manuscript. I would have pushed it with publishers. Some of them do listen to me.'

'Maybe. In any case I had sent it to them before I joined the bank. I wanted to succeed on my own,' Shreya said. She looked at him and then at the letter on the table and tears started to flow again. However, this time she was not hysterical, nor was she sobbing. Aditya went closer to her and hugged her. She hugged him back. 'Thank you, Aditya,' she said.

'Send me the manuscript.'

'I will after refining it a bit. Now that it has to go to the biggest author in India. Might as well rework it and bring it up to his standard.'

'Whenever you are ready,' he tightened the embrace.

She felt his grip tighten around her and, after momentarily jerking her body, eased into his embrace. They stayed there for a long time, Aditya stroking her back and Shreya lying with her head on his shoulders. His shirt had become wet with her tears, where her head rested. He didn't care. Her hair cascaded down, right next to his face. It smelled wonderful. He inhaled the fragrance and then in a momentary lapse of self-control, planted a kiss on her bare neck. She let go of him instantaneously as if hit by an electric current and pulled back. She looked at him, right into his eyes. Her face was in front of his. For a fleeting moment he glanced down, just to escape looking at her face and could see her nipples taut against the thin cotton of the t-shirt.

He moved his glance upwards to meet hers. This time, her eyes held a soft appeal. An invitation he couldn't resist. He inched closer. She waited. He moved a bit forward. She closed her eyes. Their lips met. As if on cue, she parted her lips and kissed him passionately.

His hands had moved to her lower back. He subtly tugged at the t-shirt, which slid up her velvety skin as his hands felt her cool, bare back. Their lips were still glued together. His hands slipped under the T-shirt and worked their way up making her shiver in excitement. Her hands moved from his back to his chest. From there they slid slowly downwards. She tugged at his belt, but couldn't pull it open. She let it be and moved further down. She could feel his excitement. The bulge was evident. Her palm came to rest on his bulge even as her fingers fumbled with the zipper. It didn't take her long to force it open. Her fingers deftly slid in through the gap and pulled at the elastic of his underwear.

That's when Aditya snapped out of the trance-like state he was in.

He suddenly let go of her and stood up. 'No, stop. This is not right,' he whispered. He walked to the window at the far end of the room. The sun had set by then. 'No . . .!' he screamed. He strode back to where she was sitting, picked up his bag, his jacket and walked straight out of the room, without saying a word. He owed it to Maya and Aryan. At least for their sake, he could not stray. He repeated this over and over again to himself, as he got into his car and drove home.

He parked in the basement car park and sat there for ten minutes as the events of the day played out in his mind, as if on loop. A couple of times he shook his head and muttered a few expletives under his breath. Finally he stepped out of the car and rode the elevator to his tenth floor residence. The bag was in his hand and the jacket was neatly folded over his forearm. He casually looked at himself in the elevator mirror. He could see a few strands of white hair. And then he saw it . . . He froze.

In his reflection he could see a small patch on his shirt. The portion of the shirt around his shoulder had become damp because of Shreya's tears. Not only was it damp, it had also become blackish, for some of Shreya's mascara had run onto it. He panicked. He tried to rub it off, but it only got worse. The lift stopped on the tenth floor. Sensing no other option he hurriedly wore the jacket and buttoned it up, so as to obviate any possibility of the damp patch showing up. The jacket hid the patch. In any case the shirt would go for dry-cleaning. So, as long as he was able to hide it when he got inside the house, and dumped the shirt into the dry-cleaning basket, Maya would be none the wiser.

When he nervously rang the bell, Maya opened the door. After hugging her briefly he quietly escaped to the safe confines of the bedroom to change.

'Should I set the table?' Maya queried as he was entering the bedroom. 'Yes. I'll be out in a minute,' he said and shut the door. Once inside the room, he hurriedly removed the suit, dumped the shirt and changed into his regular shorts and t-shirt. The problem was solved for now.

Maya was waiting for him at the dining table. Aryan had gone for a sleepover.

'So?'

'So? What "so"?' Aditya asked.

'So your girlfriend kept you busy today?'

The colour drained from Aditya's face.

23

'WHAT ARE YOU talking about?' he asked even as beads of sweat formed on his forehead.

'I just asked if your girlfriend is keeping you busy these days,' Maya reiterated.

'Rubbish. I don't know what you are saying,' Aditya responded. If he could, he would have run away from the table. He couldn't look Maya in the eye. He looked around the room—the table, food, a copy of *Business Today* magazine, an AC remote and a few unopened mails.

'Well you only said that your girlfriend is keeping you busy these days.'

'Me?' He was surprised. 'When did I say anything like that?' he feigned irritation.

'Here?' she handed him a copy of *Business Today*. Nervously Aditya took the magazine from her.

Maya had opened a page for him. The Grishams of Banking was the title on the page. It was an article on how Indian bankers were taking to writing books as if it were going out of fashion. There were interviews with Ravi Subramanian, Amish Tripathi and himself, all bankers. He knew this story was to come, but didn't know that it was slotted for the current issue. On the marked page was a Q&A with him. Question number six had been highlighted with a blue highlighter.

> **Have you ever considered becoming a full time author?**

Maya had highlighted the response too.

> **My job is like my spouse and writing is like my girlfriend. When I started writing it didn't take up much time. But now with a lot of time being dedicated to promotions, my girlfriend has started demanding more attention and is taking up the bulk of my time. But my spouse is not complaining yet. The day the spouse starts complaining, the day I feel I can't handle my job along with my writing, I will have to make a choice.**

It was the last line, which Maya had circled and highlighted. **As of now I am very happy managing both my wife and my girlfriend.**

He looked at her and smiled, relieved.

'Why were you so shocked when I asked you about your girlfriend?' Maya asked.

'What else? I come home and the first thing you ask me is about my girlfriend. I got worried as to what happened to you.'

'Oh my baby!' Maya hugged him and led him to the table for dinner. 'I am so lucky we have each other. It's going to be fifteen years this August.'

'Seems like yesterday, baby,' a relieved Aditya echoed her thoughts.

24

THAT NIGHT, WHILE working on his book, Aditya kept going back to his phone to see if there was a message from Shreya. There was none. Was she angry? Was she upset? Would she complain about him to HR? She hadn't invited him home that evening. He had sought her out and gone.

But then wasn't she the one who initiated the kiss? Or was it his doing? Irrespective, she was a willing party to it. His final reaction, though, had been sudden and rude. He should not have just picked up his bag and walked away like that. Poor thing . . . she was in grief. Rather than help her settle down, he made it worse for her by rushing out of her house.

He picked up the phone and typed a message.

<I am sorry. I behaved weirdly today. I should not have kissed you.>

He pressed the send button and looked at the clock on the screen. It showed 11.42 pm.

Till 12.58 there was no response. He typed three follow-up messages and deleted all three before he could send them. He didn't want to push her. Till the time he went to sleep at 2.30, Shreya had not responded.

When he woke up at six he found a message waiting for him.
<We will talk.>

25

WHEN ADITYA WALKED into office the next day, his eyes went to the corner where Shreya's workstation was—the only corner where the lights were on. To g[...] he had to cross a stretch wherein Shre[...] directly. There was no way he was goi[...] walked on and looked at her as he pa[...] stared back at him. Without saying a [...] straight to his room.

After dumping his bag, he sat do[wn...] mind was blank. The best-laid plans can be foiled by the trepidations of an anxious and nervous mind.

He took out his laptop and kept it on his table. His mind was away, revisiting the incidents of last night again and again, when a knock on his cabin door, brought him back to reality.

'You didn't like the kiss?'

The question was like a bolt from the blue. 'What?' he asked.

'You heard me. You didn't like it?' Shreya asked with a straight face.

Aditya looked at her, confused.

'Why else would you not even acknowledge my presence and walk in without even saying hello?'

'Oh. No . . . I don't know . . . last night . . . I am . . .'

'Aditya,' she called his name firmly, 'relax.'

Aditya stopped talking and looked at her. It was difficult to make out who the boss was.

'What happened last night was in the spur of the moment. why are you killing yourself over it?'

have happened, Shreya. I am your

ecause you are my supervisor, we can't

nt, Shreya. I am married. I have a family.'

10re worried about it than you?'

Aditya was surprised at her belligerent approach.

'I am not saying it's a desirable scenario. Neither you nor I had any control over it. I always prefer going with the flow rather than planning ahead. It's always worked well for me in life. See, yesterday you promised to get my book published. It means more to me than anything else in life. I would in any case have kissed you out of joy.'

Aditya was speechless.

'Do you love your wife any less because you kissed me?' she asked him.

Aditya thought about it for a few seconds, and then some more. Finally he shrugged his shoulders and shook his head. 'No.'

'Then why do I sense regret?'

'Hmm . . .' Aditya didn't know what else to say.

'Anyway, think about it. I'm going to HR. I'll come back and talk to you.'

'HR?' For a moment Aditya was terrified.

Shreya giggled. 'Not to complain, silly. They called for some forms. I'm going to complete them.'

'Oh. Okay,' he smiled for the first time that day.

'And by the way, don't forget your promise of helping me get published.'

'Of course. I will do whatever I can,' Aditya said, as Shreya turned to go back to her desk to pick up something. Before the door to the cabin shut again, she pushed it open winked at him and whispered, 'Did anyone tell you that you are a fabulous kisser? Don't know how you felt, but I loved what you did last night.'

'Me too,' Aditya said. He felt like an idiot having worried the whole night before about what Shreya might think of him.

Though he briefly regretted what had happened, his mind was a whirlpool of emotions. He couldn't deny that he had liked it too. However, he was grappling with the effects that the counterfeit pleasure of an adulterous affair could have on his family.

Shreya was back in half an hour.

'Coffee?'

'No, Shreya. Give me some time. I need to send out this report.'

'Can I help?'

Aditya smiled. 'It's okay. I have come to terms with last night. So you don't need to indulge me,' he said.

'Ever considered the fact that I might like indulging you?' Shreya drawled, and as an afterthought, added, 'Irrespective of last night.'

'I didn't know kids these days were so smart,' Aditya winked at her.

'Kids? You go around kissing kids the way you did last night, Aditya?' she said with a naughty look on her face.

The kiss had suddenly become a tool to tease each other.

'Haha! Mad girl,' Aditya laughed it off.

'What did you do last night, after you went back? Don't tell me you were thinking of it all through?'

'I was. In fact, while waiting for your response, I wrote the last chapter of my book.'

'Wow. Finished?'

'Hmm,' he nodded his head.

'When are you giving it to me to read?'

'It's only the first draft.'

'How does that matter? I want to see how star authors write. Whether their first draft is very different from what lesser mortals like me produce.'

'Shut up. Just say that you want to read it before the others.'

'Whatever gets you to sleep well at night. Have it your way. Happy? Now tell me when are you giving it to me to read?'

'If you promise not to be in a hurry to judge it, I will send it to you right away.'

'If I have to judge you by your writing, you must know by now, I will start with a bias. And after yesterday, if I have to judge you by the way you handle women, you will still hold an advantage,' Shreya said. The corners of her eyes crinkled as she smiled. She winked as she shut the door and moved back to her seat.

In the next five minutes Aditya logged into his iCloud and mailed Shreya a copy of his next book. Even Maya had not read it yet.

26

'Have a safe flight,' Aditya said as he hugged Maya just before she entered the Mumbai international airport along with a team of fifty-eight students and two other teachers. Aryan was super thrilled about going with them.

After seeing them off at the departure gate of the Mumbai airport, Aditya rushed to the other side—the arrival gate. Shreya was waiting there for Sunaina who was arriving from Dubai.

'Her flight has come. She is at immigration,' Shreya announced cheerfully.

'Great. So she should be out soon.'

'Hopefully.'

'Did you read my manuscript? You told me in the morning that you have forty pages to go.'

'Yes, I did.'

'That's it? "Yes, I did!"' he exclaimed. 'Isn't there something called feedback?'

'Of course there is. But everything has a price. Take me out for a drink and I will give you my feedback.'

'Umm . . .'

'This is not the time for "Umm". When are you taking

me out for a drink? I will only give you feedback if you indulge me.'

'Well,' Aditya smiled, and with a naughty look on his face said, 'care to elaborate on what you mean when you say indulge me?'

Shreya waved her hand, 'Just, tell me when?'

'We could have gone now, but your friend is here.'

'Tomorrow? What say?' Shreya asked.

'Whenever you say and wherever you want.'

'Let's go to some nice place, where we can sit, chit-chat, be ourselves.'

'No better place than home. At least we don't run the risk of people seeing us,' Aditya offered.

'Not my place. There are other people around.'

'The last I checked, I had a house in Mumbai too.'

'Aaaah . . . that way. You sure you want to invite me home?' She had a naughty suggestive grin on her face.

Aditya smiled.

'You won't regret inviting me over? We do have a history,' Shreya said playfully.

'Not at all. I have never regretted anything in life.'

'Except maybe kissing a hot bitch,' Shreya laughed at him.

'You mean a super hot author.' Aditya knew she liked being called that.

Shreya latched on immediately. 'No. Not yet. I'm not an author yet. That will be once you set me up with a publisher. And from the looks of it, Mr Kapoor, you don't seem to be doing anything on that front.'

'Normally when you approach a publisher, you send a manuscript. At least that's the way it used to be,' Aditya replied.

'I will bring it when I meet you tomorrow.'

'Hey Shreya!' A loud exclamation broke up their discussion. She turned and looked towards the arrival gate.

'Sunainaaaaaa!' Shreya screamed and ran to hug her. 'So good to see you, babes. Was beginning to miss you,' Sunaina reacted to her squeal.

Sunaina was pleasantly surprised to see Aditya at the airport. 'I haven't read your books, Aditya. You must pardon me. But let me tell you, after your visit to IIM, my friend here has become a huge, huge fan of yours. So much so, that had you been single, she would have snapped you up.'

Aditya smiled shyly. He dropped both of them to Shreya's house and left.

Once they were in Shreya's room, Sunaina pounced on her, 'Is something cooking?'

'As in?'

'Are you guys seeing each other?'

'Not yet . . .'

'What do you mean not yet?'

'Not yet means not yet. It means I am not seeing him. I am happy just being with him. He is a nice guy. He can also get me to my ultimate objective of making a mark as an author. Fighting a lone battle in this field is tough, babes.'

'So you are using him. Why does everything have to have an underlying motive for you?'

'It's not like that.'

'Just watch out, Shreya. Someone will get hurt in this relationship—if I can call it one,' Sunaina cautioned. 'Either you, or him or his wife. This can only end in heartbreak and chaos.'

'I am in control of my emotions, babe. Trust me I am,' Shreya dismissed her concerns.

27

IN RELATIONSHIPS, PARTICULARLY those that are adulterous in nature, the first time is always the most difficult. That's the point in time when one's conscience makes its presence felt the most and people are consumed by regret. Once that bridge is crossed regret is often forgotten.

Aditya spent the entire Saturday in anticipation. He cleaned up the house to make sure that it was in good shape to welcome Shreya. He checked with her and made sure her favourite vodka was in stock. He ordered food from Little Italy well in advance. This was the first time she was coming home. He had even stocked up on condoms.

At 7 pm, he showered and started getting dressed. He sprayed on his favourite deodorant, and changed into his Armani jeans and a Tommy Hilfiger tee. He switched off the harsh chandelier and switched on the soft mood lights and waited for Shreya. The Italian pianist Einaudi's music was seductively streaming through his Bose home theatre.

It was 8 pm, by the time Shreya rang the bell. Aditya was surprised to see Sunaina in tow and could barely hide his disappointment. Sunaina sensed Aditya's displeasure. 'Just came along to say hi. Not staying back, so don't panic. I'm headed for a movie.'

Aditya's sigh of relief was so loud that Sunaina almost heard it. As she was leaving, she looked at Shreya and asked her, a twinkle in her eyes, 'Coming back tonight?' Shreya just smiled in response.

'You look sizzling,' Aditya commented when he shut the main door and walked behind Shreya into the living room. He was not making it up. Shreya was dressed in a stunning bush shirt held at the hip by a thin black belt. It gave a sexy, curve-hugging illusion that left Aditya mesmerized. She had left her hair open and it was falling over her shoulders so very gracefully, that she looked like she had stepped straight out of a fashion magazine.

She sashayed to the couch in the living room, removed her sandals and made herself comfortable. As she slid back to rest her back against the wall, her shirt slid up a few inches, revealing milky white, freshly waxed thighs. Aditya wanted to feast on them soon.

'What?' she asked him seductively. 'Now will you please stop staring at me and get my drink, please?'

Hurriedly he turned away and walked to the bar. 'What will you have?'

'Do you have olives?'

'Hmm . . . yes.'

'I will have a Martini then.'

'Ahaaa . . . Dirty Martini.' He turned to look at Shreya. The shirt had slid up a couple of inches more than the last time. Whether it was intentional or not, he couldn't tell. 'How dirty do you want your Martini?' he asked as he glanced back, simultaneously opening the bottle of vodka.

'How about,' she paused, looked at the ceiling and added, 'how about you make it ... filthyyyyy?' Filthy Martini was nothing but Dirty Martini with capers instead of olives, but the way she dragged the word, seemed to imply something much more.

He walked back to the couch with two glasses in hand—single malt on the rocks for himself and Filthy Martini for Shreya.

'There you go,' he said, handing over the glass to her. 'If you need anything more filthy ... I am here,' he said, laughing. She giggled.

Shreya took the glass from his hand and kept it on the side table. She dug into her bag and pulled out a large envelope. She handed over the packet to Aditya, 'My story.'

'Aah ...' Aditya suddenly got excited. 'So this is the one which created such a ruckus in your life.' He took the papers out of the envelope and flipped through them.

'You will help me publish this, right?'

'If I am not able to, no one else will, sweetheart.' As he said this, she extended her arms towards him. He slid next to her and hugged her. This time around, the hug was more intimate than the one in her house a few days back.

'But you read it first, before you send it to anyone else. And then tell me if it is worth getting published. Tell me if I have a future as an author.'

'I will, I will. But that reminds me, someone was to give me serious feedback on my book, over a drink.' He released her from the hug and his hands came to rest on her smooth thighs. 'If in the next thirty seconds you don't start, then don't blame me if I get seduced. You are looking like a naughty, sexy angel.'

'Okay enough,' she pushed him back. 'If you want me to give you serious pointers, then sit at least six feet away from me. No touching. No kissing.'

'What? This condition is unacceptable,' he thundered.

'You want me to tell you or not?'

'Okay. Your wish is my command,' he said and stepped back and sat on the sofa.

'All right,' she began. Aditya took a deep breath. He was nervous.

'I loved the manuscript.'

'Really?' Aditya grinned. Every author loves someone telling him that they loved his book.

Shreya nodded. 'Yes. I loved it.'

'And?'

'Hold on. Don't rush it.'

'Cool,' Aditya rested his back on the sofa and sat back. 'I won't interrupt.'

'I loved it because a) it is a great story b) it's brilliantly paced c) it ends very well d) the language is simple and easy and e) the characters are relatable. But . . .'

'But what?'

'I am a nobody here, Aditya . . .'

'As in?' Aditya looked at her suspiciously, wondering what was coming.

'I meant to say that you are obviously way more knowledgeable about this than I am, but I noticed some places where I felt that the sentence construction was not appropriate; some minor errors. I have made a few changes and I also felt that in one aspect, you need to fundamentally change your approach.'

'So the management trainee is going to give some English lessons to the business head?' Aditya cocked his head.

Shreya looked away. 'Okay, forget it. I will not send you those corrections. I should've known better than . . .' she didn't finish her sentence and looked away.

Aditya looked at her fondly and smiled. 'Thanks, Shreya. Send it to me on a soft copy. I will take a look.'

Shreya's face lit up. 'Really? You will take a look at it? Wow! I am so thrilled.' A big smile adorned her face. 'I've already made the changes on the printout. You can go through them. This is what sets you apart. You are so open to feedback, something which no other author of your stature will be.'

'Doesn't feedback help you improve? Anyway what about that one fundamental change in approach or something you mentioned?'

Shreya looked at him, and without demonstrating any emotion said, 'The sex in the book is cold. It is *thanda*. I wonder how a person, who is such a fabulous kisser, writes such drab sex scenes.'

Aditya didn't say anything. This was feedback he had not expected. He tried to rationalise. 'I guess I am uncomfortable writing about sex.'

'Then why write about it? I am sure you can figure out a way to make it classy without talking about it.'

'I kind of just touch upon the topic and move on. I leave it to the reader's interpretation.'

'Not having erotic content is better than having a horribly written sex scene. Bad sex is a huge turn off.'

'Is it really that bad?'

Shreya nodded her head, 'Yes, it is.' She thought for a while and said, 'Clumsy, yes, clumsy is the right word.'

'I tried a lot, Shreya. I even rewrote every sequence multiple times. But, I don't know why, it never comes out right for me.'

'Apart from that everything in the book is super; a winner all the way. Figure out a way to fix it,' she said.

'Let me rework those portions. I will critically re-examine them,' Aditya said as he walked to refill his glass of whisky. 'Another Filthy Martini?'

'Halfway through mine. Maybe later,' Shreya said. 'Tell me, Aditya, that day when you kissed me, did you think of me when you came back home?'

'How could I not? You kiss fabulously and I haven't been kissed like that in a while.'

'Really?'

He turned from the kitchen counter and took one hard look at her. Is this luck? Or do relationships grow like this organically? Her comment about the sex in his books being cold was bothering him. Was her interpretation of the sex in his books an extension of her impression of him?

'What is taking so long?' she asked from the couch.

'In a minute,' he replied.

As he walked back into the room, she noticed a slight frown on his face.

'What's that frown for?'

'I am not frowning.'

'Yes you are,' she insisted.

'Am I?'

'Okay, now you are in denial. What's bothering you?' she pursued the conversation, but got no response. She smiled. 'I think I know,' she said.

'What do you know?' he asked, curious. How could she know that he was upset at her calling the sex in his book *thanda*.

Before responding, she turned, and began by first stretching her legs, letting her dress ride up further, and then folding her knees, bringing them to her chest, giving him a good look straight down her legs, and between her thighs.

He took in a long breath. Surely she knew what she was doing. The glint in her eyes confirmed that.

'Do you like what you see?' she asked.

'Shreya!' He let escape involuntarily, as he walked straight upto her and knelt down by her feet. 'You have the most awesome legs that I have ever seen.' He ran his fingers up her velvety thighs.

She slapped him on his fingers. 'Stop teasing me. You pervert!' she laughed. 'And move your hands off my thighs. You are tickling me.' Aditya didn't say a word. He just sat down at her feet and continued running his hands up her thighs.

'I am sorry I upset you by saying your sex was cold,' Shreya began. 'It was your book. You are amazing.'

Aditya looked up. Shreya's face was very close to his. 'I

know my sex is not cold. It could well be that I didn't have the right inspiration while writing!' he quipped.

'Oh really!' she said, setting her glass aside. 'Sing for your supper! Seduce me!' she responded.

'I hoped you'd say put your money where your mouth is,' he replied cheesily, and began to laugh.

She began to laugh too and dragged him down by his shirt, covering his mouth with hers. Their moans resonated in the room. 'Kiss me baby,' said Aditya, passion dripping from every word.

As he fell into her arms, kissing her hungrily, he didn't notice her take something out of her clutch, and leaving it on the side table, a small red light blinking on the device.

She pulled back for a brief second, 'You are indeed a damn good kisser. Fuck!' she said.

'It is the inspiration,' he laughed again.

'Tell me how you would make love to me,' she said.

Like a dog in training, he immediately began, first by planting small kisses on her neck, then her collarbone.

'Stop, stop, stop,' she said. 'Keep the commentary on. I like to listen.'

'I will . . .' he was breathing heavily.

'You will . . .?'

'I will kiss you on your neck, the side of your neck, down to your shoulders,' and he paused, for he was licking his way to Shreya's shoulder bones. 'I will slide down your body, licking my way down to your breasts—your glorious mounds of flesh.'

'Oh baby!' Shreya moaned as Aditya slid down her body,

reaching between her breasts. 'Aah,' she moaned, as he began to unbutton her shirt, slowly, one button at a time, stopping at the thin belt that held it in place. 'Hold on, baby. Don't remove my shirt. Slow.'

'I want you naked in my bed,' Aditya said as he ignored her protests, which were in any case cursory.

'Go on then!' she instructed impatiently.

'Shush!' he said and then let his lips linger on hers. 'I will silence you with my kiss,' he murmured as he smelled the vodka on her breath. Strangely it turned him on further. 'For the first time vodka tastes so intoxicating,' he whispered. She adjusted herself beneath him to give him leeway to manoeuvre himself.

'Oh my gawddd,' he exclaimed as he opened her shirt, discovering she wasn't wearing a brassierie. 'You are faster than I thought, my pussy cat,' he exclaimed. 'You just saved me the trouble of ripping off your bra.' Glee spread across his face, like a little boy who had just been given candies to suck on. Without any delay, he bent down and took her right nipple in his mouth, wetting it and rolling his tongue gently in circles. 'Go slow on my nipples baby, they are sensitive,' Shreya's voice was hoarse.

'I can see that. Oh my god! he exclaimed. 'Look at them. Ohhhh! How much I love them,' he muttered as his tongue unleashed a fierce lapping on her right nipple as his hand mauled the left one.

'Fuck!' she exclaimed. 'I have unleashed a monster.'

He lifted his head up and said, 'You haven't seen him yet!' and grinned.

She giggled and began to ruffle his hair, and pushed him back down her body.

He obliged, immediately, leaving small kisses down her abdomen, and lifting her shirt over her hip, reached the edge of her panties.

She sucked in her breath loudly.

'I love lace,' he said and inserted a finger on either side of the panties. Just when he was ready to pull them down . . .

'Stop!' she said, 'Aditya, stop!' There was a firmness in her voice. She meant what she said.

'Something wrong?' he looked up with a start.

She was smiling, which perplexed him a bit, but she began pushing him back, and then proceeded to sit on him.

'You are good!' she said. 'Your lips on my nipples felt like heaven, Aditya.' He smiled back, and pulling her down kissed her hungrily. She gave in. She unbuttoned her shirt further, and pushing him down again, ran her nipple along his lips. 'Oh my god. These are awesome. Your boobs are the best I have ever seen,' Aditya panted.

'How many have you seen, lover boy?' she asked teasingly.

Aditya ignored the question and reached out with his right hand. His left went behind her and caressed her butt.

That was when Shreya stood up. 'I want this badly, but we have to stop now,' she said.

Aditya was aghast. 'WHAT, Shreya?'

'Yes, my darling. I wanted to show you that you can seduce a girl into doing what you want. And that if you think about it, you can write it like it is too! And if you still feel words fail you . . .' She reached back to the device she had left on the side table, 'Here! Replay the audio, and write it as it is,' she said and gave him the small device, an audio recorder which was connected to her iPhone. 'Connect it, download it to your iPhone and listen to it whenever you need inspiration to write a sex scene. If you write the way you make love, no one can beat you at erotica, Aditya. Not even EL James.'

There was a flood of emotion in him, going from surprise, to anger, to confusion, back to anger again, which she noticed.

She responded by taking his face in her hands. 'Don't be angry, Aditya, please don't. Think of it as great foreplay. And you are a super seducer. I promise we will pick up where we left off!' She stood up and began to button up her shirt. In no time she had worn her clothes and was out of the house. A stunned Aditya didn't even have time to react.

She had only been out of the house for five minutes when she SMS'd him, <Let's not hurry it up. The fun is in the chase.>

<Of course> was all he could say.

His iPhone beeped in a few seconds. Shreya had messaged again.

<Don't forget to read my manuscript and send it to the publishers. Your word will matter.>

He replied: <YWIMC>

<??>

<Your Wish is My Command :)>

28

MAYA CALLED SOON after Shreya left. Aditya freaked out, thanking his stars that she hadn't called when Shreya was around.

'Everything okay?' she asked him.

'You mean except the fact that you are not here?' Aditya flirted.

'Shut up, I am sure you must be having a lot of fun with that girlfriend of yours,' Maya joked. Aditya managed a chuckle. Aryan came on line. They coochie-cooed for a bit, and then hung up.

After taking a bottle of water from the refrigerator, he switched off the lights and was walking towards his bedroom, when he saw the neat spiral-bound copy of Shreya's manuscript lying on the dining table and picked it up. It was a short manuscript. His estimate was that it would make a 175-page book, were it to be published in the form that it was in.

It was a story set against the backdrop of the Maoist insurgency. The story was about a girl from a small village in Chhattisgarh; a girl who at the age of twelve is raped by the village chieftain and then saved by an NGO worker. It was a tragic story, where the NGO worker's wife eventually dies and he ends up marrying the same girl whom he saves. Very different from the thrillers that Aditya was used to writing, or reading.

★

Aditya was woken up by the incessant ringing of his doorbell.

Hurriedly Aditya got up and ran to the door. Sunaina and Shreya were standing there with a couple of bags in hand. Aditya looked around, just to make sure that none of the neighbours had heard the girls scream and jump in the corridor.

'Breakfast!' Shreya held up a bag, as she walked in. Sunaina just shrugged her shoulders. 'I was just dragged by your friend. Don't blame me for intruding.'

'Not at all. You are a friend too,' Aditya responded, though the conviction was missing. He excused himself and walked into his bedroom to freshen up.

When he came out, he walked up to them and sat down on the chair next to Shreya. Aditya opened the casserole and pulled out two *aloo paranthas* and served himself.

'So?' Shreya asked.

'So?' Aditya looked at her surprised, wondering what she meant.

'So, how is it?'

'The *aloo paranthas* are awesome!'

'No, not *aloo paranthas*. The book . . .'

'Aaah . . . I will tell you. Let me first finish my breakfast.'

'Shut up and tell me now,' she pulled Aditya's plate from him, much to Sunaina's amusement.

'What makes you think I have read it?' Aditya put up a facade.

'Because you were "last seen" on your WhatsApp at 3.50 am, and there is no way you would be up for anything else for so long.' Shreya was determined.

'Okay, okay. You ask the questions, I will answer.'

'How was it, damn it?' she yelled.

'I loved it,' Aditya said, licking his fingers.

'Really?' Shreya's hands went up to her face and cupped her cheeks. Her eyes glistened with tears of joy.

'It's a nice story, very emotional. I loved the way you have depicted the girl's life—her thoughts, her fears, the trauma and finally the ecstasy when the NGO guy proposes marriage.'

'Why then did the publishers reject my book?'

'One did, right? Where did the plural come in from?' Aditya corrected her. 'We need to take it to other publishers, the bigger ones.'

'YOU will take it to them. Not WE.'

'Yes, fine. I will. Send me the soft copy and a brief bio of yourself.'

'A biodata?'

'Yes. Publishers love marketable authors. If an author is an MBA, or well qualified, foreign educated, young, well-networked, he or she finds many backers. This is because the publishers know that they will be able to sell a significant number of copies in the author's own personal network.'

'Sounds elementary when you hear it, yet nobody thinks of these things,' Sunaina stepped into the conversation.

'That's why we have the biggest commercial fiction writer in India backing us,' Shreya said, as Aditya's chest swelled a few inches with pride. 'I am just going to sit back and watch the famous Aditya Kapoor take me under his wings and make me fly high.'

Aditya smiled at both of them and said in a mock-serious tone, 'Your dreams are mine now.' Everyone started laughing.

On the way back, Sunaina again confronted Shreya. 'He is completely besotted with you. Don't lead him up the garden path.'

'Not at all, Sunaina. What makes you think so?'

'You guys fooled around?' she asked abruptly.

'What? Oh wow! That was pretty straight,' Shreya was taken aback at the sudden question. 'You want to know if we had sex?'

'Yes, I do. So tell me?'

'We flirt a bit, we kissed once but no sex yet.'

'You kissed? Shreya, you kissed him?' Sunaina was surprised.

'Infact, he kissed me. In one of those weak moments I kissed him back too. What's the big deal?'

'No sex?'

'Nope. Just a little petting.'

'Why?'

'What is this? An interrogation? An exposition of my sex life, Sunaina?'

'Just felt like asking. Chill!'

'I have a feeling that the day we have sex, the day we fuck, regret will kill him. He wants me, but feels guilty about our relationship. He is into me, but he is not out of his family. He wants the best of both worlds.'

29

SHREYA CAME IN late that morning.

'How was the apartment? Any good?' Aditya asked her. He knew that Sunaina and Shreya had gone to check out an apartment to rent.

'It was kind of average. One of the bedrooms is small. Sunaina is fine with it. But rent is an issue.'

'Rent?'

'The *Indian Express* does not really pay her too much. So she will have a problem with the rent.'

'Tell me,' Aditya interrupted her, 'why on earth did she join the *Indian Express* after an MBA from IIM Bengaluru? Do you want me to check out something for her here? In the bank?'

'Can we talk about that later?' Shreya said, irritated at Aditya's sudden surge of interest in Sunaina.

'Sorry, sorry,' Aditya smiled as he patted her on her back. 'What were you saying?'

'I told her that since she will be taking the smaller room, I will pay a larger portion of the rent. If we do that, it will work out for her.'

'Great. So a big issue is settled for you.'

'The biggest remains . . .'

Aditya looked at her with apprehension. He didn't understand what she meant.

'The book?' Shreya rolled her eyes.

'Oh yes,' Aditya gave her a big smile. 'Don't fret over it. I will get it done. I am sending it out to publishers today.'

'Thanks, Aditya. I owe you a big . . .' The ring of Aditya's phone cut short her commentary.

'Someone here to meet you,' the receptionist's voice came on the line.

'Who?'

'A Mr Nikhil Raut?'

'I don't know him.'

'He says he wants to meet you.'

Aditya's mobile phone beeped. It was a message. Aditya read it and went back to the phone.

'Ask them to wait. Get Sanjay to come down.' He hung up the phone.

'What happened?' Shreya asked him. From the expression on his face, she knew something was wrong.

He showed her his phone. On the screen was a message from the reception desk.

<He is here with some sixty people. Is threatening to forcibly enter if you don't come down. I have asked Chris to also come ASAP.>

★

By the time Aditya came down from his room, the crowd had swelled to over seventy-five people. Strangely they were all standing quietly. Sanjay had also come down by then. The receptionist pointed towards the largest conference room on the ground floor. Both of them walked towards it.

Nikhil Raut was a dangerous-looking man. He looked every inch a *pehelwan* from the *akharas* of Lucknow.

'Maharashtra Rakshak Sene,' he thundered. 'I don't think we need an introduction.'

'What is it that you want?' Aditya asked him. The door opened and Christopher John, head of branch security, walked into the room. He strode up to Aditya and stood by his side, arms crossed.

'I believe you are sacking some 500 people.'

'We hire based on growth requirements and let go of our employees based on business compulsions. It is a regular process. Why should it concern you?' Sanjay countered.

'How many Maharashtrians are there in the list of people being sacked?'

'Looks like you did not hear what our HR head just said. We cannot confirm anything,' Christopher stepped in, trying to take charge.

Nikhil leaned forward and read Christopher's name off his badge and said, 'Mr John, I would suggest you take a walk around and then decide whether you really want to answer my question or not.' As Christopher did not budge Nikhil Raut continued, 'There are over a hundred people patiently waiting outside for my instructions.'

Sanjay, Aditya and Chris, all knew that MRS was a local hardline political party which had taken the aggressive, nuisance-creating way to popular appeal. By espousing the cause of the Maharashtrian population, and by claiming to be the custodians of their well-being, they had appealed to the senses of the masses. They were here, supposedly, to support the cause of the employees being sacked. Clearly some disgruntled soul from National Bank had gone to them.

Christopher took the lead in the conversation. 'Let me explain. There seems to be some confusion,' he attempted.

'How many Biharis are being sacked? And how many Maharashtrians?' Raut demanded.

'Mr Raut, we do not tolerate any external interference in our internal issues. We don't discriminate based on regional affiliations. If at all we sack anyone, it will be as per our internal approvals and we will also be compensating people for their loss of jobs. We take care of our people, you see,' Sanjay was curt.

'Don't give me this bullshit!' Nikhil roared, prompting Sanjay to cast a worried look at Christopher, who simply nodded his head, as if imploring Sanjay to keep calm. 'Can I get you some tea?' he asked Nikhil Raut, ignoring his tirade. 'We can then sit and talk peacefully.'

'Look here, Mr John. I came here to meet you guys and tell you that even if one Maharashtrian is harmed, we will make sure that your bank is thrown out of this country.' He raised his index finger and pointed at Aditya and Sanjay, 'Take that as a warning.'

At that precise moment, the door opened and two people walked in.

'Back to your old ways, Mr Raut?' One of the two looked directly at Nikhil Raut and addressed him sternly.

'I will not allow a single Maharashtrian to lose his job,' Nikhil Raut said, but in a lower pitch and politer tone.

'Has anyone got sacked?' the man asked Nikhil. Christopher John smiled. He knew the man who had walked in.

'Not yet, but soon. They will get sacked soon. That's their plan,' Nikhil spat out.

'We will see when they get sacked. Right now, ask your rowdies to clear the main gate,' the man said. He seemed least interested in what Raut had to say. 'If they don't, I will ask my team to drive them out,' he said firmly.

Realising that the person meant business, Nikhil repeated his warning once again and walked out of the door promising to be back again.

'Thank you, sir.' Christopher John looked at the person who had helped them take on Nikhil Raut's aggression. He looked at Sanjay and Aditya and introduced them. 'Meet Sanjay, our Head of HR and Aditya Kapoor, Head of Branch banking.' He turned towards Aditya and Sanjay and said, 'Meet Sh. Ramesh Karia *ji*, the Commissioner of Mumbai Police.'

'Thanks for coming, sir,' Sanjay said.

'I was on my rounds of various police stations when the call came in. I decided to accompany the ACP to the bank,' Karia volunteered. He then turned towards Aditya and smiled. 'Well, who doesn't know Aditya Kapoor?' Ramesh Karia started off, much to Aditya's surprise. 'You are the person my police force needs to learn from. I keep telling them. These days it is important to learn from authors like you. What is important for the police is to start thinking creatively, as creatively as the criminals. That's where your crime thrillers come in handy. I've read all your books and I am a fan, Mr Kapoor.'

'Thank you, sir,' was all Aditya could say.

For the next twenty minutes the five of them talked about the core issue at hand and what precautions needed to be taken.

'As far as Nikhil Raut is concerned, if he creates any further issues, please call me directly. Cops and politicians have a lot of secrets. We need them, but they need us too. Nikhil Raut has many skeletons in his cupboard. I can get him to back down,' he assured them. He gave Aditya his personal number, shook his hand again and left. Aditya was floored by Ramesh Karia's humility, as were the others.

'I think he came only to meet you,' Sanjay said after the police commissioner had left the room.

'Well I am glad he did. It was his presence which neutralised Nikhil Raut,' Christopher John commented. 'Raut is known to be a chronic trouble creator. Hope he doesn't come back again.'

'Well, if he does, we will ask our friend here to call the commissioner of police,' Sanjay said and looked at Aditya, who just smiled at him.

30

'When will you make sure the Commissioner reads my book?' Shreya asked Aditya with fluttering eyelashes, the moment he told her about Ramesh Karia's dramatic entry.

Aditya laughed, 'I get the hint. I told you, didn't I, that I will send your manuscript out today?'

Shreya smiled and walked out of the room.

As she left, Aditya made a few calls. The first one was to his editor at Kiwi Books, Vaishali Mathur.

'I'm sending you a manuscript titled *The Girl from Chhattisgarh*, written by a colleague. I read it and found it interesting. It's definitely worth a try. Would you want to look at it?' he said after the customary greetings.

'You liked it?'

'I thought it was unique. Good story, nice pace and written well. The language is very good too. I would say it is much better than many of the crappy books that you publish these days.'

'You're forgetting we publish you too.'

'Hahaha! You know what I mean, right?' Aditya enjoyed a great relationship with Vaishali . She had been his editor for a few years now. More than an editor-author relationship, theirs had grown into a personal friendship. Vaishali knew Maya and Aryan, and would often visit them whenever she was in Mumbai. Professionally too, Aditya's growth as an author had rubbed off on her stature as an editor.

'Yes, I know. Anyway, let me read the manuscript and get back to you quickly.'

Aditya hung up and called a few other publishers and literary agents, post which he sent out Shreya's manuscript to all of them. He marked Shreya on the mails that he sent out.

Within five minutes, Shreya was at his door. 'Thank you,' she said peeping into the room, 'for sending out the manuscript. Hope something works out.'

'It will.'

'By when will they get back? When will you chase them up? I will keep reminding you.'

'I don't know, Shreya. But all I can tell you is that the publishing business works differently. Publishers are like potential love interests. The more you chase them, the more they run away from you and the more you let them be, the more they are drawn to you.'

'Okay. So?' she rolled her eyes.

'So we must let them be. Let's not chase them. They are not Aditya, who is so impressed by Shreya that he finished reading the manuscript overnight. They will take their own time. Let's wait. Chasing them reduces our ability to negotiate a deal.'

'Oh, okay. You are the boss,' Shreya said, making Aditya smile.

'Do we have a plan this evening?' he asked.

'We can make one,' she smiled and was leaving the room when she hastily turned and walked straight back. 'Before I forget . . . This mass retrenchment is really impacting our staff.'

'Isn't that expected? If I was a wealth manager, I would be worried.'

'I was standing outside with Sunaina at the tea shop across the road. We overheard a few of our staff standing there. They were saying that some people in the mainline branch banking team will also be losing their jobs.'

'No one but the identified wealth managers will lose jobs.'

'Yes, but this lady Diana Moses has apparently told some wealth managers that she will get some people from other parts of branch banking removed to accommodate them in those roles. They were saying to one another that Diana Moses has told some of them that she is going to play a key role in the realignment of people. That's what we could pick up . . .'

Aditya was surprised. So Diana was at it again. He decided to take it up with Sanjay.

31

THE MEETING WITH Tim was scheduled for two hours. The first hour was meant to be a steering committee meeting where all of Tim's direct reports were to be present. Worried about rising costs in the retail bank, Tim had constituted a task force, headed by Diana that was to work with all his direct reports, including Aditya, and come up with a recommendation on expense reductions.

The second part of the meeting was to be on the wealth management downsizing. But because of Nikhil Raut and his gimmicks the entire time was taken up by just downsizing talks.

Sanjay and Christopher updated Tim on Nikhil Raut's threat, and Ramesh Karia's intervention.

'Thank God at least there is one benefit accruing to the bank on account of your writing skills, Aditya,' Tim commented.

Aditya chose to ignore the barb. He turned and looked at Sanjay and said, 'No change in our plan because of Nikhil Raut or any of those jokers. We go ahead as usual.'

'Agreed.'

'You know, Tim, we cannot prevent these idiots from

creating nuisance for us. We need to be seen as a fair organisation. The worry could be that all the three hundred who are losing jobs are middle and junior management. If we are shutting down a business line, shouldn't we be seen as being fair to the staff across levels, and put a few senior managers on the line too?'

'But it's difficult to isolate senior managers who are in the wealth management vertical alone. We have to run the business in maintenance mode. We are not shutting it down completely,' Tim said.

'That's why, Tim, we need to cut dissonance by adding a couple of dispensable seniors to the list.'

'Okay, give me some names.'

'Diana Moses, and maybe one or two others.'

Sanjay was shocked. 'We are waiting for the right assignment for Diana Moses,' he argued. 'The moment we have one, she will be moved. She is a part of the Country Talent Pool,' he finished. The Country Talent Pool at National Bank was a pool of high-potential talented employees who had been identified as leaders for the future.

'But so are seventeen of the wealth managers who are being sacked. Think about it, Tim. She doesn't have a critical role right now. The product management role can be done by anyone significantly junior to her. It will be easier for us to sack her and justify the fact that we have been fair to seniors and juniors alike,' Aditya shrugged.

'Let me think about it,' Tim responded. 'We have just handed her the cost control project.'

'Till the time we agree on what to do with the seniors,

Tim and Sanjay, I would recommend that the decisions on people and their movement rest with the three of us,' Aditya asserted.

'Fair point,' Tim said.

As they exited the room, Sanjay looked at Aditya and said, 'What the fuck is your problem, Aditya? Why are you messing with Diana? If in your mind she is a demon, there is little anyone can do.'

'Well she has been going around telling people that she is the one in charge of redeployment of staff and hence people aligned to her will be the obvious beneficiaries,' Aditya retorted.

'Says who?'

'How does that matter?'

'Somebody might be misguiding you, Aditya. It's not like Diana to do such things.'

'Oh is that so? Why don't you ask her?' Aditya gritted his teeth in anger. 'If she wants to play god who everyone has to pray to for survival, then I am an atheist.'

'Of course I will ask her,' Sanjay said, as he walked away.

By the time Aditya got back to his office he realised Shreya had left. She had sent him an SMS just before leaving.

<8.30 pm, Out of the Blue. Cya.>

32

SHREYA AND SUNAINA were already at Out of the Blue when Aditya landed up at 8.45. The girls were feasting on their sangrias. Apparently it was their fourth already.

'Someone is looking gorgeous,' Aditya commented when he hugged Shreya. She was looking festive and lovely in her black and orange dress, which went well with her hair which was streaked red. The short-sleeved dress did nothing to conceal her ample curves. The dress featured a cut out at the shoulder and the back. With boots to complement her look and hair tied into a neat pony at the back, she looked a sight for sore eyes.

'Hello,' Sunaina waved her hands in front of Aditya's eyes. 'If you have finished admiring her, I am here too.' Aditya smiled and gave her a quick hug. They settled down and Aditya ordered his single malt. These days, with the younger generation, he knew that for girls, girlfriends were a lot more important than men. Men would come and go; girlfriends stoically remained at each other's side.

'Top it up, please,' Aditya instructed when the steward brought him his whisky. He always had single malt on the rocks, with ice cubes filling the glass.

Shreya looked exceptionally happy, almost like a kid at a birthday party. She was full of excitement and energy, laughing at every joke he cracked, fussing over him and taking care of what he wanted to order. All the attention that was being showered on him made him feel young all over again.

'You should tie up your hair like this even at work. It looks very elegant.'

'Really?' Shreya asked.

'Oh yeah. It looks awesome and quite classy. Isn't it easy for you to tie it this way? You have seen how that girl in the marketing team ties up her hair. She puts in so much effort and yet it looks repulsive.'

'Who, who? Which girl in marketing?' Shreya was curious.

'Oh that girl . . . what's her name . . . the one who handles deposits. She ties up her hair like . . .' Aditya lifted his hands and brought them up to his head, and twirled them in a crazy manner. While turning his head to the right, with hands over his ears, he saw someone and immediately stopped. 'Give me a minute,' he said as he got up.

'What happened?' Shreya wanted to know.

'Nothing. Just wanted to say hi to that guy . . . be right back,' Aditya responded. He walked to the table at the far end of the room.

Shreya and Sunaina looked at each other, perplexed, wondering who it was he was meeting. The suspense didn't stay for long as Aditya immediately returned and said, 'Give me ten minutes, I will be back.'

'Who is it?' Shreya asked.

'Anurag Kashyap.'

'Anurag who?' But by the time she finished her question, Aditya had already disappeared, back to the table in the corner of the room.

When he did finally come back after about twenty minutes he found Sunaina alone. Shreya was nowhere to be seen. He asked Sunaina, 'Where is she?'

'She left.'

'What?' He was taken aback. 'When?'

'Just a short while back.'

'Why?'

Sunaina just shrugged her shoulders.

Aditya hurried out of the restaurant. The traffic was heavy. He searched frantically, just in case Shreya was still around. He saw her. She was about thirty metres ahead of him trying to flag down an autorickshaw. 'Shreya!' he called out. She heard him, looked back and saw him. He waved. She ignored him and got into an autorickshaw and disappeared.

Aditya came back. Sunaina was still there. She didn't look half as stressed and anxious as he felt.

'It's okay. Chill,' she said. 'Let her be. She will be back to normal tomorrow.' Sunaina smiled reassuringly.

Aditya was a bit taken aback by Shreya's behaviour. He tried calling her but her phone was switched off.

'It's off, right?' Sunaina asked him. She had a wry smile on her face.

'Hmm.'

'I told you. Wait till tomorrow. It will automatically resolve itself. When she is angry, it's better to stay away from her.'

They finished their respective drinks, settled the bill and walked towards Aditya's car. Aditya dropped Sunaina back, and in deference to Sunaina's request didn't come up. He went back home. He messaged Shreya but she didn't respond.

33

VAISHALI CALLED HIM the next morning when he was on his way to work.

'Aditya, something is weird here. Actually many things are weird here.'

Aditya stretched back and ran his hand through his hair. It was growing unmanageably long. He needed a haircut. 'What happened?'

'I have read this manuscript before.'

'Maybe she did send it to Kiwi.'

'Maybe. But I can't trace it. A hard copy had come in. I guess we would have decided not to publish it and someone might have put it in the shredder.'

'Possible,' Aditya agreed. 'Don't know why she did not tell me that she had sent it to you already. In any case, what's weird about it?'

'Who is she, Aditya?'

'Oh, she is a colleague; a fresher, just out of college.'

'How does she know so much about naxalites and Chhattisgarh? This sounds like a true story. The earlier one did even more.'

'Earlier one?'

Vaishali ignored Aditya's question and rattled off another one. 'Aditya, are you in a relationship with her?'

'What? Hahaha . . .' Aditya laughed nervously, as if he had been caught with his pants down. 'No, no. Why do you ask?'

'Sorry. Even if you are, it is none of my business. I'm only asking because the earlier manuscript was slightly different.'

'English, sweetheart. Publishers must learn to speak in a comprehendible manner,' Aditya's tone was sarcastic.

'Okay, so there are three key differences from the earlier manuscript. In this one the male protagonist's name is Aditya. It was different in the earlier one. I would have let it pass, had it not been for a second reason. Aditya, the character, was the rapist, in the initial manuscript. In this he becomes the saviour. And to top it all, in the earlier manuscript he was single. In this, he is married and his wife leaves him after he becomes the protagonist's saviour. She eventually dies and he marries the protagonist. Do you get what I'm trying to say here?'

'I noticed the fact that the male lead was called Aditya. He is a good man and the female lead gets married to him in the end. I didn't have this backstory that you are giving me now, but despite that I don't think there's too much to it. I had mentioned to her that a tragic story with a happy ending will do well. Maybe that's why she changed the plot a bit. And I am her supervisor, Vaishali . She probably is just trying to keep me happy. Don't waste too much time thinking about it. Sucking up to supervisors for benefits is quite common in the corporate world. Don't tell me it doesn't happen in the world of publishing.'

'Hmm.'

'And what is an author without a few quirks. We have seen worse, haven't we? I know of at least two authors who insist on having a character named Aditya in their books. Don't I insist that we price my books in such a manner that the sum of the digits in the MRP of the book is five? Let her evolve her quirks, Vaishali . It's harmless.'

'I just wanted to let you know ... Sorry if you think I intruded,' Vaishali didn't sound entirely convinced.

'Don't worry, Vaishali . In any case, what do you think of it?'

'In its current form it is promising.'

'Make it happen, Vaishali . Please. I will put my weight behind it.'

'With you backing it, there is a good chance that we will buy it. Let's see.'

'Great!' he said as he entered the basement parking of his office building and Vaishali hung up.

34

Aditya had barely settled in his chair, when Shreya was at the door.

She knocked; something she usually didn't do.

He looked up and nodded.

'I am sorry, Aditya,' she said as she walked in.

'Sorry for what?' He didn't look irritated at all.

'For what I did yesterday.'

'It's okay. Long forgotten.' He smiled. It didn't look like he was pretending.

'No. I am an evil bitch. I . . . I . . . don't deserve to be forgiven.'

'But it's . . .'

'No. I was very selfish.'

'Fine. You were. But it's forgotten.'

'Don't you want to know what got me pissed?'

'Does it really matter? Something I did got you worked up. Now you feel you shouldn't have reacted quite so severely. So we are quits now, the matter dead and buried.'

She smiled. Her smile alone could light up a room, Aditya thought to himself.

'Did the publishers call back?' she asked all of a sudden.

'Oh.' He was about to tell her about the call with Vaishali but changed his mind. 'Actually, not yet . . . no.' Seeing the smile disappear, he added, 'In any case, we only sent it the day before. Give it at least a couple of weeks.'

'Do you think endorsement from a production house will help?'

'You mean a movie deal?'

'Hmm . . . yeah.' Almost as an afterthought, she added, 'That's what upset me yesterday. You went and met Anurag Kashyap alone. You could have taken me to meet him. It was a golden opportunity to tell him about my book. Before I could even tell you to introduce us, you had disappeared. At least the thought should have struck you.'

Aditya could see her eyes glistening. He knew that she was about to burst into tears. He walked up to her and put his arms around her. Through his peripheral vision, he was constantly on the lookout to see if there were any people around.

'Shreya. You need to relax. You have it in you to be a great author. Chill. Everything has a time and place. Had I got you to meet Anurag yesterday, it wouldn't even have registered. He was three drinks down. I would rather speak to him about the manuscript and the possible film options once things work out on the publishing side. Going to him now will be premature. You need to trust me.'

She looked up and smiled. 'I don't have anybody to trust but you, Aditya. I don't know anyone else.' She planted a quick kiss on his lips, before he even had time to react. 'I will make up for my behaviour yesterday,' she said as she walked back to her desk.

A few minutes later, a message sprung up on his office chat. 'Thank you for being such a wonderful person. I am glad I have you in my life.'

'In your life?'

'Shut up, not over here. On SMS'.

And within seconds his phone beeped.

<As if you don't know what you mean to me. Last night I felt so horrible, never felt like that before.>

<I have forgotten last night. Did anything happen? Remind me.> He messaged back.

Aditya went on flirting with Shreya, enjoying their time together.

Maya and Aryan came back that week from the US.

35

THE FINALISTS FOR the Crossword Book Awards, one of the premier book awards in India, were announced. Aditya's book had made it to the shortlist. He was on cloud nine. It was normal for any author who had reached the pinnacle of commercial success to look for critical recognition. Aditya was no different. And for him this was a big one—a shot in the arm for his self-esteem. The actual awards ceremony was still a month away. The moment he got to know of it, he wanted to call Shreya. He pulled up her number from his contact list and stopped. He did not press the dial button. He called Maya instead.

When he told Shreya about it later, she was super thrilled.

'Wow, Aditya. This is such great news. I am sure you will rock it,' Shreya enthused while Aditya just smiled.

'Is everything okay, Aditya? You are behaving very strangely these days. You still haven't forgotten the Out of the Blue event, right? I said I am sorry,' Shreya made a face.

'You are mad. I was just wondering how nice it would be if your book wins the award some day.' He tried to divert her attention.

'Oh, Aditya, I love you,' Shreya squealed with joy. 'I so wish your prophecies come true.'

'But for that, you must focus on getting the book in perfect shape. Focus. Focus gets results.'

'Of course, grandpa. I will do it after two weeks.

'Why? Why after two weeks?'

'I am off this Thursday for two weeks. The management trainee induction starts this weekend. While I am away I can't do anything on the book. I told you. You don't listen to me at all these days.'

'Oh yes. I completely forgot about that. I am so sorry.'

It was Wednesday. A day more, and Shreya would be gone for two weeks.

Vaishali called Aditya later that evening. 'I wanted to talk to you about two issues, Aditya. We are announcing your next book to the media in two days. The press release is going out. All the videos that we have shot with you for the book will be live this weekend. Amazon, Flipkart and all the other ecommerce sites will put it up for pre-booking this Sunday.'

'Isn't it too early?'

'Not at all. It will be on pre-order for three months. We will work overtime to get it ready in time for the committed date. Be prepared. Life is going to be terrible for the next few days.'

'Hmmm . . . and the second thing?'

'We need to throw a success party for your nomination for the award. And we need to do it before the winner of the Crossword Awards is announced. We will get a fair bit of media attention and that will overshadow the winner, just in case it's not you.'

'Do we still need to do this, after all these years, and all these books?'

'Aditya, irrespective of how big you become, it's important to stay engaged with the media. Authors thrive on media hype. You know that.'

'Of course, the one who is seen more, sells more—the age-old adage.'

'So when?'

'You decide.'

'Too little time this week to do justice. We need time to make sure that everyone who matters is there. The media needs to come too. Will next weekend do?'

Aditya thought for a moment. 'Fine.'

'Cool. I will be in touch. I'll let our CEO know. She will have to plan a trip to Mumbai around the same time.'

*

That night at around eleven, Aditya was on his computer working on his edits when he decided to check his Facebook account. Without social media interventions, books would take half the time to get written. He had just logged on to Facebook when he got a ping.

'Hiiiii!' It was Shreya.

'Hi Shreya.'

'What are you doing?'

'Edits. The boring stuff.'

'Not thinking about me?'

'Haha . . . you think that is possible?'

'You know what I am doing?' she asked.

'Tell me.'

'Drinking.'

'What?'

'Beer. Me and Sunaina.'

'What's the occasion?'

'Your award nomination. We are celebrating. The one who has been nominated is not giving us a treat. So we are celebrating amongst ourselves.'

'Of course there will be a treat for you, baby.'

'When?'

'Once you are back from your training.'

'Why not today?'

'Today?'

'Yeah. Why not today.'

'You know the time?'

'How does that matter?'

'How will I get out of the house at eleven? What will I say?'

'I don't know. That's your problem.'

'Shut up now, Shreya. Go to sleep. You have work tomorrow.'

'Are you coming with me to celebrate or not?'

'Not today, baby. Let's plan for later.'

'Later is not today.'

There was radio silence for some time. There were no further messages from her for the next three minutes.

'You there?'

'Wait,' she responded.

And then after a painful wait for five minutes, she typed, 'Sunaina says that she doesn't want to come.'

'That's why I am saying let's do it tomorrow.'

'I am going. If you don't want to come, don't. I will celebrate your award nomination on my own. I'm going to Marine Drive. Will hang around there for some time and come back.' The moment he read this message, Aditya panicked. Marine Drive was about ten kilometres from where Shreya lived and almost equidistant from his house. Going there at that hour, that too alone, was not safe.

'Shreya, you are drunk. It's a bad idea.'

'I think it is a good idea. The bad idea is that you don't want to come along. But it's okay. I will celebrate today's success, today.'

'Baby, wait.'

'Bye. See you tomorrow.'

Aditya was worried. Going to Marine Drive at that hour in a cab was asking for trouble. He didn't know what to do. He pinged her a few times on Facebook. Every time he got a *seen* receipt, but she didn't respond. After five minutes even that stopped. She had gone offline.

He walked to his bedroom and glanced inside. Maya was fast asleep. He shut the door and walked to the other end of the house and dialled Sunaina. She didn't pick up the first two times her phone rang. Finally on the third attempt she answered.

'Where is she?'

'Hi, Aditya. How are you?' The slur in her voice was unmistakable.

'Where is she, Sunaina?'

'She is changing. Getting ready to leave.'

'Are you going with her?'

Sunaina laughed. 'I can't walk a step and you want me to go to Marine Drive? And by the way congratulations, Aditya.'

In a split second, Aditya made his decision. 'Hold her there. I am coming,' he hung up. He was worried that Shreya would end up harming herself if she went alone. But what would he tell Maya? Obviously he couldn't be going to work at midnight.

He walked back to his bedroom and shook Maya slowly to wake her up. 'There has been an incident at the Andheri branch—a small fire in the basement. I need to go.'

'Oh my God! I hope it's nothing serious.' Maya woke up with a start.

'Will have to go and find out. Though from what the branch manager told me, it doesn't look too bad.'

'You want me to come with you?'

'No it's okay. No point in waking up Aryan. You stay here. I will be back soon.'

'Take the keys with you,' Maya said.

Aditya hurriedly wore his clothes and rushed out of the house. This was the first time he had ever lied to Maya to leave the house at night.

36

ADITYA DROVE LIKE a maniac through the deserted streets of Bandra and Khar to reach Santa Cruz, where Shreya stayed. It took him eleven minutes to cover the distance, which during the day would have taken him thirty.

Shreya was standing at the gate, waiting for him. Sunaina was nowhere to be seen. He presumed that she was drunk and not in her senses. Shreya too looked fairly zoned out. Dressed in a tank top and mini skirt, she looked straight out of any man's fantasy.

The moment he saw her his anger melted. He stopped his car and got off. Shreya saw him and smiled. He walked up to her and hugged her. His hands roamed freely over her back and for a fleeting moment caressed the swell of her hips.

'Naughty boy,' she chided him. He smiled and held the car door open for her to get in. Once she was settled in her seat, he started driving.

'Where to?'

'Wherever you want to take me. The idea is to celebrate your nomination.'

Aditya grinned. He had calmed down by then. 'Let's go

where you wanted to go,' he said and turned the car towards Marine Drive.

'Did you expect to be nominated for the award?' she asked him the moment the car hit the Bandra Worli Sea Link.

'I wanted it, for sure.'

'I'm so happy for you, Aditya,' Shreya said as she bent over to her right and kissed Aditya on the cheek. As she stretched, her skirt rode up a few inches. Aditya could see her lacy panties. He was getting turned on. As it is her cleavage was making life miserable for him.

He slowed down and extended his left hand which now rested on her inviting thighs. Shreya made no attempt to shake him off. An emboldened Aditya started caressing her thighs, even as he drove at over 100Kmph on the sea link.

'What are you doing, Aditya? Focus on the road,' Shreya chided. Aditya looked at her lustfully. But he didn't remove his hand. In fact it moved up a few inches. He could now feel her panties.

'Aditya' Shreya whispered. 'Don't.' Her breathing was heavy. 'Not here. There are cameras on the sea link.'

Aditya removed his hand and stepped on the pedal. The moment they got off the sea link, he turned into Pochkanwala lane, which was deserted at that time of the night, and parked in a secluded corner, under a tree, hidden from the streetlights.

'No cameras here,' he said, as he turned towards her.

'Weren't we going to Marine Drive?' asked Shreya. Her breathing had come down to normal.

'We will, we will,' whispered Aditya. 'What is the hurry?'

He leaned towards Shreya and kissed her on her lips. His hands had snaked under her skirt and moved her panty aside. 'You are wet,' Aditya stopped kissing her and mentioned, matter-of-factly.

'What did you expect, Mr Writer?' Shreya moaned as she took his face in her palms and ferociously kissed his lips, as if it was the last kiss of their lives. After savouring his lips, she pushed him back on his seat and moved her hand down his chest, further to the buckle of his jeans. She just fumbled for a moment as she unbuttoned him, even as she lifted herself off the seat, providing Aditya the much needed manoeuvrability to pull off her panties, at which he had been tugging for a while.

Aditya glanced at the side mirrors just to make sure that no one was approaching. By then, Shreya had freed his manhood from the dark confines of his jeans and Calvin Klein underwear. Her eyes lit up as she bent down and started teasing it with her lips. Aditya moaned in ecstacy as he stretched back on his seat.

In one defining moment, Shreya swung her leg over the gear shaft and even before Aditya could realise it, she was on top of him. Hurriedly he glanced at the rear view mirror again; no one in sight. Shreya's top was open and her fabulously delicious globes were in front of him. He reached out and licked her nipples while Shreya guided his manhood into her. She put her arms around his head, held him tightly against her breasts and began to ride him. She loved it when his stubble grazed against the sensitive skin of her breasts. She also wanted to be as close to him as possible to avoid even the remote chance of her back coming in contact with the steering wheel and hence the horn. Who would want a midnight love-making session to be disturbed by a blaring horn?

'This is my gift to you, on making it to the shortlist,' Shreya whispered into his ears once they were done and had cleaned up. They stayed there, in the car, for a long time, possibly an hour, after which Aditya drove up to Marine Drive. He picked up his phone and looked at it. There were five missed calls from Maya. He had intentionally disconnected the bluetooth connection betweeen the phone and his car. Otherwise the ring of the phone would have been heard on his car speakers and would have surely interrupted them. He decided not to call her back. She would be fast asleep.

After driving around Marine Drive, Aditya drove Shreya back to her house. She was more sober than she had been when he had picked her up earlier that night.

Before getting out of the car Shreya looked at Aditya and said, 'Vaishali called,' much to Aditya's surprise.

'Today?' he asked.

'Yes, a few hours back.'

'What did she say?' Aditya asked.

'She wants to meet me,' Shreya looked at Aditya intently and added, 'next week. Apparently she is coming for your success party.'

'Hahaha! Oh that!'

'How could you even think of having a party when I am away?' She was angry and it showed.

'Relax. No one is having a party.'

'Well, that's what Vaishali told me. Friday evening . . . next week. She even gave me the precise date. You have started lying to me too?'

'No, Shreya, Vaishali wants to have the party on that day. Maya is not available. She is travelling on her community work. In any case it will not happen.'

This peeved Shreya even more. 'So, if Maya had been fine, you would have gone ahead with it? Even for a moment you did not think that this could have been a wonderful forum for me to meet people who matter—people from the trade, production houses, publishing industry . . . all of them together at the same time.'

'It's too early, Shreya. Why don't you understand that? First meet Vaishali , sign the book deal, get the manuscript in shape . . . there's still lots to do. Once you are close to the book release, that's when you need to worry about all this.'

'Okay, fine. If you are hesitating to introduce me to them then tell me. I will figure a way out.'

'What?' Aditya couldn't be sure if Shreya was behaving the way she was because she was drunk or whether she was actually upset.

'You heard me,' she walked out of the car, slamming the door in his face. A beautiful night had come to an end.

Aditya was shocked at her demeanour. After all, wasn't he the one doing Shreya a favour? And if she knew about the party and was angry, why hold it back till the end of the evening? Was this celebration a façade? She could have easily confronted him on the phone. She made him come all the way, spent the evening with him and then at the end, pushed him off the cliff. As he was driving back that night, Aditya couldn't help but wonder if she was really in a relationship with him, or she was faking it all just to achieve her goal.

Maya was awake when Aditya returned. 'I tried calling you so many times,' she complained.

'I was tied up, Maya. And by the time I saw your missed calls, it was too late. So I didn't call you back.'

'Sanjay called a few minutes after you left.' This sent shivers down Aditya's spine. Sanjay was not aware of Aditya's lie.

'He wanted to talk to you. Apparently your phone was out of range.'

'Did he say why he wanted me?'

'Not sure. I told him that you had gone to attend to the fire in the basement of the Andheri branch. He didn't seem to have any clue about it.'

'Oh okay. I am sure it wasn't anything important or else he would have called me again.

'I hope so,' Maya said. 'But strange that the HR head wouldn't know of a serious incident like a fire in a branch.'

'Well you know it better than I do. Only if there is a serious impact on people are those guys told. In any case the incident report will go to them,' he concealed his lie. At the same time he made a mental note to update Sanjay on his lie. He would understand.

37

Aditya called Sunaina the next morning and asked her to meet him in his office. Sunaina dropped by after Shreya and the entire management trainee team had left for Lonavla, the camp for the induction programme.

'You don't seem too surprised,' he observed when she didn't show any reaction after hearing the happenings of the previous night.

'When it comes to Shreya, nothing surprises me,' Sunaina shook her head. To Aditya it sounded like a strange statement coming from Shreya's best friend.

'Was she like this on campus too?'

'Far worse than what she is now.'

'As in?'

Sunaina sighed. 'You know her background, don't you?' Looking at the near blank look on Aditya's face, she continued, 'Shreya comes from a family where she was the only child and yet no one loved her. Her parents were constantly at each other's throats, always screaming and shouting. She was extremely traumatised.'

'I knew she was from a troubled family, but so are many others these days. That doesn't really justify anything. Where are her parents now?' Aditya asked.

'Her father is in Dubai. Don't know what he is up to . . . I know he has some investments in properties which came his way when he was in a government job—he has two apartments in Mumbai. But Shreya doesn't want to take any favours from him.'

'Mother?'

'She remarried a rich divorcee and is settled in Delhi. She took care of Shreya's financial needs, paid for her education, but could never be with her. I am not sure if it was because she never felt for Shreya or her new family constrained her.'

'How long back was all this?'

'Shreya was ten years old when her parents separated. The only person emotionally available for her was their family help; it was she who gave Shreya her strength. She calls the maid *amma*, a term normally reserved for your mom. But more importantly the behaviour you see is, in my opinion a result of the chaos in her life. Her arrogance, her belligerence is a means to hide her insecurities. Whenever she sees love, which hasn't been too often, she gets stuck like a leech. When she gets it, she doesn't want to let go. She keeps saying that her mother had taught her that relationships with the right people are the key to success. That's why, I guess, she is desparate to form the right equations in life. The right connections . . .'

'Hmm . . . Where is the maid now?'

'She died of old age when Shreya was in her first year at IIM. Shreya is what she is because of her. She loved her more than anyone would love their own mother. She is not evil, Aditya. That's why I put up with a lot of rubbish from her. Because I know she loves me, though her way of expressing it is different from other people. And more importantly, she loves you, Aditya.'

'Why didn't you tell me this that day when she walked out of Out of the Blue?'

'She has not shared this with anyone. I am the only one who knows. I thought she would tell you herself, when the time was right. Do not misunderstand her actions, Aditya,' Sunaina urged.

Aditya didn't know what to say. He was overwhelmed by what she had just told him. It put Shreya's actions and reactions in context. He thanked Sunaina.

'Please make sure that Shreya is happy in life. She needs you, Aditya. It feels wrong to say it, but that's how it is,' Sunaina said.

Aditya nodded.

'I just have one worry,' she said with a concerned look on her face. 'She cannot take rejection well. She is very focused on what she wants to do. But if she doesn't get what she wants, despite her efforts, she cannot take it. She is a bad loser. A relationship with her is a one-way street.'

Aditya smiled at her indulgently. 'Any relationship is always a one-way street, till it isn't. After which you think there is no way out, but mysteriously the walls diffuse and pathways open up.'

'With Shreya it is very different,' Sunaina said with a deep breath.

Aditya understood what she was hinting at. He didn't

know of any woman who would take a break-up calmly. Shreya was no different. But why think of that when the relationship was just starting? He just had to be clear with her so as to set the right expectations.

'Have you ever been in love, Sunaina?'

'Once.'

'And?'

'It didn't work out.'

Aditya looked at her intently, waiting for her to continue.

'He is at IIM Bengaluru now. He'll pass out this year. We were in a relationship, when he just walked out on me. No reasons given. No explanations offered. It's okay, Aditya. Que sera sera.'

Aditya could see that Sunaina was saddened by this topic and decided to drop it. 'Thanks, Sunaina, for coming. You helped me make up my mind.'

*

That night Aditya called Vaishali . 'Maya is not in town next weekend, Vaishali . We need to put this off, at least for a couple of weeks.' He knew that after two weeks Shreya would be back from her programme. Vaishali was unhappy but didn't have a choice when Aditya put his foot down.

Aditya waited for Shreya's call or message till Sunday morning. She had been gone three days. When he didn't hear from her, he sent her an SMS:

<I have told Kiwi to have the success party after you come back from Lonavla. You take care. Stay calm. I am with you.>

Still there was no response. He tried to call her but couldn't get through. He tried calling Sanjay but couldn't get through his phone either. He assumed that they would be in the training programme. He stopped calling.

Later that evening, Shreya replied. <You are a sweetheart. This is why I love you.> Aditya didn't respond. He felt confused. Sunaina's disclosure had muddied the waters for him.

The next day, all newspapers carried the announcement of the imminent launch of Aditya's next book on their first page.

The brouhaha surrounding the fifth book had begun.

38

THE SUCCESS PARTY for Aditya's book was a bumper one. Kiwi Books had invited over 200 people—authors, publishers, people from the film fraternity, as well as the trade and media. It was a packed house at the banquet hall of Taj Lands End. Aditya and Maya were personally welcoming all the guests.

Sanjay walked into the hotel lobby around the same time that Shreya arrived. He hurried to the banquet hall where he walked up to Aditya. 'You invited Shreya for this party. Are you mad?' he said.

'Calm down, Sanjay. It is okay. She is going to be a Kiwi author soon. They invited her. It's a different matter that had they not, then I would surely have.'

'So you are okay with her meeting your family? Meeting Maya?'

'I shouldn't be?'

'Don't be an ass, Aditya. You know what I mean.'

'We will see, Sanjay. Don't get paranoid.' Aditya was very chilled and relaxed.

'Well, all I can say is that you are playing with fire. What if Maya comes to know about you and her?'

'Maya comes to know what? What are the two of you conspiring?' Maya was standing right in front of him.

'Haha... Maya!' Sanjay nervously laughed. 'Can anything be hidden from you? We were just talking about the ... about the ...' he started to stammer. He didn't know what to say.

'About the fire at the Andheri branch, Maya. Not upgrading our fire safety requirements is like playing with fire. That's what Sanjay was saying,' Aditya finished as he glared at Sanjay.

'Exactly. That's what I was saying.' Sanjay looked relieved.

'So what's the harm in me knowing about it?' Maya had a grin on her face. 'Anyway, I can't understand you guys. Ever!' she complained and walked towards the main door of the hall.

'What the fuck is wrong with you, Sanjay? Couldn't you see her coming?' Aditya whispered in anger the moment Maya's back was turned towards them.

'Relax, dude,' Sanjay replied and patted him on his back. 'You are lucky that you have a wife who trusts you blindly. I wish she didn't trust you as much as she does though,' he winked at Aditya.

Aditya smiled and gave him a quick hug. 'Go in. Tim is here and he is feeling restless and bored. Manage him,' Aditya said and ushered Sanjay into the room. He made a mental note to have a chat with him later. Things were no longer the same. Aditya had become a lot more careful in his dealings with Shreya and Maya but Sanjay was yet to adopt caution. He had posted the *Times of India* article, with Shreya's picture on Facebook. That was unnecessary, especially after the interview where Sanjay was literally arm-twisted into hiring Shreya. He had also called Maya on the night of the fake fire at the Andheri branch. What was the need to tell her that he was not aware of any fire? He could have quietly got out of it and not sown seeds of suspicion in Maya's mind. And then again today, he should have seen Maya walking towards them and checked himself. Aditya decided he needed to talk to him to ensure that he wouldn't jeopardize anything.

Shreya and Sunaina walked in next. Aditya met them at the gate. He had just finished complimenting Shreya when Maya walked up to them. Aditya introduced her to Shreya, and also gave her a brief outline about Shreya's interest in writing. 'Shreya Kaushik has just been signed up by Kiwi,' he said.

Shreya said a curt hello, while Sunaina extended her hand in a handshake.

How often does it happen that you meet someone and you know at that very instant whether you will gel with that person or not? The like or dislike is instantaneous. The same happened with Maya and Shreya—they disliked each other instantly. The instincts of the wife, when it comes to issues that concern her husband are stronger than those of even the best astrologers.

'Is that your son?' Shreya asked looking at the boy standing next to Maya and tugging at her dupatta. Aditya nodded.

Shreya looked at Aryan and smiled. 'Look at that smile, and those glittering eyes,' she admired Aryan. 'I'm sure he will grow up and turn out to be a compulsive flirt,' she looked at Maya and then at Aditya, '. . . like his father.'

Maya looked at her with irritation. 'Aditya? A compulsive flirt? Are you sure we are talking about the same individual, Miss . . .?'

'Shreya,' she reminded Maya of her name. 'I was just kidding, ma'am. You have a cute son. Very cute.' She bent down and kissed Aryan on the cheek, before she walked in to the party area.

That evening, Maya had eyes only for Shreya. She kept following her wherever she went. She noticed that Aditya introduced Shreya to everyone who mattered.

Maya didn't confront Aditya. Just because someone had called Aditya a flirt was not a good enough reason for her to question him, but something about Shreya kept bothering her. She looked familiar. Aditya had introduced her as a management trainee at National Bank but she didn't behave like one. She behaved like someone who knew everyone very well, someone who derived her confidence on account of her closeness to the seat of power. Even Sanjay was being nice to her, and she knew Sanjay was extremely hierarchy conscious. What was it that she was missing? She couldn't put a finger on it.

Later that night, she got on to Google and did a search on Shreya Kaushik. It threw up 2,66,000 results. She went to the search box, added a comma after Shreya Kaushik and typed 'Aditya Kapoor'.

And there it was, on the very first page. A blog post of Aditya's talk at IIM Bengaluru, posted by a student who was present there. It had a vivid mention of Shreya and Aditya's discussion. It even had a picture of Shreya standing there in the audience engaged in an animated discussion with Aditya. So Shreya was the same girl who had asked Aditya the question about books being products. Maya was surprised that Aditya didn't mention this when he introduced them.

The problem with trust is that if it is broken, then all acts committed by the perpetrator come under the purview of suspicion. She went back to thinking about everything that Aditya did in Bengaluru. He had gone for the placement interview, hence it was likely that he had hired her for National Bank. But if he was upset and angry with Shreya, why would he agree to hire her? That's when she recollected that Aditya had also done a book reading at EaslyLib around the same time.

She hurriedly went on to Sanjay's Facebook page and looked for the article about the EasyLib event in TOI which he had tagged Aditya in. She found it easily enough and clicked on the link. It opened up on the TOI website. Shreya was in the photo with Aditya and the EasyLib team.

But it was not her presence in the picture which irked her. She had asked Aditya about the picture and he had told her that all of them were employees of EasyLib. He had lied to her. If he had nothing to fear or hide, then why would he lie?

She hated lies.

And more importantly, she hated liars.

39

Maya could contain herself no longer. She stormed up to Aditya and asked him, 'Isn't Shreya the same girl who asked you that arrogant and snide question in Bangalore?'

'Oh yes. She is,' Aditya acknowledged. 'And it was not an arrogant or insulting question. The manner in which she asked the question was inappropriate, not the question itself.'

'Semantics,' Maya argued. 'Why didn't you tell me she was the same girl?'

'It wasn't that important.'

'She was there at your book event at EasyLib too?'

'Yeah, she was. Why? What happened?'

'But when I had asked you about the people in the picture that TOI carried, you told me that they were all employees of EasyLib. But this woman was there too. You lied to me,' Maya was peeved. Her face had gone red and she was beginning to stammer. 'Why?'

'Did I?' Aditya asked coolly.

'Yes!'

'Maya,' Aditya spoke in a very loving and assuaging tone, 'come, sit here.' He patted the seat next to his. When she sat down, he put his arms around her shoulder and asked, 'What is the issue? What's on your mind? Out with it.'

'You lied to me about her. Why would you do that?' She was angry, upset and irritated.

'Look. I didn't lie to you. The TOI picture had seven or eight people. Everyone else apart from her and me was from EasyLib. In fact till you told me right now, I was not even aware that she was in the picture. I didn't even see the snap closely to look at the others. I just looked at myself and saw if I looked okay. I did, so I moved on.'

'Why is she in your team? I thought you didn't like her. Wasn't that what you told me?'

'Sanjay hired her. HR allocated her to my team because we wanted the wealth management project to be handled by someone confidentially. And what better way to manage confidentiality than have a new resource who will do as told and has no internal alignments? She is writing a book, so she asked for my help. That's it. As for the party today, Kiwi invited her, I didn't. You know Vaishali . Pick up the phone and ask her.'

'Did you rehearse these lines knowing that I will ask you or are these impromptu?' She wiped the tears which had rolled down her cheeks.

Aditya knew that he had managed to calm her fears. She had been won over for the time being.

'Be careful, Aditya,' Maya said. 'She isn't harmless. Stay away from her,' she warned. Aditya just nodded his head and kept quiet.

That night he was about to sleep when he got a message on his mobile. <You looked great. Indian attire suits you. Muaaah. Loved being there today.>

Maya heard the phone beep and looked at him.

'Who is it?'

'Sanjay. He just dropped off Tim at his house. SMSing to say thanks.'

Despite his calm exterior Aditya was worried. He was lucky that Maya hadn't seen the phone screen.

He immediately brought up Shreya's contact on his phone and altered her name to Ram Kumar. Henceforth even if Shreya messaged him late and Maya inadvertently saw it, she wouldn't know it was Shreya, for it would show up as Ram Kumar.

Matter resolved for the time being.

40

'Last night after the party, Vaishali and I went out for coffee. She wanted to spend some time with me; gave me a long list of changes she wants done to the manuscript.' Shreya didn't even wait for Aditya to walk into his cabin the next morning.

'Good. So things are moving.'

'Good? What do you mean good? Why should I make the changes she wants?' Shreya was indignant.

'That's the way it normally works, baby. These editors know what are the flaws in a book. For a newcomer, it is always safe to trust your editor. And Vaishali is a seasoned editor, she is good.'

'Will you first read the changes she is recommending,' Shreya said, forcibly handing him a printout, 'before you begin your lecture?'

Aditya looked at her. He didn't like the way she was speaking to him, but then their relationship went beyond that of a subordinate and supervisor.

He started reading the sheet that Shreya had given him. On the top of the page were the words 'Suggested alterations for Shreya Kaushik's untitled book.'

a) Change Aditya's name to something more rustic. The name does not suit the character.

b) Detailing of locations in the book needs to be fleshed out. As of now it is very elementary. The average reader will have to be told what those locations stand for. Take a relook at pages: 4, 89,112 and 165.

c) The book is short. Can we look at adding another 15,000 words? We need to have a book of at least 200 pages. Readers will hesitate paying a good price for something less than that.

d) Reduce the gore in the rape scene. While it is very hard-hitting, it might put off many.

There were a few more easy-to-manage points on the list. He read through everything and looked at her.

'What is wrong with this?' asked Aditya. 'Everything she says is reasonable.'

'Another 15,000 words? It will kill the pace of the book, won't it?'

'It might not. Provided you add some incidents, which add some texture to the story or characters. Not too difficult. It might kill the pace in a thriller but not in a book like yours. A little bit of focus on prose and detailing may only add to the value of the book. Vaishali is right.'

'It will take a lot of time. Where will I find time to do all this, Aditya?'

'Don't worry. This will not take too long, max two weeks,' Aditya reassured her.

'Hmm,' Shreya looked dejected.

'I will help you with this. Let's start with the easiest.'

'Easiest?'

'Yes. Think of a name for Aditya. Do edit-find-replace in the word document,' Aditya laughed. 'Isn't that the easiest thing to do?'

Shreya made a face and walked back to her seat. Once there she dialled him on the intercom. 'Coming home this evening?'

'Yes. Provided this asshole Tim doesn't screw it up.'

'Language, Aditya.'

'Haha,' he laughed. 'You just reminded me of Maya.'

Shreya banged the phone down.

*

That evening after work, Shreya left on time and went home. Aditya left half an hour later and followed her to her house.

Shreya was alone at home when Aditya reached. 'Isn't Sunaina here?' he enquired. The excitement in his voice was palpable. Of late, this had become a daily affair. Every day, on his way back, Aditya would spend some time with Shreya at her home and then head back to his house. Invariably one thing would lead to another and they would end up in bed.

'She has gone to Kolkata on an assignment. The *Indian Express* is covering the Trinamool Congress annual celebrations and felt that it would be a good learning ground for new journalists. So they sent her to be a part of it.'

'Wow.'

'What's on your mind, lover boy?'

'Shall we focus on the book before we digress into something else?' Aditya had a wide grin on his face. Shreya's attire was distracting him. She was wearing hot pants which tantalisingly ended a couple of inches below her butt. Whenever she got up and walked away from him, it drew his gaze like a magnet.

'Sure, but if you don't stop focusing on my derriere, Mr Kapoor, there is no way I am going to be able to focus on what I have to do to please Vaishali ,' Shreya teased.

'Have you considered the fact that someone here also needs to be pleased?' Aditya was at his flirtatious best.

'Like how?'

Aditya pulled her towards him in a seamless motion. Before she could even realise it, she was on his lap. Aditya didn't have to put in much effort to take off the clothes that didn't want to be there in the first place.

'What about the book?' Shreya whispered, her breath coming in short gasps.

'We will see, once we are done with the author,' Aditya commented as his hands slipped past the unbuttoned shorts into the elastic of her panties. Shreya moaned. Aditya's lips had engulfed her right nipple even as he stood up. He struggled out of his trousers and managed to kick them off. With his lips still sucking on Shreya's erect nipples, he led her to the bedroom.

A tired Shreya fell asleep in his arms almost immediately after their steamy session. Aditya stayed there for about an hour, trying to make sure that he didn't move and wake her up. She was lying naked in front of him. He thought about how Shreya's life had been deprived of love. He was not in a position to give her long-term solace. He could only ensure that she was happy as long as the relationship lasted. But after that, what?

A hand snaked up to his cheek and went on to play with his hair. Shreya had woken up. 'Where are you lost, baby?' she asked.

'It's nothing,' Aditya smiled as he got up to wear his clothes.

'Stay back,' Shreya implored. Aditya looked at her. She was patting the side of the bed that he had just got up from. He smiled. 'Got to go . . . people are waiting.'

'I know,' she made a face but then she quickly changed her mood. 'It's okay. I should be happy that we are able to spend this time together.' She got up and hugged him. 'It's just that when you are with me, I feel that my life has a purpose. I feel closer to my dream. I feel that I will become someone that I will be proud of.'

'I know,' Aditya hugged her back.

'We never discussed the book,' she complained.

'Tomorrow. Stay away from me and we will close it.' Aditya kissed her and left the house.

41

Aditya was on his way back from Shreya's house when Vaishali called to confirm that everything was as per schedule for his book launch. August 8th was fixed as the date for the launch of Aditya's fifth book. It was a month away.

'I am comfortable with that. We then get the entire season for the book,' he said. August onwards was considered the peak season for book sales in India.

'Correct,' Vaishali responded. 'We need to close out the book launch details. Where do you want to do it? A bookstore, mall, college . . . where? I can get the marketing team to get cracking on it.'

'Obviously a bookstore. Where is the doubt?' Aditya loved the quaint romantic appeal of a bookstore. 'Bookstores have made me who I am. We owe it to them, Vaishali . We must help herd crowds back into the stores, or else the bookstores will all play the vanishing act soon. As it is Reliance TimeOut shut shop two years back. We don't want Crossword and Landmark to down their shutters. Without these bookstores, there will be no books, and without books, there will be no culture. So . . .' he paused and took a deep breath, 'bookstores it is.'

'Noted. Will be executed accordingly,' Vaishali replied.

'When is Shreya's book launch?' Aditya asked.

'Targeting for November. Need a clear three months between your book and hers.'

'You think my book will eat into her sales or vice versa?'

'Neither actually,' Vaishali responded calmly. 'We need you to help promote her book. And for two months you will be busy with your own book. That's why November. Might slip to December depending on how your book tour works out, and how punctual she is with regard to her commitment.'

'Aaah. Now I get it. Fine by me.'

★

'Had dinner?' Maya asked as she opened the door for him, 'Or should I warm it up for you?'

'Not too hungry. I'll have it in a while, baby.'

'What took you so long? I was waiting for you to come.'

Whenever Maya said something like that, it meant she was waiting to tell him something important. 'Tim had called for a meeting, and you know how he is,' Aditya lied. 'Why? What happened?'

Maya smiled. 'Our school has been selected to represent India in the *World Emerging Trends in Education* conference. And . . .' she fluttered her eyelashes like a hummingbird flaps its tiny wings, '. . . and guess what? Nita Ambani wants me to go.'

'Wow! That's great news. So where is the conference?'

'Paris.' Her eyes lit up.

'Amazing! I will also come. When is it?'

'Next month.'

'Oh shit. Hope it is not on 8th August.'

'Why? What happened?'

'My book launch. Kiwi called today. And also, towards the end of August is when we will be doing all the people actions—sacking 290 people in my business. I will be a bit messed up.'

'Oh. This programme is in end August too. Bad timing . . .'

'Damn. We will have to figure out something for Aryan.'

'But then it's okay,' Maya immediately responded. Her mind was clear. 'If it comes to that, I will tell them that I can't go. We'll manage; you don't stress over it.'

'Rubbish. You have to go. I don't want you to give up this opportunity. If nothing else, I will drop Aryan at your parents' in Delhi. He can spend a week there. In any case he hasn't missed much at school this year.' Aditya stepped into the kitchen and held her by her shoulders. 'I don't want you to give up more than what you already have, baby. You gave up your career for me and Aryan. That bothers me till this day.'

'I didn't do it for you, Mr Kapoor. I was fed up of the rat race.'

'As if I don't know,' he smiled as he hugged her. 'We will figure out a way for you to go.' Maya hugged him back, a smile on her face.

'So one more round of shopping?' Aditya asked her as they settled down for dinner. Aryan had not returned from his play date.

'As of now, there is only one thing that I want.'

'And that is?'

'An iPhone6!' she squealed. 'I will pick it up either from Paris or from the duty-free in Dubai, if we transit through Dubai, that is.' Aditya could make out the thrill on her face as she said this. Maya loved Apple.

42

THERE WAS ONLY a month left for the retrenchment. Everyone involved was getting jittery. No one wanted a collateral damage on the brand and so the approvals were slow in coming. Things were progressing, albeit slowly.

'Is everything under control?' Tim asked Sanjay and Aditya when the two of them met him that afternoon.

'Yes. As of now it is. We have covered everything from a legal and HR standpoint,' Sanjay answered.

'What about regional office approvals for the severance packages?'

Sanjay nodded. 'Work in progress. It's expected to come through this week.' He pulled out a piece of paper and handed it over to Tim. 'Three months' notice pay plus three months' severance pay, and on top of it every employee will get one month's pay for every completed year of service,' he outlined their recommendation, which had become a standard practice across the group.

'Good. How many people have we managed to find jobs for internally?'

'Thirty-eight. Of the 297 whose jobs were on line, we have saved thirty-eight jobs. We could have saved more, but we hired forty management trainees. So, most of the entry-level job openings are taken.' The moment he said this, Sanjay realised it was a mistake.

'That's unfair.' Tim's face turned red. 'On one side we are sacking 297 people and on the other side, we go and hire forty management trainees?'

'We had made campus offers to them earlier, Tim.' Sanjay reasoned.

'Offers could have been withdrawn. When did they join?'

'End of May.'

'And when did we get to know that we have to wind down the business?'

'End of April.'

'So we had time to withdraw the offers?' Tim asked him.

'Would we have wanted to?' Sanjay said cheekily. He didn't need to be as restrained as Aditya was, as he didn't report to Tim. Moreover, Tim had known about the management trainees all along. Then why create a ruckus at this stage?

'Damn well sure I would have wanted to,' Tim was furious. 'How many of them are in Retail Banking?'

'Not sure, but around twelve of them, I think.'

'I don't need a single MT in my team,' he said, looking at both Aditya and Sanjay. His face was red with anger. 'Do you get it? I do not need a single management trainee in my team. All the roles that have been given to MTs need to be reallocated to the people who are being sacked.' He looked at Sanjay. 'As of this month-end, terminate all the management trainees in Retail Bank. I will speak to the CEO.'

'But, Tim, the management trainee programme is very prestigious. We will lose face in the management institutes. The preferential treatment we get at the campuses will stop. Hiring good talent from institutes will become difficult.'

'I would rather pay and hire experienced people from the market, than hire duds from campuses and train them.'

'But these guys have already joined,' Aditya reasoned even as he looked at Sanjay.

'That is an HR problem,' Tim thundered.

'Yes, Tim. Let me see what can be done,' Sanjay said and got up and walked out. He had had enough of Tim.

The moment they got out of the cabin, Aditya angrily whispered to Sanjay, 'What is wrong with you? You should've never agreed to Tim's idea.'

'Relax, Aditya, Shreya is safe. She is on HR head-count. Even if we execute Tim's diktat, Shreya won't be touched.'

'Aah then it's okay,' Aditya was relieved. 'I wouldn't have been able to face her had Tim had his way.

'Is there anything else you think of these days, Aditya?' Sanjay shook his head. He looked upset. 'Irrespective of what he feels, I do not think Tim can carry out this weird decision of his. Global HR will have to be involved. And they will actually fuck Tim, if he even utters these words in front of those blokes. Management trainees just can't be sacked at one's whims and fancies.

43

ADITYA'S BOOK WAS launched on 8th August, at a well-attended event at Crossword Bookstore at Kemps corner, Mumbai. Over 500 people attended the event, in a store which would burst at its seams if 250 people came in at the same time.

Shreya was the first guest to arrive, much to Maya's chagrin. She even sat in the first row, just a seat away from Maya. It was a big day for Aditya. Karan Johar, who announced on stage that he had bought the film rights for the book, for an undisclosed sum, launched it along with Ramesh Karia, the Commissioner of Mumbai Police. Aditya had been in touch with Karia since they first met. Who could have been better than the commissioner of police to launch a crime thriller written by India's number one writer?

In the first week of sale, the book rocketed to No.1 position on all the bestseller lists across the country. As Vaishali had often told him he was a brand unto himself. The numbers proved it, beyond doubt.

His first stop after Mumbai, for the book promotions, was Pune. At the Pune Crossword, he got a reception normally reserved for a film star. The event lasted for forty-five minutes after which he signed books for about an hour.

He thanked the organisers and got into his car. The car went ahead a few metres and then turned right into the main road. The moment the car turned into the road and he was sure that he was out of sight of the organisers, he tapped the driver on his shoulder. 'Stop, stop,' he said urgently. Within thirty seconds the car door opened and someone got in.

Aditya smiled, 'Was I good?'

'Fabulous! No one could have done it better. The Q&A round was super.'

'You are biased, Shreya,' was all he said, before asking the driver to head back to the hotel.

The two of them came back to Mumbai on Sunday morning. This had become quite a staple. Shreya would accompany Aditya to all his book launches around the country and sneak into the event, a scarf covering her face, to stay unrecognized. Afterwards, they would lock themselves inside their hotel room, undisturbed.

Oblivious to all this, Maya was preparing for her trip to Paris.

44

THE WEATHER IN Paris is at its best in August. With summer just bidding adieu, and an average day temperature around 20 degrees, it is one of the best times for anyone to visit France.

Maya landed in Paris on a Friday morning. A representative of the Global Education for Progress Foundation, the conference organisers, was at the airport to receive her. The drive from the airport to the hotel was about an hour and the organisers had clubbed her travel with the participants from Egypt.

As soon as the Cairo flight arrived, the three participants, Maya and two others from Egypt were ushered into a minivan and driven to the Hotel de Crillon, the venue for the conference.

On the way, Maya got chatting with her co-participants. Both of them were from Cairo and had interesting but diverse backgrounds. The guy, Adly Mansour, a career educationist, in his fifties, ran a school for the disabled in the upmarket area of the city. The lady, Minouche Shafik, in her early thirties, was the Patron-in-Chief for a school for Syrian and Palestinian refugees who had fled the neighbouring strife-torn state of Syria. Operating in the Beheira Governorate, and largely funded by her diamond trader boyfriend, she was also instrumental in improving the overall condition of the refugees in the province—an effort recognized by Amnesty International. Minouche was the more impressive of the two and Maya instantaneously struck a chord with her.

At Hotel de Crillon, they were among the first few delegates to have checked in, and they managed to get rooms next to each other.

'See you in the restaurant in an hour,' Minouche said just before Maya opened the door and got into her room.

Maya showered, changed and connected to the Wi-Fi, and sent Aditya a WhatsApp message informing him that she had checked in. She even sent him the hotel numbers. It was standard operating protocol for her whenever she travelled.

Aditya didn't see her message for a long time. He was busy somewhere else.

With someone else.

45

THE FIRST DAY at the conference was just an icebreaker; the real sessions were to start on Saturday. It was an early night. The two of them, Minouche and Maya, returned to their rooms by 9. They settled in Maya's room and started talking about life back home in Cairo and Mumbai.

'It must be an amazing life, married to a writer. All the fame, the adulation . . . I would love it,' Minouche rhapsodised.

Maya smiled. 'I love to lead a life of my own, Minouche, away from all the attention, doing my work. I don't like being dragged into Aditya's life as a celebrity,' she said.

'I would have used the fame to raise money for my cause,' Minouche commented. When Maya showed her a family picture of Aditya and Aryan on her phone, Minouche promised her that she would come to India and spend some time with them on her next vacation.

Minouche's was a slightly more poignant story. Her boyfriend's family was not in favour of them getting married. Though he stayed with her most of the time when he was in Cairo, his family persistently targeted her. She had even been attacked a couple of times. 'Maybe his family is worried that I desire to be with him because of his wealth. Anyway, we hope to marry by end of this year,' she said as she brought out his photo and showed it to Maya. 'He will be here on Wednesday. We will be spending the rest of the week shopping for the house we are building in Cairo.'

Finally around midnight, Minouche walked back to her room. Maya checked her phone before going to sleep. There was a message from Aditya. It had come around fifteen minutes back. So lost was she in her conversation with Minouche that she hadn't noticed it.

<We gave out termination letters to 120 people in Mumbai yesterday evening. It was so heartbreaking. Going to Kolkata Sunday night. Tim wants me to go as HR expects some trouble there. Hope all goes well.>

<It will. You don't worry. Sad as it is, it is not your fault that these guys are losing their jobs. Be in touch with Aryan. He will miss you.> She had dropped Aryan with her parents in Delhi before coming on this trip.

*

The sessions the next day were interesting. Listening to how underprivileged children across the world were treated gave her many ideas on what could be done in India.

That evening, Minouche and Maya visited the Eiffel Tower and the Arc de Triomphe. She took a few pictures to show Aryan. On the way back, they stopped at the flea market and picked up some curios. By the time they decided to head back to the hotel, it was seven in the evening.

Both of them debated whether it was worth going back to

the hotel for dinner or grab a bite at a roadside café. What's a visit to Paris without spending time in its legendary bistros? That clinched the deal and they decided in favour of the sidewalk café. They settled down for a bite at a place overlooking the Seine River. The discussions over coffee again veered towards family. Minouche expressed a desire to read Aditya's books. Maya had taken a couple of them with her. She always did that on her trips. She gave them to Minouche, after she promised to read them.

While leaving her room, Minouche smiled and said, 'For the first time, I am going to read an Indian author.' She raised her eyebrows and looked at Maya from the corner of her eyes, 'Are they any good?'

Maya laughed. 'At least this one is,' she said as she shut the door behind Minouche.

46

MAYA WAS SUDDENLY woken up from her sleep by the ringing of her cellphone. The clock on her bedside table showed the time. 2.14 am.

'Hey. All okay? What happened?' she groggily whispered into the phone.

'Can you come to my room right now?' a faintly audible voice said. Her breathing was heavy, as if she was in some trauma. Maya was worried. 'Minouche. What happened?' she panicked. Something was terribly wrong. Minouche could barely whisper.

'Now. Can you come quickly? Please . . .' there was a pause interspersed with heavy breathing. 'Hurry!'

Hastily Maya wrapped a stole around her night dress and rushed out of her room. She knocked on Minouche's door and waited. Within seconds, she heard someone stumble up to the door. She pushed it open, just in time to see Minouche collapse on the floor. Her T-shirt was wet with sweat, despite the AC being on full throttle. And the room was stinking of vomit.

Maya panicked. 'Minouche! What happened? Oh my God!' She reached out to help her get up. Holding her by the hand, she led her to the bed and supported her as she lowered herself on the mattress. She wiped the sweat off Minouche's forehead and gave her a glass of water. Holding her hand softly, she settled down next to her. Once she calmed down a bit and her breathing became more steady, Maya rested her palm on Minouche's forehead and slowly ran her fingers through her hair. 'What happened, Minouche?' she asked.

'I am so sorry I troubled you in the middle of the night, but I didn't know what to do. I have thrown up four times in the last ten minutes. Now it seems like my guts will come out. It pains like hell when I vomit. For a moment, Maya, I thought I was going to die. I was scared. That's why I called you,' Minouche said through gasps. She had tears in her eyes.

Maya cradled her head in her arms and stroked her hair. 'Don't worry. It must be something you ate at the café. You will be okay by morning.'

Minouche asked Maya to pull her medicine kit out of her bag and popped a couple of tablets. The tablets put her to sleep. In no time she was purring away like a child.

Maya decided to hang around and sleep on the couch, just in case Minouche had a repeat bout of vomiting.

In the morning when she woke up, Minouche was still asleep. Effects of the sedative had not worn off. Casually, she walked up to the bed and touched her forehead. It was burning hot. She was worried. She tried to wake her up, but Minouche was delirious. She was groaning in her sleep. Maya couldn't make head or tail of what she was saying.

She called the session coordinator for the conference, who arrived almost immediately and took over. When Maya didn't leave, the coordinator told her that he would manage and asked her to go ahead as the conference was to begin in thirty minutes.

'What about her?' Maya asked. 'I would prefer to be around.'

'Your flight is in the evening, madam. You have to check out of the room and head to the conference. But don't you worry; we will take care of her. Once the doctor sees her, we will decide on the course of action. I will ask her to call you once she wakes up.'

'Please do,' Maya said and walked back to her room with a heavy heart. As she exited the room, she saw Aditya's book on the side table, a bookmark lying somewhere midway through the book.

Till the time Maya took her flight out of Paris, Minouche hadn't called. Maya kept checking on her and was told that she had high fever. The doctors had sedated her to get the fever under control.

Maya left Paris, worried about her new friend.

47

It was a torrid Monday for Aditya in Kolkata. A number of staff members gathered outside the room of the regional head, shouting slogans against the retrenchment decision. At one stage it looked as if cops would have to be called in. But thankfully some politically savvy staff members averted that situation.

Aditya was mentally drained by the time he got back to his hotel room. He quickly showered and changed into jeans and a t-shirt. He had fixed up with Sunaina for dinner. She was doing her political reporting in Kolkata.

Sunaina landed up in the hotel at 8.30 in the evening. Aditya met her in the lobby and they headed to the Italian restaurant.

'You look tired,' Sunaina started off. Even though she was coming straight from work, laptop bag on her shoulder and book in hand, she looked quite fresh.

'Been a bad day. We gave out termination letters to forty-two people in Kolkata. The look in their eyes when they got those letters was killing, Sunaina. Grown-ups shedding tears; I have never seen that before. This was the first time for me in my entire career. There was a guy in there who got terminated today, who is getting married two weeks from now.'

'Was there no way to save them?'

'No. But please let's talk about something else. I wanted to meet you because I wanted to forget all this crap.'

'I guess this is what made Shreya come to you,' Sunaina said. Aditya looked at her, blankly. 'You are so intense that it reflects in your writing. She became your fan the night she read your book,' she said with a smile. 'Though she never read it with that intent.'

'What do you mean?'

Sunaina recounted the entire story of how and why Shreya read Aditya's books for the first time.

'What a bitch!' Aditya laughed out. 'But for all the bitchiness she has turned out well, hasn't she?'

'You do love her, don't you?' Sunaina asked Aditya. He looked at her and smiled. Some questions don't have an answer. This was one of them. 'You are completely into her,' Sunaina looked at him with admiration. 'I hope she finds someone like you to settle down in life with—someone who has time for her tantrums and her idiosyncrasies. The way you handle her is amazing, Aditya.'

'There's nothing to it. I just listen to her.'

'More importantly, she listens to you. That's the key. Else she is quite pig-headed. The way you handled her when she wanted to go to Marine Drive, in the middle of the night was just so adorable.' The look on her face turned mischievous. 'The way she helped you write that erotic chapter in your book was just so romantic. I loved it.'

'What?' Aditya was shocked. 'How the hell do you know about that?'

'How else, Mr Kapoor? Girlfriends share all their secrets, including the length of their boyfriend's . . . you know what! Hehehe . . . just kidding! Shreya and I don't keep secrets from each other. She told me how you managed to pacify her the night she showed you the rejection letter. Her love and respect for you grew manifold that day.'

Aditya just shook his head. 'Yes, I know. I wish sometimes that Shreya and I had a future together.' He casually flipped through the book that Sunaina was reading—Wendy Doniger's, *On Hinduism*. Aditya knew that it was a controversial book withdrawn by the publishers, though he had never read it.

'Hmm . . . I know. I think she understands too. She knows that family comes first for you. She is happy with the way you are with her. She likes it that way. She has her independence as well as someone who loves her. Best of both worlds.'

'It worries me to think what would happen when either of us would want both worlds to converge,' Aditya sounded grim.

'And also that she is a determined young soul who will wreck your life professionally and personally if she doesn't get you. Right, Mr Kapoor?'

'Hahaha . . . that's not what I meant at all,' he tried to cover up. 'How do you read books like these?' asked Aditya, trying to change the topic. 'Don't you find them too heavy?'

'Nope. It's brilliant. You should read it.'

'I just don't seem to be able to find time.'

'I will give it to you once I am done. You can peacefully read it and give it back to your girlfriend. I borrowed it from her.'

'Oh. It's hers, is it?' Aditya flipped through the book again. 'Too big for me. There is no way I will be able to read it.' While flipping through the pages he saw that the reader had scribbled a lot on it; doodled in fact. 'I hate it when someone tortures a book like this,' he said. He pointed to the doodles on almost every page of the book. Someone had taken a pen and scribbled random designs. The designs were very distinctive. He casually concluded that it must be the work of a bored reader. 'I hate it when people don't give a book its due respect—most of all, people who are, or want to be authors. Please tell your friend,' Aditya finished with a smile.

48

BY THE TIME Maya came out of the airport it was 1.30 am. Sanjay was there to receive her. Since Aditya was in Kolkata he had requested Sanjay to pick her up. He didn't want Maya travelling alone at night.

'Want to grab a drink?' Sanjay asked her.

'I thought you had a call early tomorrow morning,' Maya responded. Sanjay had told her about his conference call with the regional office early next morning, wherein he was to give a progress update on the retrenchment project.

'I do,' he shrugged his shoulders, 'but I thought you might be jet-lagged and find it difficult to sleep. And a drink with you is always a pleasure.'

'Haha!' Maya laughed. 'No, I'm fine. I do not want Tim and Aditya screaming at me for delaying you nor do I want you to land up groggy.'

'Whatever you say,' Sanjay grinned. 'I feel like having a drink but I guess I'll have to make do with one at home.'

*

Maya dumped her luggage in the bedroom and plugged her phone for charging. She waited and the moment the phone turned on, she sent an SMS to Aditya.

<Reached home. Wish you were here.>

Aditya called back immediately.

'You still awake, Adi? I didn't want to wake you up so I sent you an SMS. What are you up to?'

'I couldn't sleep. You know how it is for me when I am alone in a hotel room. Did Sanjay reach on time to pick you up?'

'Of course he did. I would have killed him otherwise.'

'He won't mess around when it comes to you. How was Paris?'

'Lovely. Didn't get a chance to do much, but whatever I saw was breathtaking. Missed you there, baby. It is no fun without you,' she lamented.

Aditya laughed. 'What all did you shop for, baby? I lost count of the credit card alerts that I got.'

'Rubbish. I didn't shop using your add-on card, only because I didn't want you to get the alerts. I used my own card. In any case, not much shopping happened in Paris. The big purchase was in Dubai.'

'So you bought your iPhone6?'

'Yessss!!! It's lovely. Come fast and set it up for me.'

'Ma . . . ya!' Aditya dragged her name a bit, pretending to be cross. 'You are an IIM graduate. You travel the world. You win international awards. And you want me to come and set up your phone. Just do it yourself. Don't be such a techno-retard.'

Maya was about to respond when she heard a call waiting tone. It was not her phone. It had to be on Aditya's. 'Who is calling you at this time?'

'Wait,' Aditya paused for a moment before coming back on line, 'It's Sanjay. He is trying to call me. I guess he wants to tell me that he has dropped you off safely.'

'Okay. Speak to him. Thank him again. Poor guy gave up his sleep for me.'

'Okay, baby. Goodnight. I'll call you tomorrow.'

After disconnecting the call, Maya got up to make sure all the lights were off and windows closed. The moment she got up, she felt dizzy. Holding on to the corner of the table, she balanced herself and sat down on a chair. She waited for a few moments and allowed it to subside, till she felt a little better and got up again. Low BP probably, she thought to herself and walked to the kitchen to get some water. She added a spoonful of sugar to it, just to get the glucose levels going.

Back in her bedroom, she tried to sleep but couldn't. Her eyes were wide open. She mulled over her brief discussion with Aditya. It was not that she was a techno-retard; far from it. She just loved Aditya doing things for her. She decided to surprise him by setting up her iPhone6 herself. She connected her existing phone to their home laptop and backed it up. Then she connected her new iPhone6 to the laptop and restored it from a backup. It didn't take her much time to get the iPhone6 up and running.

She walked to her bed, admiring her new phone. It looked sleek, comfortable to use and had a large screen to boot. The screen clarity was out of the world. She fell in love with her phone. She played with the icons, opened the Kindle app and tried to check out her books. She couldn't.

They were missing. She logged off and logged into Kindle again, using her ID. She checked the music on her phone. Her iTunes match was on, so all the music that she had on her laptop was on her phone too. She looked at the messages, just to make sure she had not lost any of them.

And she froze.

49

HER MIND WAS blank. She didn't know what to think or do. She sat on the sofa for a long time. Not able to decide on her next course of action. Finally, after a lot of deliberation, she decided to call Aditya and dialled his number. His phone was busy. So he was awake—speaking to someone and that too at 4.00 am!

She flicked open the messages folder, selected a number from there and called it. It went to call waiting again. Given what she knew, it was safe to hypothesise that Aditya was speaking to the person whose number she had dialled.

But how and why? She didn't know this side of Aditya. Was Aditya gay? She didn't have anything against homosexuals, but for god's sake, not Aditya. How could he be gay? Aditya couldn't be cheating on her, that too with a guy. She was furious, and upset at the same time. Was he bisexual? It's not that they had a very active sex life, but whenever they did have sex, he was good at it. He never gave the impression that something was amiss. Her life was lying in front of her, in tatters. Would she be able to pull back from the brink that it had been driven to? She didn't know whether to be angry, or feel sorry; whether to be aggressive or understanding; whether to call him again right now and scream or wait for him to return to Mumbai.

Her phone rang. The name Ram Kumar flashed on her screen; it was the same name that she had called some time back. Probably Ram Kumar had seen her call and was calling her back. She picked up the phone and didn't speak.

'Hello . . . Hello . . . who is this?'

As soon as she heard the voice on the other side of the line, everything came together in a flash. She understood the entire game. She had been cheated. She disconnected the phone. Her head was spinning like a top. She got up, struggling to balance herself. The corner of the table came to her rescue again.

She picked up the phone and dialled another number. It continued ringing. No one picked up. She called again. This time someone picked up the phone.

'I need to talk to you,' she said, 'now.'

'Maya? At this hour . . . what happened?' Sanjay stammered. He had not woken up fully. 'Is everything okay?'

'Will it be possible for you to come over,' she was breathing heavily, 'right now?'

'Now? What happened? Is everything all right?'

'Are you coming?' Maya kept her composure.

'Can we talk over the phone?' He sat up rubbing his eyes.

'Are you coming now or should I get into my car and come over?' It was a threat she knew would work.

'Hold on, I am coming,' Sanjay said, alarmed. He got out of his bed. 'Give me thirty minutes.'

In a little over thirty minutes, Sanjay was back where he

had dropped Maya a few hours ago. He had tried to call Aditya on his way, but he didn't take his call. He was probably fast asleep.

Maya opened the door within three seconds of him ringing the bell. She appeared to have been waiting for him.

'Maya . . .' he had hardly begun when he noticed the anguish on her face. He fell silent, waiting for her to talk.

'Did you contact Aditya after you dropped me?'

Sanjay looked confused. 'I sent him an SMS that I had dropped you home, yes. Why?'

'Did you call?' she asked firmly.

'No. I thought he would be sleeping. He pulled out his phone from his right pocket and looked through it. 'Here it is,' he said. 'At 2.47 am I sent him the message. Why? What's the problem?'

It didn't come as a surprise to her that Aditya had lied about being on a call with Sanjay earlier that night. She wanted to make sure that her hypothesis was correct. 'On the day of the Crossword Books' award party, did you drop Tim home?'

'Tim?' Sanjay sounded surprised. 'Why would I need to drop Tim in my Innova when he has his own Mercedes GL?'

So her assumption was correct. 'What's going on, Sanjay?' There was a tremor in her voice—the kind that creeps in when one is angry and frustrated but forced to keep calm.

'As in? What are you talking about?'

'Stop faking it, Sanjay. Tell me what's going on between Aditya and that bitch.'

'I don't know who you mean, Maya . . .'

'Sanjay,' she cut him short, 'stop covering up for him. What the hell is going on between my husband and that bitch?' Maya's patience was at its lowest ebb and she was ready to burst.

'Whom are you talking about?'

'That management trainee from Bengaluru, Sanjay,' she raised her voice.

'Ohh . . . Shreya.'

Maya didn't respond. It was as if she didn't even want to utter her name. Her piercing gaze made Sanjay uncomfortable. He was searching for words. He looked to his right, then at the table in the centre of the room, his restless mind unable to decide what would be the appropriate thing to say.

'Sanjay,' Maya said, this time a strange fear in her voice. 'You are making me nervous.'

'Well there is nothing to be nervous about. I don't know why you are worried. Aditya is a dedicated guy. He has always been committed to you and Aryan.'

'If that is true then why is your face staunchly refusing to endorse your words?'

'What gave you the impression that something is going on between the two of them?'

'This.' She gave him her iPhone. On the screen was the message string—explicit romantic messages between Aditya and someone else. 'How do you explain this?'

'Whose phone is this?'

'It's my new iPhone.'

'How did these messages get in here?'

'How important is it for you to know that? Can you please just tell me what is going on?'

'Just asking!' Sanjay reasoned.

Maya felt bad that she was being rude to him, to someone who she was counting on to tell her the truth. 'I was setting up the new phone that I bought. I backed up my old iPhone on iTunes and then connected my new iPhone6. When I restored the new one from a backup, accidentally I chose an older backup of Aditya's phone. His phone was a hand-me-down—a phone that I had used for a short while.' She looked at the phone in his hand. 'An iPhone5, the same one that you have. It is also registered as Maya's iPhone5. So when I selected a file to restore, I mistakenly restored from the backup of his phone. All his messages, contact list everything came into my phone. That is when I saw the messages.'

'But these are from some Ram Kumar. Where does Shreya fit in?'

'Do you have Shreya's phone number?'

'I do.'

'Read it out loud please.'

Sanjay looked into his phone and brought up Shreya's number. The number matched the number saved in Maya's phone as Ram Kumar.

'Now tell me, Sanjay, apart from the explicit messages, why would Aditya save Shreya's number as Ram Kumar's, unless he has something to hide. Now will you tell me the truth or should I call this Ram Kumar and confront "him"?'

Sanjay knew that she was serious. 'Look, Maya. There is

nothing going on between the two of them. Just a little bit of healthy flirting, I'd say.'

'Flirting? Healthy flirting? Really Sanjay . . .' she rolled her eyes in disgust. 'That's what you men call it.' She threw up her hands in utter exasperation. 'That's what you call it . . . Healthy flirting. There is nothing healthy about flirting, Sanjay, not for a married man. Healthy flirting is a term introduced by perverted men who want to lend legitimacy to their extramarital dalliances. Flirting invariably has a sexual connotation to it.' She got up from her seat and walked around the room gesticulating and muttering something to herself. Suddenly she stopped, turned back, looked at Sanjay and asked, 'Did my husband sleep with her? Did he ever tell you anything about it?'

'No,' Sanjay immediately responded, and then after a moment's thought, added, 'Not that I know of at least.'

A look of resignation came on Maya's face. 'Sanjay,' she pleaded, 'how deep in this shit is he? Please don't lie to me. I have Aryan's future to consider. I can't compromise that because of a wayward father. Please, Sanjay. Don't lie to me.' There were tears welling up in her eyes. She was brave, but every brave act has a breaking point. She was fast reaching that point.

'Maya . . .' Sanjay wanted to console her.

'You are not telling me the entire truth. You were in Bengaluru with him when he went for the placement interviews. Who hired her?'

'Maya, you must relax. Let Aditya come back. We will sort this out,' he stopped when he saw her angry face. 'Or rather let me call him now. We can kill it right now.'

'No!' Maya yelled. 'You will not call him now. You will not call him on this ever. I will deal with this. He has cheated on me. I will not tolerate it. I have given him my entire life. I would have tolerated him sleeping with her once. It would've hurt me but I could've explained it to myself as an impulsive reaction. But getting into a long-drawn emotional tangle with her could not have been without him considering the repercussions. So it is obvious. He made a choice. He chose her over our relationship. From this very instant he is gone for me. I don't need him in my life. A man who does not consider the ramifications of his actions on his six-year-old child is not worth wasting my time on. He is dead to me. He does not deserve Aryan and me. He is dead.' Maya started shivering.

It was clear that she was upset. Her hands were shaking with anger. She picked up the glass vase kept on the centre table and flung it with all her might. It hit the wall and shattered into a thousand pieces. She was getting hysterical now, screaming expletives, abusing Shreya and Aditya. Sanjay was worried. This was not the Maya he knew. He walked up to her and held her by her forearm.

'Maya, please calm down . . . Maya!' he screamed. But Maya kept shouting. Her body was shivering violently. Sanjay finally held her tightly, hugged her and sobered her down. He made her sit and gave her a glass of water. She drank it while Sanjay patiently held her hand. Even though Maya had calmed down, the shivering hadn't stopped. Sanjay realised that she wasn't shivering simply out of anger. Her body was burning. She had a fever. He estimated it to be around 103 degrees.

'Maya, you don't seem well,' he said in a concerned tone.

Maya just looked the other way. 'Does it matter anymore? When my life is getting torn to smithereens, does a simple fever matter?'

'Come on, Maya. You need to take some medicines.' Sanjay walked to the cabinet, pulled out a Crocin and gave it to Maya along with a glass of water.

'Thank you, Sanjay.' Even in a moment of extreme angst, Maya didn't forget basic courtesy.

'Maya, you must go to sleep now. Let Aditya come back. We will sort this issue out.'

'No. He will not come here. I don't want to even see his face. When he comes back, I am going to throw him and his luggage out through the front door.' She seemed determined. 'And before you go, Sanjay, promise me that you will not utter a word about this to him. I want to confront him when he is unprepared. When he is least expecting this.'

Sanjay promised not to tell Aditya and returned home.

Sleep had deserted Maya and she lay on the bed staring blankly at the roof. Her future seemed bleak. Her personal life was in tatters. What had she done? Rather what had she not done that things had come to this stage? She had always given Aditya his privacy, his space; never ever doubted him or his intent.

She didn't realise when her eyes shut involuntarily and she dropped off to sleep. She slipped into a dream in which she was wandering around in a desert, chased by someone riding a horse. The man's face was covered. He ran his horse tantalisingly close to her but never knocked her down. She was tired and thirsty. Profusely sweating, she considered giving up and surrendering to the horse rider. Just as her senses were giving way, she saw a pool of water. She ran towards it. The man on the horse kept following her. She reached the oasis and hurriedly scooped some water and gulped it down. It tasted like nectar. She kept drinking, oblivious to the fact that the man on the horse had closed the gap. By the time she saw his reflection in the water, he was standing right over her head. The cloth covering his face had slipped. She was surprised to see who he was—Aditya!

What was he doing chasing her through the desert? Why didn't he offer her a ride? Before she could figure out answers to these questions, the rider pulled out a sword, its edges glistening in the sun, and in a rehearsed motion, brought it down smooth and fast, the blade slicing through her abdomen like hot knife on butter. She clutched her abdomen and screamed, 'Aaaaaaah!'

She woke up with a start and sat upright on her bed. The desert was a dream, the man on the horse was a dream, the sword was a dream and the murderous attack was a dream.

The pain wasn't. It was real.

And when the same pain hit her again, she clutched her abdomen and rolled over in a foetal position. It was unbearable. She couldn't move. For an instant she felt that she was going to die. And then, like it had hit her all of a sudden, the pain subsided on its own.

She got up from her bed, wondering what was happening to her. She couldn't stand straight. Her head was spinning.

Worried, she sat down, which was just as well for she felt weak and could have crashed to the floor.

'Oh my God! Why are you doing this to me?' she cried. She could feel the pain coming back. Deep inside her, the stirrings of pain which would soon shoot through her body, were beginning. This time the pain was different. It was accompanied by a churn in the stomach, like someone had set a centrifuge inside her. She rushed to the bathroom, clutching her stomach. The pain was unbearable now, and the churning was uncontrollable. Doggedly she held on, but for how long . . . The moment she opened the door, she let go, spraying vomit all over the floor and some bits inside the washbasin. She collapsed on the marble floor and started crying.

She couldn't bear it any more. Yet, the pain in her abdomen seemed a lot more bearable than the pain that Aditya had gifted her.

50

Aditya returned Sanjay's call the next morning. 'Sorry, missed your call last night. I was talking to Maya.'

'Really?' Sanjay was not in a mood to humour him.

'Hahaha!' Aditya laughed, which only irritated Sanjay even more. 'So, why had you called yesterday?' Aditya continued.

'I just wanted to tell you that last night I had a long call with Tim. He wanted us to finish the entire retrenchment exercise by today. Just get it over with and come back.' He didn't tell him about Maya's conversation with him honouring Maya's wishes.

'And for that you called me so late at night?' Aditya was curt. 'In any case, everything is done. The letters have been handed out yesterday. If today there are no issues with the teams in Kolkata, no protests that is, then we can assume that everything is done and dusted.'

'Let's hope for the best. We'll talk during the day.'

'Thanks, Sanjay. By the way, I have been trying to reach Maya. She is not picking up the phone. Maybe she slept off after a tiring flight. In case she calls you, just let her know that I have been trying to reach her.'

'Why will she call me?' Sanjay barked, unable to hide his anger.

'Just saying, in case she does . . .' Aditya knew that Maya would call Sanjay in the morning to thank him once again for the trouble he had taken the night before. She was particular about these things.

'She will see your missed calls for sure.'

'What's the matter, Sanjay? Is everything okay?' Sanjay's curt responses confused Aditya.

'Oh yes, yes. Just stressed a bit about the lay-offs,' Sanjay lied. 'You are taking the last flight out today, right?'

'Yes. Just riding the day out here, hoping there is no further complication.'

'Hmm . . . Be careful. Union issues can get pretty rough. See you soon, Aditya. God bless.'

What a strange way to end a conversation, Aditya thought. Sanjay never said 'God bless'.

After he disconnected the call, Sanjay dialled Maya. He wanted to update her about his conversation with Aditya. The phone kept ringing, but no one picked it up. Maybe she was tired, emotionally drained and fast asleep, Sanjay assumed. He kept the phone aside and started ironing his shirt. Once he was done, he called Maya's number again. The phone rang. No one answered. He let it ring on speaker and started buttoning his shirt. He was hoping that after ten rings or so, the call would automatically get disconnected. At the eighth ring, he got lucky.

'Hello?'

It was not Maya.

51

Sanjay disconnected the call and ran, stopping only to wear his shoes and to gather the car keys.

On the way he called Aditya's number. Thankfully he was not busy on another call.

'You need to get back here right away, Aditya.'

'What happened?'

When Sanjay told him, Aditya freaked. 'Oh my god! How did this happen?'

'I am going there to find out; will keep you posted. But you take the earliest flight out. I will manage Tim. Just brief the Eastern India HR head and he will take over.'

After he hung up, he called Diana. She was at home. He asked her to be on standby just in case he needed her help.

Sanjay reached Maya's residence in a little over fifteen minutes. The maid was waiting for him at the door. He pushed the door open and hurried in.

Maya was lying on the sofa. She looked pale, as if all the blood had drained out of her face. Her skin was beginning to sag, and her eyes were drooping. Her entire frame had sunk into the sofa. She had no energy to even lift herself. Quite a contrast to the bubbly Maya he had picked up from the airport less than twelve hours ago.

'Maya, what happened?' Sanjay rushed to her side and sat down on the sofa. Maya looked at him, with extremely tired eyes. Lifting her eyelashes to bring them in line with what she wanted to see was an effort.

'*Memsaab* was lying on the floor of the bathroom unconscious when I came in. I have my own keys,' the maid volunteered. 'I sprinkled some water on her face, and helped her drag herself to the sofa.'

'Maya, what happened?' Sanjay repeated his question.

'I don't know. I think I was sleeping, when I had this shooting pain in my abdomen. I threw up and passed out. I don't know for how long. The only thing I remember is the maid waking me up,' she took a deep breath as she finished.

'Did you call a doctor?' he asked. Maya shook her head to indicate that she hadn't. 'Let me do it,' Sanjay offered and took Maya's phone to search for the number.

The moment his hand brushed against hers, he was shocked. 'Maya,' he said with a touch of concern in his voice, 'it feels like you are on fire. We need to go to the hospital.'

'No, Sanjay. I think it is just exhaustion from the trip. And probably something we ate in Paris did not agree with my system. I will have another Crocin.'

'You had one only four hours ago. Are you sure?'

'I probably vomited the Crocin out. Thanks for driving all the way. I have troubled you so much over the last twelve hours.' She looked at the maid and asked her to get her two slices of toasted bread and the medicine box.

'I have spoken to Aditya. He is coming back in the afternoon today. He has been trying to call you.'

Maya suddenly sat up straight. 'Let him come, he has a lot to answer for. He better have his defence ready,' she said, despite the fact that words were barely coming out of her mouth.

The maid brought her some toast. Maya quietly nibbled on it. Sanjay called Aditya and briefed him when Maya was having her breakfast. He was already on his way to the airport.

Maya popped another Crocin and sipped water to wash it down her throat. Sanjay sat down next to her. He picked up the newspaper and started reading it. Maya stretched out on the sofa and curled up around a cushion and closed her eyes. Sanjay was worried. The fever did not seem like a normal one.

And then it started, all over again. Maya clutched her tummy and ran to the washroom. The maid ran after her. This time it was worse than before. Sanjay stayed in the living room, wondering what his next step should be.

When Maya came out after fifteen minutes, looking even paler compared to her earlier state, he decided to call the doctor. This time Maya didn't object.

The doctor came within forty-five minutes. He stayed nearby and had known the Kapoors for a long time. By then Aditya had reached the airport in Kolkata. He had managed to get a seat in a flight and was waiting for boarding announcements when Sanjay called him again.

'It's severe gastroenteritis. That's what the doctor said. He has given her some medicine. It will slow her down a bit for the next few hours and then we will see what needs to be done. He has said that even if she doesn't eat, it's fine.

'Where is she now? Give her the phone. She has not been taking my calls.'

'She has just closed her eyes. Let her sleep, Aditya. She has been through unmentionable trauma all night.'

'The boarding announcement has just been made. I will be home in four hours,' Aditya said.

52

MAYA WOKE UP after three hours. She was weak, though a lot better than how she had been in the morning. The antibiotics and sedatives that the doctor had given her seemed to have had an impact.

Sanjay was with her. He was worried and had decided to wait till Aditya arrived. He had even got the conference call with the regional office postponed.

He was in the living room watching some mind-numbing programme on television when Maya walked in and sat down on the sofa.

'When is Aditya's flight coming in?'

'He should be landing any time,' Sanjay replied. He could see that Maya had calmed down. She now wanted answers. What was it that was lacking in their lovely family that made Aditya do what he did?

'I think I should go and take a shower,' Maya interrupted his flow of thoughts. 'I'm feeling very yucky. I constantly feel that I smell of puke.' She got up and went inside.

Maya showered, changed into fresh clothes and came out to join Sanjay in the living room. By then Aditya had landed and was on his way home. Maya casually picked up the newspaper and started to glance through it.

The doorbell rang. 'It must be Aditya,' Sanjay said.

The maid walked towards the door. Maya didn't even bother to look up. She continued reading the newspaper. She was on the seventeenth page of the *Times of India*. The maid had reached the door and was about to unlatch it when Maya screamed.

'Savitha, wait!' she called out to the maid.

The doorbell rang again. Savitha turned and looked at Maya but she was lost in her newspaper. She was looking at a picture—a picture which she recognized. She lifted the paper, brought it to eye level and read the entire article in a flash. Sanjay and the maid looked at her, waiting for the next set of instructions. The doorbell rang a couple of times in the interim.

Maya read through the article and kept the paper down. She got up to walk towards the door. Her eyes were red with anger. She looked hurt, sad and furious all at once. She opened the door and looked at Aditya through the grill door.

'Hey, Maya. What is this? Why are you not taking care of my baby?' Aditya gave her a big smile. He was genuinely happy and relieved to see her. He bent down just a bit to pick up his bag, which he had kept on the floor, in anticipation of Maya opening the door.

'Why have you come here, Aditya?'

'What? What do you mean, Maya?' Aditya had a look of surprise on his face. He looked at Sanjay who was inside the house and asked him, 'Is there a problem?'

'Look at me, Aditya. Why are you looking at him?'

Aditya turned towards her. 'What were you thinking

when you got involved with that woman,' she turned to Sanjay and asked him, 'What's the name of the girl? Aaah Shreya!'

'I am not involved with her. What is going on?' Aditya was completely taken by surprise and didn't know how to react.

'What is she to you, Aditya? Does she mean anything to you?'

'She is just a colleague who works in my team. Listen, Maya, I am sure there is a misunderstanding. Open the door. I will clear all confusions. She does not mean anything to me. Believe me.'

Maya held her phone in her hand and started reading, '"Baby, come over. I am alone and missing you."' She moved the phone away and looked at Aditya. 'Is that what you would say to someone who doesn't mean anything to you?'

'What?' Aditya attempted to look disgusted. 'What did you say I said?'

'Baby, come over. I am alone and missing you. There are more. Want me to read them out to you?'

'I never said anything of that sort. There is a misunderstanding,' he lied, confident that there was no way Maya could possibly know of his affair.

'Oh really?' Maya seemed perfectly okay now. The way to kill pain is to inflict a bigger pain on one's self. 'Then what is this?' She lifted her phone and showed the message through the grill to Aditya. 'And this,' she said as she swiped through a few screens and pressed a button on her screen.

Shreya's voice could be clearly heard, 'And tell me Aditya, that day when you kissed me, did you think of me when you came back home?' There was a sound of some liquid being poured into a glass and then Aditya's voice came on line, 'Of course yes. How could I not? You kiss fabulously and I haven't been kissed like that in a while.'

The entire recording of Aditya and Shreya's sexual escapade started playing on the phone. Maya had tears in her eyes.

Aditya was shell-shocked. How on earth did Maya get hold of the recording? This was the recording that Shreya had made the first time she had come over; when she had told him that the sex in his book was *thanda*; when she had helped him spruce it up. But even in his wildest dreams he couldn't comprehend as to how that recording could've ended up on Maya's phone.

Maya was shattered. The look on her face said it all. Unable to tolerate the audio recording, she shut it off. 'Aren't you ashamed, Aditya?'

Aditya didn't know how to respond. The evidence was there, for everyone to see. There was no way he could have refuted or denied a dalliance. 'There is some confusion. Let me come in. We will talk it through. I can explain, Maya,' was all he could say.

Maya could feel the pain building up inside her again—deep inside her gut, a dull pain. That's how it had begun the earlier few times. And then it had rapidly grown in intensity till it seemed like an elephant was sitting on her and squashing her, blowing the wind out of her lungs.

'Don't even try to lie, Aditya,' she raised her voice. 'I always had a suspicion. But I invariably gave you the benefit of the doubt.' She clutched her stomach and bent forward, her breathing laboured. Aditya could see that she was in enormous pain. He was helpless. He couldn't do anything till she opened the door.

Her breath was now coming in short spurts. She was panting and had begun to sweat.

'Maya. Give me a chance to explain, baby. You are in bad shape now. Let's get some help. I will work it out. I love you, Maya. I really love you. No one else matters to me. Trust me on this.'

'Liar! You are a liar,' she screamed through her pain. It was getting unbearable, as if she had been stabbed right in the abdomen and now someone was turning that knife three hundred and sixty degrees, slowly, inch by inch. The air was gushing out of her lungs and she was finding it difficult to breathe. She was struggling as if she was fifty metres under water. 'You cheated on me. You cheated on Aryan. I hate cheaters. Now get the hell out of here,' she said as she turned to rush to the washroom.

'Where will I go, Maya? I don't have anywhere to go except our home—the home that you and I built. Where will I go?' he yelled, as Maya rushed away from him.

She stopped for an instant as she reached the washroom and looked at him for that brief moment. 'For all I care, Adi, go to Hell. Until then, may I recommend the Hyatt.' She banged the toilet door behind her.

'Sanjay, dare you let him in,' were her last audible words.

Sanjay walked up to the door. 'I think she needs to let out some steam. You go home. I will calm her down. Till then, it is better you stay away.'

'Which home? This is my home.'

'Go to my house, Aditya. Stay there. The maid is at home. I will call you once things are under control.'

'But she is so unwell. How can I stay away?'

'Trust me. Your being here will do more harm than good. I am going to give her the next dose that the doctor had given this morning. Hopefully she will calm down. Once she does, it will be easy for me to bring around reconciliation.

Aditya didn't know what to say. He was quiet. The only sound he could hear was Savitha knocking on the door of the bathroom. Maya was vomiting her bile out. Aditya had tears in his eyes.

The washroom door opened and Maya stumbled out. Her eyes were red. Water was flowing in a steady stream. She was struggling to walk. Savitha rushed towards her, wanting to support her and extended her hand.

'No. I can manage,' Maya said. She looked at Aditya who was still waiting for her to open the door, and then at Sanjay who was standing where Maya had been standing till a few moments back.

She looked frail, as if she were about to collapse. But seeing Aditya at the door had given her renewed energy and vigour. She wanted to let him know what she thought of him for cheating on her.

'Till I am alive, Aditya,' she declared, 'you will not enter this house again. You have lost my trust. You have taken advantage of Aryan and me, our blind faith in you. I will never forgive you for it,' she sank to the floor. 'Ever,' she added before she turned over and clutched her stomach again.

Sanjay ran to call the doctor.

'Shut the door, Savitha,' Maya let out a scream. A hesitant Savitha walked to the door and gently shut it on Aditya's face.

'The doctor is on his way,' Sanjay announced as he ran back to help her gain balance.

'No. Stop!' Maya yelled at the top of her voice. 'Don't come near me. Stay away.' Sanjay stopped in his tracks. Gasping for breath, she was about to faint. She was still holding her abdomen but the pain had now spread to her chest too. Sweat was glistening on her face. It looked as if she had washed her face and forgotten to wipe the water off. She pointed to the table. There was a glass of water on the table. Sanjay hurriedly picked it up and extended it towards her.

'No', she shook her head, struggling to even breathe. 'The paper,' she whispered, pointing to the newspaper lying on the table.

Sanjay looked at the open newspaper. Page seventeen—the international news section of the *Times of India*. He looked at the picture staring out of the newspaper. He had no idea who it was. But it was not the picture. It was the news that accompanied the picture which scared him. Sanjay began to panic.

53

Woman detained in Paris, tests positive for Ebola Virus

An Egyptian educationist Minouche Shafik, who arrived in Paris three days back and who was rushed to a Paris hospital on Sunday evening, has tested positive for Ebola, giving France its first Ebola case. The educationist is believed to have been infected by her fiancé, a diamond merchant with business interests in Egypt, Sierra Leone and Nigeria. The diamond merchant (refer inset) passed away on Saturday morning in an isolation camp in Sierra Leone. Health authorities are worried that Minouche Shafik, might have passed on the Ebola Virus to various people she came in contact with during the course of the Global Educational Conference she was here to attend. Health authorities are in the process of identifying and isolating the individuals she may have infected. The concern arises from the fact that it was a global conference with delegates from all over the world . . .

Sanjay turned and looked at Maya, scared. Wasn't this the conference that she had returned from?

54

IN NO TIME an ambulance screeched to a halt in front of the housing complex. The area had already been cordoned off and access to the 10th floor had been restricted. The elevators had been stopped, causing a fair bit of problems for the residents. But this was serious.

Three men in yellow biohazard suits stepped out of the ambulance. Seeing the men in full body suits, head gear, face-masks and eye-covers, a crowd had gathered outside the apartment complex. The three men accompanied by six assistants and an equal number of constables hurriedly took the lift up to the tenth floor apartment. Outside the main door, they found a desperate looking Aditya waiting for them. After the initial introductions, Aditya guided them inside. By then Diana too had reached Aditya's residence.

The three men in body suits entered the premises. They took over one of the lifts. They were carrying disposable stretchers—these would be thrown away after use. The three people in the house—Maya, Savitha and Sanjay—were made to lie down on the stretchers and wrapped in some cheap-looking tarpaulin. All three were carried down to the ambulance. Once they had been transported to the ambulance, the apartment was sanitised by spraying a combination of bleach and water. The entire process was repeated for the elevator too.

Aditya tried to get into the ambulance with the three patients. He was advised against it.

'Not in the ambulance. We can't take any chances,' the doctor informed him.

A worried Aditya ran to his car and followed the ambulance. Diana followed him in her car.

Just as the ambulance was driving off, Aditya saw the first media van arrive.

He followed the ambulance to the isolation ward at the Government Hospital (GH) in Jogeshwari. On the way he called Shreya and told her about Maya's sickness. He also told her about Maya finding out about the two of them. Shreya fell silent.

'Now what, Aditya?' she spoke finally.

'I don't know what to say, Shreya. I am not even thinking about anything right now. I just want her to get okay. She was so upset; I just can't get over the look in her eyes. She was in agony. I could see that the pain was not because of the illness. It was the pain of realising that I have cheated on her. She trusted me, Shreya, and I failed her. I failed her, Shreya.'

'You have been an amazing husband, Aditya. Despite everything not once did your commitment towards your family waver. I am sure you can explain things to her.'

'Bullshit!' Aditya screamed. The panic over Maya's condition was evident. 'There is no logic for what is going on between us. There can be no explanation. It is an inappropriate relationship and both of us know that. Yet we have gone ahead with it.'

'So what are you saying, Aditya?'

'Nothing. I will talk to you later. I'm very disturbed right now.' He hung up. Shreya called him back a few times as he was driving. He didn't pick up the phone.

55

IN A MATTER of minutes, the news channels got wind of what was the first suspected case of Ebola in India. OB vans from all news channels rushed to the General Hospital in Jogeshwari—the only hospital in Mumbai with an isolation ward for Ebola patients. Aditya would find out only later that a few bigger hospitals like Lilavati and Jaslok in Mumbai were not approved for patients placed under quarantine or isolation for Ebola.

Sanjay's parents had been informed and they were rushing to Mumbai, from Kolkata. Aditya did tell them that it would not be necessary for them to come to Mumbai at this stage as Sanjay was only under quarantine, pending the blood test results. But in India, no one particularly understood the difference between isolation and quarantine. Isolation separates sick people with a contagious disease from people who are not sick, to prevent them from infecting others. Quarantine separated and restricted the movement of people who were exposed to a contagious disease to see if they become sick. In this case Maya was the one who was in the isolation ward. She was sick. She was the one suspected to have Ebola Virus Disease (EVD). Sanjay and Savitha had just been quarantined to see if they would show symptoms of the disease and if they would eventually fall sick. They were the ones who had come in close contact with Maya.

A general advisory was issued by the government, and the authorities started getting in touch with everyone who was on the flight with Maya, to inform them of the risk and put them under quarantine in their own houses. The French authorities had apparently communicated with the Indian agencies on the possibility of an Indian having contracted Ebola, but the Indian agencies on their part had been extremely lax and did not display the same agility in reaching out to Maya in time.

At the Jogeshwari GH, a steady stream of visitors trickled in to provide moral support to Aditya. The CEO of National Bank, people from his team, colleagues from Maya's school, a few friends; soon it became a carnival. The TV cameras only added to the entire cacophony. They debated if Maya should have been held back at the airport when she came in from Paris. Shouldn't the security checks at the immigration point be strong enough to detect possible cases of Ebola and detain those infected?

No one really cared about what was going through Aditya's mind. If guilt could kill, that day Aditya would have died a thousand times. He loved Maya. He couldn't help thinking that the knowledge of his affair had precipitated her illness. She was sick and heartbroken at the same time. It was a strange twist of fate. But the fact was that Aditya liked Shreya too. Whether he loved her enough to leave Maya for her, he was not sure. He had also told Shreya many a time that for him family was a priority, and that he would never be able to leave them for her. Whenever they had this discussion, Shreya always told him categorically that she had no such expectations from him either.

Sunaina called him that night.

'Shreya called me, Aditya. She told me about Maya. It is really unfortunate.'

Aditya was listening. He didn't say anything.

'She was in tears, poor Shreya. She is very worried for you.'

'I spoke to her when I was driving to the hospital,' Aditya said.

'She also told me that she is not going to the hospital to see you, because she won't be able to see you unhappy and stressed. She didn't want to complicate your life at this stage. She wanted me to tell you that she will be waiting for your call, whenever you are free. She doesn't want to disturb you or put pressure on you.'

'Thanks for that, Sunaina. I was very worked up at the time I spoke to her.'

'She was panicking about what you told her. Apparently you were very curt. She is scared that she is about to lose you.'

'I was disturbed, Sunaina. Isn't that to be expected?'

'I am in Mumbai tomorrow, coming for a couple of days. I'll come and see you.'

'Sure,' he said and hung up. He could see the Medical Superintendent walking towards him. He stood up from his seat and waited for the doctor.

'Will you please come with me to my cabin?' the doctor directed. Aditya accompanied him to his cabin at the end of the corridor. The Medical Superintendent made Aditya sit down on a sofa in his room. Maya's parents, who had followed Aditya, sat down next to him. They had flown into Mumbai immediately on hearing about the scare, leaving Aryan with Maya's sister who stayed with them.

Dr Krishnan, the Medical Superintendent, looked at the three of them through his rimless glasses and began, 'I am sorry.' Aditya's heart sank as he heard those three words. 'The news is not good. The medical reports have just come in. It's EVD.' He looked at Maya's parents and said, 'Ebola Virus Disease.' He even explained to them the possible connection to Minouche.

'Has she regained consciousness?' Aditya interrupted.

'Yes, a few minutes ago. She apparently helped the Ebola patient wash up and get into bed after she had thrown up. That's when she must have come in contact with the body fluids of the Ebola-infected person and contracted it. Ebola manifests itself in the patient within two to twenty-one days of contracting it. In Maya, it has been quick to show up; within two days, and that is not a good sign.'

Aditya clutched his head in his hands and looked towards the floor. He was about to cry.

'What about the other two?' Maya's father asked.

'No signs of Ebola. We will keep both of them quarantined; under observation for three days and then let them go. The good thing with Ebola is that the virus cannot live for long outside the human body. So it is not airborne or contagious as many other viruses are. Only when the person comes in contact with the Ebola patient's body fluids or blood or faeces, is there a chance for transmission. That said, it is always better to be careful, given the 90 per cent mortality rate.'

There was a stunned silence in the room.

'Are you then saying,' Aditya asked, horror writ all over his face, 'that Maya has only a 10 per cent chance of survival?' He knew that Ebola patients had high mortality, yet someone laying it out in black and white could be nerve-wracking.

'Can I meet her?' Aditya asked Dr Krishnan.

'No,' Dr Krishnan's reply was firm. Aditya held his head in his hands and started sobbing.

56

Dr Krishnan waited for some time, letting Aditya calm down, after his outbreak.

'It is a bit risky, Mr Kapoor. We are under strict instructions not to allow anyone but the designated medical professional to meet the patient. It is in your own interest.'

'I really don't care about myself. I need to meet her.'

'We care, Mr Kapoor. Not only about you, but about others you might infect in case you contract the disease. We do understand the sentiment, but we don't have a choice.'

'Can I at least speak to her?' Aditya was desperate. Maya's parents were sitting in one corner just listening to the conversation, stupefied.

'She is extremely weak and under sedation. Let her condition stabilise. Once she improves, you will be able to speak with her.'

They spoke for a few minutes, after which the Medical Superintendent got up and walked towards the door. 'I have to make a statement to the press on this. I will send you a copy of my release. Please stick to it when you speak to the press.'

Later that night, a request did come for Aditya to meet

the press. He turned it down saying that he was not in the right frame of mind.

Shreya called him that night. Aditya hadn't called her the whole day.

'Hi Aditya. How are things there?'

'She is in a bad state, Shreya, a really bad state. She has been sedated, and injected with fluids all day. She hasn't spoken a word to anyone. I don't know what's going on. How am I going to get through all this?'

'You want me to come over and be with you?'

'No, Shreya. It's okay. There are enough people here. There isn't even a proper place to sit.'

'You are there. If you can be there, how difficult will it be for me?'

'Maya's parents are also here. It will be embarrassing in front of them.'

'Are you cutting me off, Aditya?'

'Come on, Shreya. Don't be ridiculous. Why would I do that?'

'Do you love me?'

'Is it necessary to answer that right now?' he countered. The timing of the question bothered him.

'Maybe it is?'

Aditya was not in a frame of mind to respond to Shreya. 'I will talk to you tomorrow.' He was about to hang up when Shreya squealed, 'Wait, wait. Don't hang up. Sunaina is coming tomorrow. Is it okay if I come and see you with her?'

'Okay,' Aditya gave in. It wasn't that he didn't want to see Shreya. The fact that just as she got felled by Ebola, Maya got to know of Shreya, was killing him. He was worried that just in case something happened to Maya, her last impression of him would be one of an infidel and cheat. Shreya was the first dalliance in his life. He was worried that he would never get a chance to clear the air with Maya or make up with her. Guilt was killing his spirit the way pain and suffering was killing his wife. Nothing in life is more wretched than the mind of a man conscious of his guilt.

Shreya realised that Aditya didn't want to talk about Maya or her illness. She changed the topic. 'By the way, Aditya, Vaishali has finished editing my manuscript. She has sent it to me—the final manuscript.'

'Great,' Aditya didn't encourage the conversation. He wanted to be by himself.

'Would you want to read it while you are waiting in the hospital? And maybe tomorrow when I see you, you can quickly tell me if it is good to go?'

'What?' He was shocked. 'Really?' he yelled into the phone, 'Really, Shreya?'

'It's okay if you can't,' Shreya beat a hasty retreat. 'I just asked. I thought it would help divert your mind.'

Aditya was disgusted at Shreya's demand. He maintained his cool. 'Later, Shreya. Not right now. I'm not in the proper frame of mind.'

'No problem, Aditya. We'll talk tomorrow.' When she sensed silence from the other end, she added, 'I love you,' and hung up.

Aditya was furious as he disconnected the phone. How on earth did Shreya even expect him to read the manuscript, sitting in the hospital? How insensitive was she?

As it is he was confused about the state of their relationship. He was now beginning to see that Shreya was with him to further her writing career. She wanted to break into the clique of top authors in the country, be known in the industry and be talked about. For her, the easiest way to get there was to be in bed with him, to be his muse. She was using him for his influence. Why else would she have even brought up this topic today, especially when he was grieving over Maya's plight? He started questioning his own judgment. But the more he thought about it, the more the truth stared at him. Every time he and Shreya had engaged in a romantic conversation, or kissed, or had sex, she had invariably brought up her book. As if she was waiting for the right opportunity to strike. But there was a small part of him which refused to believe that his assessment was true.

That night Maya's condition deteriorated.

57

SHREYA AND SUNAINA came over to visit Aditya at the hospital, the next morning. They had brought him some food from home. They walked to the small room at the end of the corridor. Dr Krishnan had allowed them to use it.

'Can we see her?' Sunaina asked, probably out of courtesy.

'No one can go into her room. But just outside her room is a small anteroom—a transition area for healthcare workers. There is a glass wall, which overlooks Maya's room. You can see her from there. Only one person is allowed at a time and that too after the Medical Superintendent's approval. To go beyond that there is a strict procedure regarding the protective suits, gloves and masks that one has to wear. Let me check with the Superintendent and come,' Aditya got up and left.

'Poor guy,' Sunaina said the moment he left the room.

'I know,' Shreya added.

'Do you know only 10 to 15 per cent of Ebola patients survive? I read up a lot on Ebola. There is hardly any hope left. It's better to be pragmatic. But it is very difficult to expect pragmatism from him at this stage. He loves her a lot.'

'He loves me too,' Shreya swiftly responded.

'I know.'

'But he is very guilty about it. He was distraught that Maya got to know about us and he did not get an opportunity to sort it out with her.'

'He will struggle a lot when she is gone.'

'I will not let him struggle. I will be with him. I am there for him, Sunaina. Perhaps all this is for the best. He will be happier with me. See, we have similar interests. We can feed off each other. The world will adore this author couple — Mrs and Mr Kapoor. It will be awesome.'

'Are you crazy, Shreya? You are in the hospital visiting someone on their deathbed and you are dreaming of the pleasant things life has in store for you once she is gone? Come on, Shreya. So much for compassion . . .'

'I am just being practical.'

'Fuck!' Sunaina looked away. 'Forget it,' she said, waving her hand in an exasperated manner. 'Let's not talk about it.' Whether she was frustrated at the direction the conversation was taking or whether she saw Aditya walk back into the room, no one could tell.

'The Superintendent wants to meet with you before you go in,' Aditya said as he entered the room.

The two girls got up. 'His office is down the corridor. I have to meet with their office staff and validate the press update. You guys go ahead. I will see you here in a while.' Aditya walked off.

Shreya and Sunaina walked out of the room to Dr Krishnan's office. He gave them some basic instructions and led them out to the anteroom.

From the huge glass wall in the anteroom, they could

look inside to where Maya was lying on the bed. They could see that she was awake. Her eyelids were blinking slowly. Her eyes were blood red. She seemed normal, except for her skin, which had become pale and wrinkled. Her face seemed at least twenty years older. Shreya noticed the blisters all over her hand. They were bleeding. She remembered reading that the Ebola virus pierces blood vessels causing bleeding from the eyes, ears, mouth and other orifices. The whites of the eyes turn red and blood blisters form under the skin.

Sunaina couldn't bear it anymore and turned back and ran out of the room, in tears. Shreya followed a few minutes later. Figuring out that Shreya might want some time alone with Aditya, Sunaina told her that she had to head out and that she would meet her back at home, and left.

'Don't worry, Aditya. Everything will be all right,' Shreya said the moment Sunaina left.

'I am not hopeful. It's got worse since last night. The blisters on her skin have started bleeding badly. The doctors are having a tough time controlling that. I want her to live, Shreya, I want her to live.'

'She will be back, Aditya, don't you worry.' She hugged him. Aditya began to sob. She hugged him even tighter. 'I love you, Aditya. Don't worry. God will make sure everything is all right,' she consoled him. The two of them walked into the hospital coffee shop.

On the way she stopped, pulled some printouts out of her bag and gave it to him. 'This is the final manuscript with all the changes. I have to send it to Vaishali day after. She will wait for a week or so is the sense I got. Read it whenever you get some time and let me know if it meets your standards.'

Aditya who had controlled himself till then, let go, 'Are you seriously out of your mind?'

'Adit . . .'

'No, tell me,' he shook his head furiously while struggling to find words, 'tell me what the fuck is wrong with you, Shreya? I am sitting here in the hospital. My wife is dying. I don't know what course my life will take and you want me to read your fucking manuscript?'

'I just thought you might be feeling bored sitting all alone, so I brought this along.'

'Damn your manuscript, Shreya. Damn you becoming an author. At this point in time, I care two hoots about it. The way you care for Maya, is how I care for your book. This is the only thing important to you, right?' Aditya waved his hands in the air furiously. 'My feelings and emotions be damned, but the book is important. You don't care if Maya dies. Actually why would you?' He furiously sniffed and moved ahead, only to stop and look back.

'Come on, Aditya, you know it is not like that.'

'Of course it is like that. You schemed. Right from the beginning, Maya, you have been scheming. I thought you loved me. I thought we had a nice thing going. I thought we liked being in each other's company.'

'That is the way it has always been, Aditya. I never schemed.'

'From the first time you got in touch with me to save yourself from the Director, to right now, when you are using me to get published, you have been lying, Maya.'

'That's unfair, Aditya. You are accusing me of being something which I am not. I love you.'

'Cut the crap, Maya.'

'Shreya. I am Shreya, not Maya. This is the third time you called me Maya.'

'Yes, yes, that's what I meant. I loved the woman in you, the person in you. But you always loved the author in me. Take the author out of me, and I am a nobody as far as you are concerned. Accept it. That's the fact.'

'No, Aditya. Please don't say that. Yes, I started loving you because of your books but now the books have nothing to do with it. Maybe I am very desperate about getting published, and that's because I am not as successful as you. But it's not just about the books any more. It's about you, Aditya. It is about us. How do I make you believe that you mean everything to me?' She had tears in her eyes.

Aditya retracted. He looked at Shreya and apologised. 'I am sorry. I am going through hell right now. I can't even think straight.' He led her to the main gate of the hospital. In front of Aditya, Shreya held back her tears, but the moment she was out of his sight, she broke down.

That night the Medical Superintendent released an update to the media.

Maya Kapoor, the first Ebola patient in India, continues her struggle with the virus. Her condition has further deteriorated over the last twelve hours. The blood vessels in her lower calves have ruptured, leading to sustained bleeding. Medical professionals are trying their best to stabilise her.

The Health Ministry, Government of India, has approved use of VSV-EBOV, an experimental Ebola vaccine, manufactured by the National Medical Laboratories of

Canada in association with Merck. Five doses of the vaccine have been hand-shipped to India and are expected to reach late tonight. The patient's family has given its consent to the use of the vaccine. It is worth mentioning that neither is the efficacy of the vaccine known nor are the side effects. WHO had recently approved the use of clinically untested vaccines for Ebola cure. The Health Ministry too has concurred with the WHO view.

It is going to be a difficult night. We are keeping a constant watch and will update you in case of a material change in condition. We request you all to report cautiously and respect the patient and her family's privacy.

Thank you
Sd/-
Dr Krishnan J
Medical Superintendent.

As he turned back to wind up his work for the night and head back to his house—he stayed within the hospital complex—he spotted Aditya. 'Don't expect too much, son,' he said. 'From what I see, it is a matter of "when" and not "if". Unless . . .'

'Unless . . .?' Aditya repeated.

'Unless the serum works. That's our last hope. It has thus far been administered to two patients—an American doctor who survived and a priest who died. So let's keep our fingers crossed.'

'If it doesn't work, Doctor . . . Then what?'

'Forty-eight hours, at best.'

If Aditya had had any tears left that night, he would have

cried. Why had this happened? Was this his comeuppance for his indiscretion? But why was Maya the one to suffer? He felt like forcing his way into the room where Maya was sleeping, oblivious to the happenings all around, and lie down next to her. He remembered the vows he had made in front of the holy fire when they had got married. He had not kept his end of the promise. But she could forgive him for Aryan. Didn't she have a responsibility towards their child? How could she shy away from that?

Dr Krishnan got up to leave. 'I will be in my quarters. Call me if you need anything?'

'Thank you, Doctor,' Aditya replied.

His mind was overflowing with thoughts of Maya, of the two of them. About the fabulous life they were leading till Shreya came into their lives and about the day he came back from Kolkata, when all hell broke loose . . . How could he make sure Maya didn't go away feeling that all the effort that she had put into this relationship with him was worthless?

Suddenly he had an idea. He turned and hurried outside the room.

'Dr Krishnan,' Aditya called out and ran behind him. When he caught up with him, he gathered his breath for an instant and then said, 'I need your help.'

58

THERE WAS HECTIC activity in the anteroom. It was five in the morning and there were seven people in the room—Dr Krishnan, Aditya Kapoor, two medical supervisors, two people from the Bio-safety department responsible for the gear, and one representative from National Medical Laboratories; who had arrived with the vaccine. The vaccine was to be given in two jabs over a twenty-four hour period. A dual dose was normally given in such cases in the hope that the second would improve the efficacy of the first one.

'It is high risk, Aditya. You are aware of the consequences?'

'Yes, Dr Krishnan.'

'Any deviation from what we agreed on and I will be in trouble.'

'Once in my life, I shortchanged the person I love and look at the price I am paying for it. Do you think after this, I will ever compromise the faith that someone shows in me, Dr Krishnan?'

Dr Krishnan came up to him and patted him on his back. 'Go ahead, young man. God listens to people with a conscience.'

The door to the patient's room opened and Aditya walked

in, complete in a moonsuit, a pair of gloves, water resistant boots, mask, oxygen supply and a hood on top. The only part of him visible to anyone from the outside, were his eyes. He walked close to the bed. He could see Maya's face now. Her eyes were closed. Despite the blisters around her ears and the crevices of her nose, she looked so pretty. It looked as if she would get up and walk into his arms right away. For a minute her face almost looked inviting. He wanted to kiss her on her lips and wake her up. He resisted the urge to cry.

'Maya,' he said, ever so softly. Nothing changed. He called out again, just a bit louder than earlier. He couldn't be sure if he were imagining it, but he thought he saw her eyeballs move behind her eyelids.

'Maya . . .' he repeated, a quiver in his voice, 'forgive me if you can, Maya. I have remained loyal to you, for almost all of the time that I have known you. But that one transgression on my part cannot be explained. Shreya and I . . . The attention she gave me, made me weak. Maybe it was pure lust which took an emotional turn, I don't know. The fact that she needed me gave me a high . . . But why am I saying all this? Whatever be the reason, Maya, logical or not, I know I've hurt you. I fell for someone else. It was not in my control. The entire world will say that it is impossible to love two people at the same time. How can you feel for two people at the same time without hurting one of them?' he choked and stopped.

'I was a fool, Maya. I was wrong. I ended up hurting you. I ended up being an infidel, a cheat, in your eyes. I should not have done that to you. If I didn't love you, it would have been different. If our relationship were not in the best of health, it would have been a different issue. But you have lived your life to help me live my dream, to make Aryan a great human being, to help your students and society. You have never given me a reason to complain. Everything you did was just perfect. There was no flaw in you. Perfection they say is a means for man to get closer to God. Is this what they mean when they say closer to God?

'Maya, you were the one who held me up. You were the one who I owe everything in life to. Without you I won't have anything left. The true test of a good human being is not the number of people who love you, but the number of people who learn how to love, looking at you. You don't have any enemies, and everyone who comes in contact with you falls in love with you. You have an unfulfilled agenda, my love. You have to turn Aryan into the most fabulous man ever. If you go away, I have to deal with the challenge alone. I don't think I would ever be able to do justice to him.

'I love you, Maya. Please forgive me. I beg of you, please forgive me. I can't live under the weight of the realisation that you believe that I am an evil man. I am not evil, Maya, I am not. Don't make me pay this price. Please come back. From this instant, I will live my life the way you want me to live. I will dedicate it to you, Maya. It's a promise I make to you. Please forgive me, please forgive me. Forgive me, Maya . . .'

Aditya broke down. He started sobbing by her bedside. He fell on his knees and held his hands in front of him, clasped together against his forehead. 'Forgive me, Maya,' he sobbed. His body was convulsing furiously in rhythm with his sobs. The stench of chlorine inside the bodysuit did not bother him. The heat didn't matter.

Dr Krishnan was standing outside and watching everything through the glass wall. 'Be ready to go in if he tries something dramatic,' he prepped his team. Despite Aditya's assurances he was not sure that he would behave sanely.

Aditya looked up. How he wished he could erase the last few months from his life. If only he had an option. 'Please give me another chance, Maya. I wish I could spend another life with you, to make up for everything that I have done.'

As soon as Aditya had said this he felt he could see her facial muscles twitching, as if she was trying to say something but couldn't. And then as if god himself was trying to tell Aditya that Maya had forgiven him, the ends of Maya's lips curled upwards as if she were trying to smile—the first time in the last three days. Her eyes were closed, her body was immobile, she was on life support, but her lips gently curled upwards.

Aditya cried out loud, loud enough for Dr Krishnan, in the room outside, to hear. He turned back and looked at Dr Krishnan, who gave him a thumbs up.

'I will always love you, Maya,' he said as he turned and walked slowly back to the anteroom.

As he was helped out of the moonsuit Aditya was happy that Maya had heard him out and perhaps even forgiven him. It was like an elephant was off his chest.

Save a miracle, Dr Krishnan was not confident that

Maya would last the day. Yet as a last resort, half an hour after Aditya's talk with Maya, she was given the first of the two jabs of the untested Canadian Ebola vaccine. The second was to be given to her in another twelve hours.

59

Further deterioration of Maya's health, which Dr Krishnan had expected, stopped. Her overall health stayed static — showed no signs of improvement but didn't worsen either. That was a big positive. The turnaround happened with the administering of the follow-up jab.

By the next morning, the whole hospital was rejoicing. The reason was that a conservative Dr Krishnan had just upped Maya's chances of survival to 35 per cent from 10 per cent a few days back.

Savitha and Sanjay were allowed to go home and were kept under quarantine for a week more. They were instructed not to venture out or meet anyone apart from close family. Sunaina went back to Kolkata. Shreya visited the hospital every single day and spent about an hour with Aditya before going back home. The meetings were not friendly. Aditya had started cold-shouldering her. He would speak when spoken to, and respond to questions in monosyllables. When Shreya mentioned this to Sunaina, she said, 'This is not the time, Shreya. You should not even bring this up with him. It will put him under extreme pressure.'

'I just wish that bitch kicks the bucket. Everything will be resolved once and for all. Aditya will be mine and only mine. I won't have to share him with anyone else.'

'Do you realise, sweetheart, it's not you who is sharing him with someone else. It is the woman lying on the bed who is unknowingly sharing him with you,' Sunaina raged.

'Well, she knows now. So why can't she just leave him and go?' Shreya responded nonchalantly.

'Are you out of your mind, Shreya? You are wishing her ill, at a time when she is struggling in the hospital. That's just evil!'

'Oh please, Sunaina! It's not like she will die because I said so.'

*

Whenever she met Aditya, Shreya would subtly try to raise the issue of the manuscript and Aditya would stoically ignore it. She was worried. Vaishali was putting pressure on her for the submission of her own manuscript. She was lagging behind on her deadline. The second half of the year was always a crowded one for books, and missing a deadline meant a cascading impact on the others too. Vaishali hated altering time-frames. Eventually Shreya sent the manuscript to her without Aditya endorsing it. She knew that if necessary Vaishali would seek Aditya's views and incorporate them.

Shreya called Vaishali the day she submitted the manuscript. 'How long will it take for the book to come out?'

'Three months. We will announce the book for pre-booking in a month and a half, once the cover is ready and we have a firm date for launch.'

'So our promotional activities have to start now?'

'Yes,' Vaishali agreed. Shreya could see her dream slowly about to turn to reality.

60

SIXTEEN DAYS LATER, on a Friday, a nurse walked up to Aditya, who was waiting outside the isolation ward and addressed him, 'Dr Krishnan wants to see you in his office.' Dr Krishnan got up from his chair when he saw Aditya rushing in.

'You wanted to see me, Doc?'

'Relax, Aditya,' Dr Krishnan said when he saw the tension on Aditya's face. 'The reports are fine. Maya can go home tomorrow.'

The smile on Aditya's face was one of joy and relief. His eyes were moist. On the verge of tears, he turned away. He did not want the doctor to see him cry.

'Aditya,' Dr Krishnan said, 'give it some time. It will all be okay. Time heals everything, including broken relationships.' In these past few days, he had developed a strong liking for Aditya. 'If you sincerely repent your wrongdoings with complete honesty, god will fix everything. Maya could have died. The only reason she didn't was because god wanted her to come back to you. Remember that.'

Aditya just nodded. Dr Krishnan's last line rang in his

mind as he walked out. He was at peace. But there was something he still had to do. On the way out, he picked up his phone and dialled a number. It got picked up after three rings.

'Hi Aditya!'

'Coffee? Now?' he paused. 'I can pick you up from office.'

'Call me when you are near and I will come down.'

In an hour's time Aditya picked Shreya up, and they went out to the Hyatt Regency coffee shop a mile from their office.

'What happened?' a visibly surprised Shreya asked him, first in the car, and then when they settled down in the coffee shop.

'Shreya, we need to put an end to this,' Aditya got straight to the point.

'What?' Shreya was shocked. There was an air of finality to what Aditya was saying.

'My family is falling apart, Shreya. I love Maya. I love Aryan. I don't want my son to grow up knowing that his father was someone who cheated on his mother. Maya has given up a lot for me. Her life, her friends, her career, have all been sacrificed at the altar of my career. I cannot do this to her.'

'When have I demanded anything from you? I completely understand that your family is your priority. I come in only after you have finished your duties and obligations. I know I can never replace them. I am very happy finding my place in your small world. I love you, Aditya.'

'It doesn't work that way, Shreya. Maya knows about us. I

have lied to her all along. I need to regain her trust. And for that I have to be honest with her, and that is not possible if we are still in this . . . this . . .' he struggled for words.

'Relationship,' Shreya completed the sentence for him. 'Why are you finding it so difficult to say the word?'

Aditya didn't attempt to answer her question. He just looked at her. And after a long stare, he firmly said, 'We need to end this, Shreya. This has to stop.'

'You thought about them but not about me? Thank you, Aditya,' she spat out. Bitterness was writ all over her face.

'I did think about you. If we let this go on, it will only lead to more pain.'

'Why do you want to live life the way the world wants you to live? Why can't we go on the way we are? Why do you want to end it?' She was now embarrassingly loud. People around were looking at them. 'Why does it have to end like this?' she yelled.

'I tried doing it gradually. I have been trying to slowly cut the relationship off but it is not working. I have given you so many hints in the last three weeks that it is over. I don't have either the courage or the will to go about this slowly, Shreya. So the only alternative is to end it.' He sat up straight and looked around. People were still looking at them. He bent and moved forward a bit. When he was close enough to Shreya, he whispered, 'Once and for all.'

'What about my book? You promised to help me all through, remember? And now you are walking away from your commitment.'

Aditya couldn't make up his mind on whether it was a

serious attempt at changing the topic or whether Shreya was actually concerned about her book, at this point.

'So it was all about the book for you, right?'

'How dare you, Aditya! Of course it is about you. The book is just a small part of who you are,' Shreya cried out, offended. 'Why do you keep bringing it up as if I am someone who is exploiting our relationship for my gains? If it is bothering you so much, I won't ask you again.'

'Forget it, Shreya,' Aditya said as he got up. 'I need to get back to the hospital.'

'Aditya, this is just not done,' Shreya yelled as Aditya got up from his chair. 'You can't leave me like this and walk away. I am not an object,' she continued. Her voice was filled with anger. Aditya turned and started walking towards the exit. Shreya chased him. 'Wait, Aditya,' she hollered. Aditya stopped and turned.

'You have no right to dump me like this.'

'We were never destined to be together,' Aditya responded. His voice was now emotionless which irritated Shreya even more. 'More than destiny I think it was a lapse in judgment. A momentary blinding of one's rationality that brought us together. I am just correcting it for the larger good of both of us.'

'Who the fuck are you to decide what is good for *us*?'

Aditya didn't stay to hear the last few words. He had already reached his car. He opened the door, got in, and waited for a couple of seconds for Shreya, so that he could drop her back to the bank. But when she continued standing on his side of the car and yelling at him, Aditya just shifted the car into drive mode and drove off. As he was driving away, he heard Shreya scream, 'You are finished, Aditya Kapoor. You are finished. I will make sure of that.'

61

MAYA WAS BROUGHT back home, the next morning. Her parents and Aditya were with her. Aditya was driving and Maya's father was sitting next to him in the front seat. Maya's mom was with her in the backseat. The drive back was a very quiet one. No one spoke. Maya had not broken her vow of silence towards Aditya even when she regained consciousness. She had refused to meet him in the hospital.

Once they reached home, Maya walked straight into her room. Aditya walked in behind her. 'I'm so happy you are back, baby,' he said as he held her shoulders from behind and softly kissed the back of her head.

In one swift move Maya jerked his hand off her shoulders and turned to face him. 'Don't touch me!' she whispered as loudly as she could. She pointed a finger at Aditya and angrily muttered, teeth clenched, 'Don't ever touch me again,' she reiterated.

'Maya,' Aditya looked at her, devastated. 'I am sorry for all that I did. It was a mistake, Maya. A mistake I will never commit again, ever. I promise.'

'Mistake?' Maya looked at him in disgust. 'Cheating is never a mistake. It is a choice, Aditya. When you made that choice, you were aware of the repercussions, yet you went ahead with it. I pity myself that I placed my faith in you. I trusted you blindly.'

Aditya tried his best to convince Maya to forgive him, to let him back in her life, to forget the past and make a new beginning. But Maya was a strong woman. She had made up her mind. Finally when the argument showed no signs of dying down, she pulled the plug. In the calmest of voices, she said, 'We can't stay together any longer, Aditya. You need to go. If you don't, I will.'

'Maya . . . please don't . . .' He had not even completed what he was saying when Maya interrupted him and turned back towards the cupboard. She stretched upwards and tried to pull out a suitcase from the loft. 'Forget it. I will leave.'

Aditya didn't know what to do. He just turned and walked out of the house. He felt that Maya was too agitated to listen to reason. He hoped he would be able to sort things out with her later.

Once he was out of the house he phoned Sanjay. He briefed Sanjay of his discussion with Shreya and about Maya throwing him out of the house and asked him for a place to stay.

That night Shreya called him a few times but Aditya refused to pick up any of her calls.

62

'If you need to come back again to pick up something, coordinate with mom,' Maya said curtly, when Aditya went there the next morning to pick up his clothes.

'Why me?' said Maya's mother in an aggressive tone. Both of Maya's parents had stopped talking to Aditya the day they got to know of his relationship with Shreya. They had always held Aditya in high esteem. He was the ideal son-in-law, the ideal husband, the ideal father—a showcase husband in more ways than one. But everything came crashing down for them, the day they heard about Aditya's affair. 'I don't even want to see his face; neither does your father.' Maya's mom was very clear.

Maya ignored the outpouring and looked Aditya in the eye and said, 'Just make sure you come and go when I am not at home.'

He took his stuff and went back to Sanjay's house. It was eleven by the time he reached office. He dumped his bag on his table and went up to Sanjay's floor. He wanted to give him the keys to the house.

The moment he stepped out of the elevator and turned towards Sanjay's cabin he stopped. With her back towards him, sitting in front of Sanjay, was Shreya. He didn't want to talk to her and turned back. He pinged Sanjay, 'Call me when you are finished with her.'

Back in his room, he got busy with some weekly reports. An hour passed. Sanjay had not returned his call.

'He is still in a meeting,' Sanjay's secretary told him, when he called to check.

'With Shreya Kaushik?' Aditya asked. The secretary replied in the affirmative.

Aditya started getting worried. Sanjay was his friend, but he was the head of HR too. And no one spends an hour and a half with the HR Head . . . without reason.

⋆

'Sexual harassment! She wants to file a formal complaint against you,' Sanjay said with a straight face as Aditya looked on, aghast. Sanjay had called him and asked to meet at the Starbucks coffee shop outside the Mumbai airport. 'I can't be seen talking to you in office immediately after she has spoken to me. That's why I called you here,' he explained before dropping the bombshell.

Aditya nearly fell off his chair when he heard this. 'Harassment?' he asked, words barely coming out of his mouth. 'We had a sexual relationship quite alright, but harassment? Did she tell you who started it all?'

'It doesn't matter, Aditya. She is a woman and if she complains, the organisation will invariably take a lenient view towards her.'

'What about evidence?' Aditya asked. 'Does evidence

mean anything? Can she prove that I ...' he hesitated, 'Forget all that. Tell me what all she said.' He looked expectantly at Sanjay. 'Don't omit anything.'

'She called me this morning, saying that she wanted to talk to me. You had told me that things were not going well between the two of you, so I asked her to come up to my cabin. I thought she might want some help in sorting out the problems that you have with her. But this one came as a beamer. She walked up to me and even before she settled down, her first line was that she wanted to lodge an official complaint against you for sexual harassment. She claims you forced yourself on her.'

'I forced myself on her?'

'Apparently you did. She has messages to prove it. I saw a few. In one of those you have apologised for having kissed her, possibly forcibly. There are some wherein you have invited her to accompany you to Pune when you were on your book tour, promising her a good time. They are extremely suggestive, Aditya, the sort that can get anyone in trouble,' Sanjay said, looking grave.

'Those were not one-sided messages. She responded equally passionately to each of those. I bet she didn't tell you that!?'

'No she didn't. But if you have them, we can counter her. Take her head on.'

'I was deleting her messages every day before I went home, Sanjay. Only on days Maya was travelling would I hold on to the messages before deleting everything once and for all.' He made a face. 'And that is proving to be my

Achilles' heel. The messages got backed up and appeared on Maya's phone.' Then as if struck by a bolt from the blue, he remembered, 'Hold it. Hold it, Sanjay. My phone backup at home will have some of the messages. We might have something to prove that it was a consensual relationship. I will talk to Maya and get those messages out from the backup in the laptop.

'I'm not sure, Aditya. If I know Maya, she will not help you with this, at least for now. In any case I have managed to dissuade Shreya for now. I have convinced her not to file her complaint. I told her that if this gets out, a lot of muck would flow on both sides. And that no one would remain untouched by it. She is a sensible girl. She agreed to keep it on hold for the time being. But . . .'

Aditya raised his eyelashes and looked at Sanjay, 'But what?'

'But under one condition.'

'And that is . . .?'

'That under no circumstance she be moved out of your team. She claims that she is not an escapist and that she would fight her way through.'

'And what did you say?'

'As if I had a choice, Aditya,' Sanjay exclaimed.

63

BEFORE LEAVING STARBUCKS, Sanjay warned Aditya to lie low for a few days. He also impressed on him the need to stay away from getting into a conflict with Shreya.

Aditya realised that the evidence Shreya had was enough to send him into professional oblivion even if he did prove that their relationship was consensual.

It was an uneasy truce for Aditya. He had to face Shreya every day in office. She would be her bubbly self, smiling and talking normally to everyone and making sure that no one faulted her for anything. She was probably being extra cautious so as to not give anyone a chance to take her to task.

Three weeks had passed and Aditya had still not moved out of Sanjay's house. Staying with Sanjay, he had to encounter Diana frequently. In fact it had helped him clear a lot of misconceptions about her. She was a regular visitor to Sanjay's house and the two of them planned to get married in another six months. In fact, Diana had already partially moved in.

Aditya was in a particularly broody mood that day. He had returned from a leadership training programme which had been conducted by an external agency. As a part of the programme, there was a team-building exercise wherein the audience was divided into six teams to perform some activities. Shreya had slimed her way into his team. Throughout the day, she was on the same table, next to him. Aditya was worried, not because she was next to him, but because despite whatever was going on between them, he had a weak spot for her.

'Is there any way you can get her out of my hair for a few hours of the day at least?' Aditya pleaded.

'You know what I have told her, don't you?' Sanjay argued.

'Give her a project. Give her something. Show it to her as a move up the chain. She is mind-fucking me. I can't handle it, Sanjay. I'm going insane.'

Diana was listening to all this. She had thus far maintained a stoic silence on all the happenings around her.

'I think I may be able to help,' she finally said. Both Sanjay and Aditya looked at her. 'Tim is looking for people to join the team driving the collaboration and the cross-sell effort between different teams of his—branch banking, whatever remains of Assets, Non-Resident Business, Operations, etc. Everyone on the team will be on project mode. They will double hat, do their current jobs and additionally work on this. I can push Tim to get her on the project. I will position it as young blood with a fresh perspective. She can't say no to Tim. It will keep her busy at least for a few hours a day. I will make her travel to other locations so that she gets away from you for as long as possible.'

'What makes you think that she will agree?' Sanjay asked her.

'Why won't she?'

'She will see through the facade. She is far too smart for this. What if she refuses?'

'We will see then. Why are you making the decision for her, Sanjay? Let her say she is not interested. We will deal with it at that point in time.'

'I have given her my word that I will not move her from Aditya's team. So I will not talk to her about this. You guys can do what you want, without involving me,' Sanjay said.

'Even if we do this, how will it serve our purpose in the long run? We can't go on like this forever.' Aditya was dismal.

'We will do this till she gets over you,' Diana smiled. 'But from the looks of it, you haven't got over her yet. Have you, Aditya?'

'I don't know, Diana,' Aditya avoided responding directly. He was scared to confess that he still pined for Shreya. Whether it was guilt at being the one to have called off the relationship or love for Shreya, was difficult to say. 'I am in a mind-fucked state right now. I can't even think straight,' he laboured to explain. 'When are you meeting Maya? I am hoping she will listen to you guys,' he added hurriedly, trying to bring the discussion back on track.

'Next week,' Diana replied.

Diana and Sanjay were meeting with Maya on the coming Tuesday to try and get her to see sense in accepting Aditya back into her life. Diana had planned to make a passionate plea to help Aditya. Maya was travelling and at Diana's insistence, Sanjay had spoken with her at length and she had agreed to meet him once she returned.

When they met, Maya refused to hear anything in Aditya's defence. 'Loyalty is the least I expect in any relationship, Sanjay. You have heard the conversation between Aditya and that woman. Why are you defending him now?'

'Doesn't he deserve another chance, Maya? He is in a pitiable state. You should see him to believe how much he pines for you and Aryan,' Diana argued.

'Remember this, Diana: once a cheat, always a cheat. In life it is always about the first time. Anyone who crosses that barrier once can do it, with no scruples, again. He might regret what he has lost and come around, but at the first opportunity he will cheat again. I don't want to have anything to do with this man. I am only staying away from a divorce for I don't want to get embroiled in legalities yet.'

The two of them came back disappointed. 'You could have pushed a little harder. I was doing all the talking,' Diana said to Sanjay on the way back.

'Women are more comfortable having these conversations with other women. And you were doing a good job,' Sanjay responded as he placed his hand over Diana's.

'I thought she was gravitating towards agreeing to getting back with Aditya. She just needs a push, some more reassurance. She is hurt, and psychological injuries take time to heal. We just have to wait it out,' Diana said.

And then, *Bombay Times* happened.

64

17 Missed Calls.
46 SMS's.
188 Tweets.

Aditya jumped out of bed when he saw all the notifications. Something had to be dramatically wrong.

The doorbell rang and rang again. He hurriedly walked to the door and opened it. It was the woman who collected the garbage every morning. He walked to the kitchen, and pulled out the garbage bag from the can and handed it over. The newspaper was lying on the floor outside the apartment door. Sanjay had gone off on his morning jog much before the papers came in. He picked it up and kept it on the dining table. His phone was hanging. Probably the sudden surge in tweets/messages was something it could not handle. The twitter app took some time to open. He cursed himself. He should have checked the SMS's first.

In the interim he opened the newspaper. He flung the supplements aside and scanned the front page of the main newspaper. Nothing in it interested him. His twitter feed came up. He touched the "notifications" icon to get to the tweets directed at him. He looked at the screen, waiting for it to come up and for a split second glanced at the *Bombay Times* supplement lying on the table. Aditya's eyes popped out. The twitter notifications too came up on his screen at the exact same moment. He started sweating. His eyes forgot how to blink. His mouth stayed open in shock.

On the front page of the *Bombay Times* supplement was a huge photograph of him. The tweets opened up on his screen. They were all about the *Bombay Times* article.

Next to his photograph was a small inset. In that was another photograph—this one Shreya's. But it was the headline which disturbed him the most: CASANOVA AUTHOR

Below it was the tagline: **India's biggest commercial fiction writer's private life exposed.** In the box that accompanied the article was the text:

At a time when his wife was struggling for life, in isolation, Aditya Kapoor was caught having fun with a young colleague. Read on for a sensational exposé on the double life of banker-author Aditya Kapoor.

'What the fuck?' he exclaimed as he hurriedly picked up the paper and started reading the article.

It was all about Aditya's adulterous relationship with Shreya. It went on to detail their sexual escapades and even carried the transcript of the audio recording, which Shreya had made in Aditya's house. The most scathing allegation was that when Maya was in hospital, Aditya was sitting outside the room with the love of his life—Shreya. The article even carried a picture of the two of them in the Hyatt coffee shop, the day before Maya came out of the hospital. It was clearly taken off the Hyatt CCTV cameras.

'This is a disaster,' Sanjay announced. Aditya looked up; he hadn't even realised that Sanjay had come in. He was standing right next to him and staring at the same article. 'How the hell did they get all the details?'

Aditya looked at him with apprehension. 'Why would she do this? What does she gain?' He shook his head in despair.

'I have no idea, Aditya. This is all over the place now. Tim called me while I was jogging. The sad part is that they have linked this to your profession as a banker with National Bank and have drawn the bank into the scandal. Tim is hopping mad. He will come after you. Watch your back. He might want you out,' Sanjay informed him.

'Crap. Just because the newspapers say something?' He got up from his chair and walked around the room, an angry look on his face. 'What I do in my personal life is my lookout. As long as it is not illegal, the bank has no say.'

'We have been through this earlier too, Aditya. The bank has a say if the bank gets dragged into it. We need to have a better explanation than that. Living in denial is not going to get you anywhere.' Sensing Aditya's confrontational frame of mind, he added, 'And please do not get into an accusatory discussion with Shreya. It will harm you more than her. She will play the victim card. And she plays that card well.'

'But . . .' he was interrupted by the ring of Sanjay's phone. Sanjay looked at him and then at his phone. 'Maya,' he said as he walked away from Aditya and pressed the answer button on his phone.

'Yes, I saw the article . . . hmm . . . This is rubbish, Maya. It seems like a planted one. Don't believe everything that it says . . . Yes, yes I know. But it is not true . . . I think you should still give it a chance . . . but Maya . . . okay. I'll talk to you later,' Sanjay let out a sigh as he disconnected.

Aditya who was silently looking at him raised his eyebrows. He didn't even have the strength left in him to say anything. Sanjay came up to him and put his arms around him. 'Relax. We will figure a way out of this.'

Aditya knew that Sanjay was avoiding the discussion. He pointed to his phone. 'What did Maya say?' he asked.

'She said she had almost convinced herself to give you another chance, but when she read this article she was devastated. When she was in the hospital struggling for her life, you were sitting outside the room with Shreya, taking her out on a coffee date. That is a fact she cannot digest. She knew about the escapades in your house when she was away in the US, but she is hurt by the fact that despite her being seriously ill—almost dead—you still did not stop meeting Shreya,' Sanjay reported.

'But that's a lie. I didn't do anything when she was in the hospital. Shreya came to the hospital on her own. That's not my fault. I didn't call her even once. And you know why I took her to the coffee shop. I told you before I took her there. Shit. How do I even explain it to her?' Aditya held his head in his hands and collapsed on the chair next to him. He started sobbing like a small child.

*

Sunaina called Shreya a little after ten in the morning. 'What the fuck is this, Shreya? Have you gone bonkers?'

'What the fuck is what, Sunaina?'

'Come on, Shreya. Don't pretend.'

'*Bombay Times*?' Shreya asked her innocently. 'What is the issue with it? I think it couldn't have come at a better time. It'll do me a world of good.'

'How shameless could you be, Shreya?' Sunaina looked appalled. She paused as she heard the tone for call waiting. She was getting a call from an unknown number. She ignored it.

'What is shameless about this, baby? Have you seen the eyeballs it has garnered? I couldn't have got this kind of visibility even if I had spent lakhs. I am not even saying if it is good or bad, but whatever made TOI carry it, I am happy they did. It's made me famous even before the book is out,' Shreya exhaled.

'Notorious is the word, Shreya, not famous,' Sunaina reminded her. 'You are impossible. Some day you will realise how wrong all this is.'

'Till that day, you don't be mean to me, Sunaina,' Shreya chuckled. A frustrated and irritated Sunaina hung up on her.

In around five minutes she got a call from the same number that had called her earlier.

'Hello,' she spoke into the phone, her tone curt.

She was met with complete silence.

'Hello. Who is it?'

'Sunaina.'

The phone almost slipped out of her hand. Sweat broke out on her forehead. Her heart started beating faster.

'Sunaina, you there?'

'Yes . . . Yes. What do you want? Why have you called?'

65

#CASANOVAAUTHOR HAD STARTED trending on twitter. Aditya opened his twitter feed on his smartphone. The number of trolls on his feed had crossed 500. How on earth would he go about explaining to everyone that it was Shreya who chased him? He was a middle-aged professional caught in his own vanity. He felt like a hunted animal.

For the first time in his life, Aditya walked into office, head hanging low. Shreya had taken the easy way out. She had decided to stay at home.

That afternoon Vaishali called.

'I told you, didn't I?' she mocked him.

Aditya was in no mood for small talk. 'What?' he barked.

'I asked you if there was anything going on between the two of you.'

'And if you didn't hear it the last time I said it, I am saying it again, no, no, NO!' He paused to take a deep breath and continued, 'Tell me why you called.'

'I called to tell you that since morning, your book has seen a 450 per cent rise in sales on Flipkart and Amazon. That's a huge jump given that it is coming on the back of an already huge sales figure.'

'Hmm . . .' Aditya was not interested. He was more worried about the rate at which his problems had now mounted and all Vaishali could think of were the rising sales numbers.

'The article has done you good, Aditya, so stop frowning,' Vaishali tried to lighten his mood.

'Really?' If sarcasm was a dialect, Aditya would have been fluent in it.

'That's what the sales team tells me,' Vaishali retorted.

'Whatever!' His tone was abrupt and caught Vaishali off guard. This was the first time she was experiencing Aditya's mood swings.

'Aditya, in our internal meeting today, Sales was of the view that we must fast-track Shreya's book and bring it out in the next four weeks.'

'Well, it's your call, isn't it?'

'It is, it is,' she agreed. 'Cover design of her book will be finalised by end of day. The book goes up for pre-booking on all the ecommerce websites in the next three days. We need to capitalise on this publicity.'

'Everything is commerce for you guys,' Aditya was cynical. 'Others be damned. Sense an opportunity, go for the kill.'

'New authors struggle to be noticed, Aditya,' Vaishali was very matter-of-fact. 'You know that better than I do. This article today has thrust Shreya into the centre stage. Why not leverage and position her appropriately? She will be a sure shot success. Her book will be a definite bestseller.'

'Your call,' he snapped back. 'But why are you telling me this? Shouldn't you be talking to her about it?'

'Because you and I had discussed that you will give a

quote which will go on the cover of the book. I need that quote today. Simple.'

Aditya remembered. Initially, when he had impressed on Vaishali to publish Shreya's book he had committed to her that he would lend his name to the book promotion. What better promotion for a new author than the country's most successful author endorsing the debutant with a quote on the cover. But that was then.

'I'm not sure if I would want to do that, Vaishali .'

'But why?'

'Even after today's article you are asking me why?'

'But shouldn't we turn this into an opportunity?'

'I am not as cold as you are sounding right now,' he lashed out. 'I've got to go, someone is waiting for me,' he lied and hung up on her. The lack of empathy infuriated him.

After he disconnected, he looked at the phone. There were three missed calls, all from the same number; an unknown number. There was also a message from the same number. He swiped his finger across the screen to see the message.

<Trying to reach you. Please call back when free. It is about today's newspaper article . . . Melwin.>

Aditya looked at the phone for a minute and dismissed it. There were more important things occupying his mind at the time. He had planned to meet Maya to convince her that he had not lied to her in any way. The newspaper story had nothing more than what she already knew. He decided to leave so that he could reach home before Maya got back. Savitha would be the only one there. He would be able to bulldoze her into letting him in and wait for Maya to return. For a second he considered calling Melwin back, but then dismissed the idea. Melwin was probably another of those presstitutes, harassing him for a quote.

66

THAT EVENING VAISHALI sent Shreya the cover design for her new book. 'It will go on pre-booking from day after. I think we should promote it aggressively on social media. I have convinced Marketing to buy space in *Bombay Times*, to do a story on the book. That should drive interest. People will relate it to today's article. It has the potential to go viral,' Vaishali 's mail had said.

Shreya saw the mail and called Vaishali . 'What about Aditya's quote?' she demanded.

'Well, we have managed to get Chetan Bhagat to give a quote for your book. He never does that but has agreed to do it for you.'

'I don't want a Chetan Bhagat quote. He might have seen today's newspaper article and jumped onto the bandwagon for some quick publicity. People who read him won't read my book. I would rather have Aditya's quote or nothing.' Shreya was adamant.

'Then I am afraid we will have to go with nothing. And just to remind you, Aditya too writes commercial fiction. Their genre is the same. If CB won't do, then Aditya too won't do.'

'But Aditya has stature. Leave that aside. Tell me, why can't we put Aditya's quote on the cover?'

'Aditya has declined to give a quote.'

'What?' Shreya was surprised. 'When did you speak to him last?'

'Earlier today.'

'But he had promised . . .'

'Well, it is his mind. He reserves the right to change it, I guess,' Vaishali was curt. She didn't like Shreya's arrogant approach. 'More so after today's *Bombay Times* article . . .' Vaishali wanted to rile Shreya and give it back to her for her haughtiness. But Shreya was cool and didn't seem to care.

'What does the *Bombay Times* article have to do with it?' she asked. Without waiting for a response, she added, 'If anything, it will give us brilliant branding. Isn't that why you are bringing forward the launch date for my book, Vaishali ? Don't deny it. Isn't it the best thing to have happened to us?' Shreya spoke like a pro. 'Hold on to the cover for a day. Will you do that for me, please?'

67

MAYA WENT BALLISTIC when she reached home and saw Aditya waiting for her. Savitha had to bear the brunt of her anger. She had been categorically told not to let Aditya come back into the house. Aditya was a persona non grata in her life, more so after the *Bombay Times* article.

'Maya, please,' Aditya pleaded, 'listen to me once. If after that you want to throw me out forever, it is up to you.'

Maya stared out into the open—a blank gaze into infinity. She too was tired of this. Her mind was in turmoil. A part of her wanted to get back with him. Aditya left his phone and laptop bag on the sofa and walked to the balcony. When he was right behind her, his arms came up and held Maya by the shoulders. She was uncomfortable but didn't move. That gave Aditya some hope.

'I am sorry, Maya. Can't you let this go this one time? I promise you, you will never have a reason to complain or regret it. Ever since I left this house I have not even spoken to Shreya. I am not in touch with her. Despite us being in the same team, I don't even talk to her. Trust me, Maya. I fucked up! But I will never ever repeat it in the future.'

Maya was confused. She turned away from the balcony,

walked back into the living room and sat down on the sofa. She was trying her best to stay calm.

'Maya, if you want, I will quit my job and get away from everyone who you have a problem with,' Aditya cried.

Maya stayed silent.

'We can leave Mumbai and go somewhere else, where we can rebuild our life from scratch.'

Neither Maya's expression changed nor her demeanour.

Seeing Maya not responding he held her again by her shoulder and shook her softly. 'Say something, Maya. Please say something. I love you, Maya. I really . . .'

The shrill ringtone of his phone interrupted his monologue. The phone was on the table in front of both of them. Instinctively both of them looked down at the number.

Maya saw the number and faced him. If there was any confusion in her mind earlier, it had evaporated. She picked up her bag from the sofa, slipped her feet into her sandals and stormed out of the house. 'Call me once he is out of here,' she directed Savitha on her way out. Just as she reached the door, she saw an envelope lying on the rack adjoining it. She stopped and picked up the envelope. Aditya didn't move. Maya turned and waved the envelope at him. 'You see the impact of your activities on my son! Someone handed this over to him outside school. Stay away from us. We don't need you in our lives,' she screamed.

While all this was happening, Aditya's phone had rung six times. Six calls, all from the same number. When it rang for the seventh time, Aditya looked at it. There were two words flashing on the screen: "RAM KUMAR". He picked up the phone and pressed the disconnect icon and walked out behind Maya.

As he was exiting the hall, he looked at the envelope that Maya had waved at him and picked it up. It just had the name, "Aryan Kapoor", written on top of it. No address. Inside the envelope was a tiny piece of paper. He pulled it out. It was the masthead of *Bombay Times*. It had been torn out from that day's newspaper.

He was furious; more so because the packet was addressed to Aryan. Why would anyone send this to Aryan? He was only six years old. Aditya realised that the envelope actually contained a veiled threat: that they would expose Aditya's doings to Aryan, and make him lose respect for his dad. Someone was trying to destroy the very fabric of his family. Only one person could have done it.

The phone rang and he looked at it. It was the same number again. This time he took the call.

'Yes?'

'I need to see you.'

'And you really think that I will come on all fours.' He was furious.

'Trust me you'll regret it if you don't. I won't take too much of your time.'

Aditya was taken aback. It took him a while to gather his wits. 'Why did you do this, Shreya? Why?'

Even before he could finish what he was saying, Shreya hung up.

68

In thirty-five minutes, Aditya was at Shreya's residence. When she opened the door, the base note of her perfume hit his nostrils.

'Why did you do this, Shreya?' he repeated. The thirty-five minute drive had calmed his nerves. He turned his gaze away from her so as to not lose focus. She was irritatingly sexy.

'Do what?'

'You know what I am talking about. Why did you have to talk to *Bombay Times*?' His breathing was heavy. He was angry, distracted, frustrated and possibly turned on, all at the same time.

'So you too assumed that I did it?'

'Could there be a better way for you to get back at me? What do you want to achieve by embarrassing me like this?'

'Have you considered that this article damages my reputation more than yours? It has presented me in a much poorer light. Why would I kill my own reputation, Aditya? Why would I do this to myself?'

Aditya hollered. 'You are a fucking liar and a cheat. You used me to get a book contract. And now when your book is to come out and you need to get into the limelight, you hit upon this wonderful plan. Kill two birds with one stone.'

Hearing his tirade Shreya steeled up. 'Yes, a scandal of this sort helps the book. It helps me get the limelight. But no woman would do this to her own reputation. Do you get that, Aditya?' she paused, 'I love you. I really love you. I wish you would see that. I want you to be with me, Aditya.'

'Even if it means sending a threat to a six-year-old?' Aditya brandished the envelope he had picked up from Maya's house, in front of her. 'How dare you, Shreya? How dare you send out a threat to my six-year-old son?'

Shreya brazenly smiled when she saw the cover. 'I have no clue what you are talking about,' she shrugged. 'What is in it?' She walked up to him and took the envelope from his hand. At the same time, the fingertips of her left hand ran seductively down his arm.

'Stop it, Shreya,' Aditya jerked her hand off and held her by her shoulders. He was at his wits' end. 'Have you really sunk that low that you would involve my little son in all this?' He looked disgusted. He waved the packet in front of her face again. 'Have you considered what would happen if I took this to the cops? Threatening a minor is a non-bailable offence.'

'I see. So now you are threatening me with a police case . . . ooooh . . . I am scared. Can't you see that I am sweating? Please help me, Aditya. Help me,' she mocked him. 'Interesting story, by the way,' Shreya continued once she had stopped her mock-shivering. 'For once you are spinning a genuine story all by yourself. Nice to see.'

'I hope you don't run out of sarcasm by the time the cops rough you up. Save some,' Aditya cynically advised Shreya. 'I will take you to task and haul your backside to court for defaming me.'

'So you really want to file charges against me, Aditya. Huh? For a newspaper report which contains nothing but the truth. Will you be able to prove that the newspaper report is false? Really, Aditya, who will believe you?' she asked nonchalantly.

'Look, I don't want to hurt you,' Aditya softened a bit. His intention was not to go to the cops in any case. 'I am trying to rebuild my family. Both of us have committed mistakes in the past. I don't want to repeat them. I want you to be happy, to have a good life. There is no end to these conflicts. It will end up hurting all of us. I don't understand why you are trying to make things so difficult.'

'If you haven't got it by now, it's because I love you. Every minute I spend with you is worth a lifetime for me. The only way for me to have a good life is to be with you.'

Aditya was convinced she was feeding him a bunch of lies. 'That's why you do all this? Mess up my reputation in the press . . . Screw up my family life . . .?'

'I did all this? Really, Aditya! You seriously believe I did all this!' She looked at him in disgust. 'Did I screw up your family life, Aditya? Did I plead with you to come to me? Did I coax you to make love to me? Did I force you to do anything that you didn't want to? Then how is it that I am a whore, the other woman, and you are the saintly godman who now deserves to go back to his normal life?'

'I am not running away from my mistakes. I am only saying that it's time to set it right.'

'That's crap. If you weren't running away from your guilt, why would you not honour the commitment you made to me? You even refused to give a quote to go on the cover of my book. Did you even think for a moment how I would have felt? You left me in the lurch, and you expect me to be nice to you. You have no spine, Aditya. You ditched me when I needed you the most. Just because,' she stopped for a second, 'just because your wife fell sick, and you had pangs of regret. Oh come on, Aditya! How convenient is that?'

'So Vaishali spoke with you?' He ignored the rest of her tirade.

'Yes. And I told her to hold the cover for a day and that you would agree to give the endorsement.'

Her presumptive nonchalance peeved Aditya. 'What makes you so confident?'

'Because I knew you will eventually agree.'

'Well, I won't. I have neither the desire nor intent to give a quote at this point,' he thundered. 'And if you do not stay away from my family, I will go to the cops. Do you get it?!'

Shreya didn't respond. She got up from where she was sitting and walked to her desk. She opened her laptop and fired a print. Her printer came alive and within fifteen seconds it spat out a printed sheet of paper. Shreya picked it up and walked back to Aditya.

'This,' she said, an evil grin on her face. 'Now will this make you give me an endorsement for the book and also promote it?'

Chapter No. In Aditya's book	Line	Copied from	Original line in book from which plagiarised
Chapter 23, 4th Para	I was wondering who is more ignorant. Is it the man who cannot define what a lightning is or is it the one who does not respect its mighty power?	*Angels and Demons*, Dan Brown	But who is more ignorant? The man who cannot define lightning or the man who does not respect its awesome power . . .
Chapter 37, 1st Para	Samhita and her husband were out of their daily walk. Whether it was the cloud-soft, goose feather bed in	*Tides of Memory*, Sidney Sheldon	The girls were out for a morning walk. Whether it was the cloud-soft goose feather bed in the guest room, last night's wonderful food

Chapter No. In Aditya's book	Line	Copied from	Original line in book from which plagiarised
	the hotel room, the wonderful food and wine they had the night before, or the simple pleasure of being in the company of old friends, Samhita didn't know. But she did feel revived and refreshed that morning in a way she hadn't felt in a long time.		and wine, or the simple pleasure of being in the company of old friends, Summer didn't know, but she felt revived and refreshed this morning in a way she hadn't felt in a long time.
Chapter 71, second last para	The real tragedy of our legal system, is not the absurdities. It is the ruined and wasted lives. Justice demands long, harsh sentences, and for the violent	*The Racketeer*, John Grisham	The real tragedy of federal criminal system, is not the absurdities. It is the ruined and wasted lives. Congress demands long, harsh sentences,

Chapter No. In Aditya's book	Line	Copied from	Original line in book from which plagiarised
	thugs these are appropriate. ... but the majority of our criminals are nonviolent, and many are convicted of crimes that involved little, if any, criminal activity.		and for the violent thugs these are appropriate ... but the majority of the federal criminals are nonviolent, and many are convicted of crimes that involved little, if any, criminal activity.
Chapter 76 9th para	Corporate Politics is like a glass. Aggressive moves by either side pour water in. The overflow is always war. When tension is at the maximum, no one can make a move without causing a war. And wars between senior	*Edge of Eternity*, Ken Follett	International Politics is like a glass. Aggressive moves by either side pour water in. The overflow is always war. When tension is at the maximum, no one can make a move without causing a war.

Chapter No. In Aditya's book	Line	Copied from	Original line in book from which plagiarised
	employees are never good for any organisation.		
Chapter 79	When things look simple, Samhita, they're usually not. Right and wrong. Good and Bad are in the eyes of the definer. Understand the agenda, babes, and watch your back. He is not going to let it lie. He will come after you.	*The Hit*, David Baldacci	When things look simple, they're usually not. Right and wrong. Good and Bad are in the eyes of the definer. Understand the agenda, Will. And watch your back.
Epilogue	Love makes you want to be a better person—right? But maybe love, real love, also gives you the permission to just be the person you are.	*Gone Girl*, Gillian Flynn	Love makes you want to be a better man—right right. Maybe love, real love, also gives you the permission to just be the man you are.

'What?' Sanjay exclaimed when Aditya replayed the entire conversation with Shreya to him. He had been getting ready to head out for dinner with Diana when Aditya had walked in and mentioned Shreya's antics to him.

'What does all this mean, Aditya?' Sanjay looked horrified. Staring at the sheet of paper that Aditya had just handed over to him, he asked, 'What is she up to?'

'Don't you see what she is doing, Sanjay?' Aditya said after a pause, which was necessitated by the palpitations of his heart. 'She is launching an all-out offensive. She has the threat of sexual harassment hanging over my head, and now she is screwing my writing career.'

Sanjay looked at the paper again. It had six sections from bestselling contemporary fiction. And against each section was a bit from Aditya's book. The similarity was undeniable. He lifted his glance from the paper and looked at Aditya. 'Is her insinuation correct?'

'Oh, come on!' Aditya moved his hands around in exasperation. 'You shouldn't be asking me that.'

'Well from the sheet of paper she has given you, her accusation seems to be correct. The lines match, word for word. I wonder how your publisher let you get away with it.'

'What do you expect, Sanjay? The lines which she accused me of plagiarising, the lines which she says are copied from other books, are the very lines which she edited into my book.' He walked around the room in an agitated fashion, hands on hips. 'She edited them into my book, fucker. She is the one who did it.'

'What?' Sanjay appeared shocked. 'Tell me you are kidding.'

Aditya was furious. 'She did a cursory edit of my book when she read the manuscript. She changed a few lines. Very minor edits one would imagine but while doing that, she inserted these lines. Given that I was blinded by her at that time and the fact that these lines do read well, I accepted all her edits and sent them to Vaishali to be included in the final manuscript. There is no way I could have realised that these were plagiarised. In any case there are over 10,000 lines in a book. Why would I, or anyone, specifically check six odd lines for plagiarised content?'

'Would you have a mail she sent you which proves that she edited those lines in? It will be handy in case things blow up.'

Aditya shook his head. 'No. She had given me a hand-corrected manuscript, where she had made the notations by hand. After transcribing them on to my comp, I shredded those papers. I can't even prove that she did it. And now she is holding me to ransom.'

'She is out to finish your career. I haven't heard of a single author accused of plagiarism who has survived the accusation. What a bitch man!' Sanjay commented.

'Well she claims that she loves you, doesn't she?' Diana spoke up. She had just walked in, all dressed up for dinner. 'The only thing which is unclear here is why you would scheme months in advance if you love someone. This plagiarism accusation shows that she was setting Aditya up right from the beginning, no?' Diana was thinking aloud.

Sanjay walked away from them, lost in thought, looking at the ceiling and talking to himself. 'You think it could be possible that she did this initially to impress you, Aditya? As in show you that she can write fabulously sexy lines for your books? And later when things didn't go as per plan, when you called off the relationship with her, she got offended. And when you ticked her off, she decided to use the same weapon to hit back at you. It's probably the same reason why she sent the envelope to your son. She wants you away from your family. If you end up losing out on your writing career too, either you will gravitate towards her or even if you don't, she would have had her revenge,' Sanjay argued. Diana nodded her head.

'In the interim it might help you to keep her humoured. Before we figure out a solution to this, we do not want her to make a move,' Diana proposed.

'As in?'

'Be nice to her. Swallow your pride. Don't get into a confrontation. Maybe help her with the book? Doesn't hurt you, does it?'

Aditya nodded his head. It seemed a reasonable way to buy time, to make sure that Shreya was kept under control, at least for the time being.

'Do you want to come with us for dinner?' Diana asked him, looking at him brood.

'Naah, it's okay. You guys carry on,' Aditya said and walked away towards the bar, as Diana and Sanjay prepared to leave.

Preoccupied, he pulled out a bottle of Laphroaig and poured himself a drink. After filling it up with ice from the ice pail lying on the bar, he walked towards the terrace. He was still thinking of what Shreya's motivation could be. Was it love for him? Was it the desperate desire to achieve stardom? Was she mentally ill? He couldn't decide.

That's when the door bell rang. Aditya walked up to the door to open it.

'Hey Sunaina. What a pleasant surprise. Come on in,' he said, when suddenly he noticed that Sunaina was not alone.

She looked at the person standing next to her and said, 'Melwin, meet Aditya Kapoor.'

70

'Did you check your mail?' Vaishali asked the moment Shreya picked up her call.

'No. What is it about?'

'I've sent you the reworked cover. Check it and give me your sign-off.'

'Cool. Five minutes.'

Shreya opened Vaishali 's mail. Attached to it was a 2.4MB image. She touched it to open it. It buffered for a while, and then her screen lit up, as did her face. The book cover looked fabulous on the screen of her phone. She zoomed into the image and looked at it closely.

Her lips curved upwards in a smile. 'What the fuck?' she muttered and brought the phone closer to her face. The smile turned into a wide grin. She hurried back to her workstation. She couldn't contain her excitement. She glanced at Aditya's office. He was in his room, head hidden behind the screen of his laptop.

She took a deep breath, calmed herself down and walked to Aditya's cabin. She knocked on the door before entering.

'Thank you, Aditya,' she beamed at him. 'You don't know how much it means to me. Your quote on the cover, your endorsement, is like a dream come true for me.'

'You didn't leave me with much of a choice, did you?'

Shreya looked at him. Even now her fluttering eyelashes made him go weak. 'You didn't believe I would compromise you, did you?'

'I don't know what to believe any more, Shreya,' Aditya said dejectedly.

'I love you, Aditya. I would never compromise you, irrespective of what you do.'

Aditya just smiled in return. 'I figured that out the moment you handed me that sheet of paper.'

'Oh, Aditya. You are holding that against me?' she walked up closer to him. Aditya stiffened. 'Please don't. I am sorry. I was too anxious. Too worried and I didn't want to lose you,' Shreya wheedled.

It was a flawed argument. The fact was when Shreya had edited those lines into Aditya's manuscript, she was in no danger of losing him. Aditya knew that, but didn't respond. Diana's words were ringing in his head. *Be nice to her. Swallow your pride. Don't get into a confrontation. Maybe help her with the book. Doesn't hurt you.*

'The book is going up on Flipkart and Amazon for pre-booking today. That's what Vaishali told me. Calls for a celebration, what do you think?' Shreya proposed.

'Absolutely. You are a debut author only once. This chance will never come again.'

'How about tonight? I owe you one for what you have done for me,' she paused. 'Please allow me to make up for being a bitch. Will you?'

'Can anyone say no to you, Shreya?' Aditya couldn't resist the jibe.

Dinner was fixed for 8.30 that night, at Royal China, a fine dining restaurant in Bandra.

Aditya left office and went back to Sanjay's house to change and freshen up for dinner with Shreya. Diana was home when he got there. She had come back early that day.

'There is a package for you. It's on the TV cabinet,' she yelled as she disappeared into Sanjay's room. Aditya lazily walked up to the cabinet and picked up the envelope which was addressed to him. He didn't like the look of it. It screamed bad news. He opened it and pulled out the contents.

When he looked at them, his head started spinning. His vision blurred as tears flooded his eyes. Maya had sent him divorce papers for his signature. To make matters worse he had to keep his dinner date.

Quietly he left the papers on the rack, changed and left. He was getting late for dinner at Royal China.

71

'Did you pre-order my book?' Shreya didn't even wait for him to say hello. She sat down in the car and looked at Aditya, waiting for him to respond.

'Is it up? That's quick work by Kiwi.'

'Yes. Let me send you the link,' she beamed, as she fiddled with her phone. 'Order it now,' she instructed him with the excitement of a five-year-old.

Aditya smiled. Her aggression was something most Indian authors lacked. 'Let me at least get to the restaurant. I can't order it while driving.'

At the restaurant they settled down in a cosy corner. Aditya logged on to his smartphone and pre-ordered the book from Amazon. 'I am sure you are the first one to pre-order. Hope your luck rubs off on me, Aditya,' Shreya screeched gleefully. Aditya did not react.

She placed her hand on his and asked him softly. 'Is everything all right, Aditya?'

'Maya has sent me a divorce notice.'

'Oh shit!' Shreya exclaimed.

Aditya tilted his head and looked at her from the corner of his eyes. The cynicism was unmistakable.

'Oh come on, Aditya. You know I want to see you happy. Whatever makes you unhappy, distresses me.' She snaked her other hand ahead and it too now rested on top of his.

'Anyway,' Aditya didn't want to carry the discussion forward. 'Today is not about me, it is about you—your success, your first book, the first day of your book going on sale.'

'Pre-booking, not actual sale,' Shreya corrected him. She was elated. Happy that Aditya was with her that night and thrilled that he was celebrating her success. Deep within, she was also ecstatic that Maya had sent him a divorce notice.

'You need to now tell me what all I need to do to kick off the action on my book,' Shreya said. It was at the top of her mind; the only thing that mattered to her.

'Let's draw up a detailed plan, Shreya. The next thirty days to the launch are very crucial. Don't let up steam. This is going to be the make or break period. Don't miss a single opportunity. And don't be ashamed to promote your book.'

'Did I miss one when I got into the car?' she laughed. She was happy after a long time. At one point in time during the evening, she held Aditya's hands, looked him in the eye and said, 'I love you, Aditya. If unknowingly I have done anything to hurt you, I am sorry.'

'I have lost count, Shreya,' he said. 'But the good thing about losing count is that I have stopped counting.'

Shreya just placed her hand on his and patted him. She didn't know what to say.

Aditya stayed on course. 'Let's try and see if we can get

some large corporate deals. Like say 500 to 1000 books. Get them to buy and gift author-signed copies.' He was trying hard to stay away from an emotionally charged discussion.

'You think corporates will do that?'

'No harm in trying. Even if they don't and we convince them to do an email campaign to their employees, talking about your book, it will be worth it.'

'Did they do it for you?'

'Our own National Bank did it. They emailed every employee. I didn't push them to buy, for that would have created an issue internally. Vested interests, some would say.'

'Hmm . . . That's nice. Do you think our bank will do it for me? My book?' Shreya asked.

'Ask Sanjay. You know him so well.'

'Sanjay? How will I ask him? I am not that comfy with him. Can you ask him?'

Aditya laughed. 'He is not going to eat you alive. What's the worst that can happen? He will say that he can't do it. If he refuses, I will step in. Happy?'

'No, no. You only ask him, Aditya. I am not that close to him.'

Aditya smiled and nodded his head. 'Fine, I will do it. But we need many such corporates to help us to actually affect sales.'

'Should we buy my book from the stores? Just to show some movement . . .?'

'Well. You can. Some authors do it too. But it is a very expensive proposition, unless your publisher supports you.'

'Why do you need the publisher's support?' Shreya asked. She was all ears.

'How else will you dispose of the books that you buy from the stores? Assuming Amazon buys 200 copies of your book from your publisher. You buy 100 off Amazon. Who will you give those hundred books to? Giving it for free to friends and relatives is an expensive proposition. One way is to give it back to the publisher who will buy it back from you at the rate they would have sold it to Amazon, and they would put those books back in circulation. So the only loss for you will be the markup that Amazon or for that matter any bookstore puts up. But there is no point discussing it as Kiwi will not support you in this. And more importantly it is unethical,' Aditya summarily dismissed the thought. 'Instead try and get some bloggers who will write honest reviews. Reviews will help promote the book, and also give you content for social media promotion. I can talk to a few of my blogger friends.' After a pause he added, 'Remind me tomorrow, I will connect you with Nirav Sanghavi of Blogadda. He will be able to help you out. I will also introduce you to Sangram Surve of ThinkWhyNot, the agency that does my marketing promotions. He will help you promote your book.'

The discussion on books and what Shreya should do to promote hers went on for an hour, during which time dinner was served.

Later, as they were walking out, Shreya looked at him and asked, with all sincerity, 'You still think I was behind the *Bombay Times* article?'

Aditya smiled but didn't respond. She slipped her arms in his as he led her out of the restaurant. His left hand went into the pocket of his trousers to pull out the valet parking slip.

The moment they stepped out, they were blinded by the glare of what seemed like a million flashbulbs going off simultaneously. The entire paparazzi that had been hungry for news on the two of them had got wind of the fact that they were at the restaurant and had gathered there waiting for them to come out.

'Get back in,' Aditya angrily muttered as he turned and pushed her back inside the restaurant. He stood there alone waiting for the car to come. The moment it arrived, the two of them got in and left. The walk from the restaurant to the car was enough for the media to get the pictures they needed.

*

It was too late for the media to carry the pictures in the next day's edition. However they did carry them the day after.

That afternoon Sanjay called Aditya on his mobile. 'Your boss has been harassing me. You refuse to stay out of the media's glare and I bear the brunt of it.'

'How about I send you a letter where I officially inform HR of this relationship—we could use that as another tool to buy time before we figure out a way to get rid of Shreya from my life? You could show the letter to Tim to calm him down,' Aditya offered.

Sanjay agreed to his proposal as an email would serve as a written confirmation for his records.

*

That night, Aditya tweeted about Shreya's book. He even posted the cover image on his Facebook page and asked his readers to pre-order the book.

Just by virtue of Aditya getting involved in the promotion the book rocketed from obscurity to #8 on the Amazon bestseller list. Shreya was thrilled. How many fabulous new authors disappear into oblivion because they are unable to market their wares to the reader base. Aditya's involvement had taken her well past that stage. Looking at the response to Aditya's tweet, it was clear that she could be a rock star author too.

Meanwhile, Aditya called Vaishali , to discuss the promotional plan. His involvement had upped the stakes for Kiwi. They were now forced to invest promotion money to back the book. Book trailers, media articles, PR stories, alliances—everything was discussed.

Once they were done discussing the plan, Vaishali asked him, 'Is there anything we are missing out, Aditya?' She was very impressed with Aditya's thoroughness.

'In fact, there is one last thing which I wanted to discuss with you,' said Aditya, leading Vaishali to let out a long sigh of frustration.

72

THE SAME NIGHT, Aditya typed out a letter and handed over the draft to Sanjay. 'Do you think this is fine?'

'It will only help cover your backside, my friend,' Sanjay responded even as he looked at the letter and scanned it from end to end. The letter acknowledged a more than personal interest in Shreya and also said that it was being tabled with HR in the interest of disclosure. It also stated that Aditya was not sure about the direction the relationship would take and also that it was dependent to a large extent on the divorce battle that seemed imminent.

'I have bought time from Tim. I told him that we will get to some clarity on you and Shreya in the next thirty days. You might as well mention that in the letter. Hopefully in the next month or so this Shreya situation will be resolved.'

'Or you will have to find me another job.'

'Haha . . . I think Tim would love that.'

'Wouldn't you?' Aditya asked in a very strange manner.

Sanjay just chuckled in reply.

'I mean it, Sanjay. Wouldn't you?'

The chuckle disappeared and Sanjay turned grim. 'Aditya, was that a serious question?'

'If it wasn't, I wouldn't have asked.'

'Shut up, asshole. Why would I be happy if I have to find you another job?'

'Diana can move into my role, can't she? If I move out . . .'

'Technically, yes,' Sanjay nodded his head, 'but both of us are happy the way things are. I think she is beginning to like you.'

'I am beginning to like her too. But at one point in time, she was screwing around with my team. Wasn't she?'

'I know you guys haven't had a great past. But now that things have started to look up between the two of you, do we necessarily have to bring up the past?'

'The vestiges of the past, unless buried, will always keep cropping up and impact relationships,' Aditya said and then added, 'But to be fair, over the past few weeks she has been more of a support than you. I think I misunderstood her.'

'I can never understand you or your thoughts,' Sanjay said as he walked away. 'Send me the final letter, once you are in office tomorrow morning.' He stopped, turned to Aditya and said with a troubled look on his face, 'Maya called today. She wanted the papers back. Signed.'

Aditya didn't like what he heard. He suddenly lost his cool. 'Why is she calling you? Ask her to call me.' Maya had stopped all contact with him. If she needed anything, she would call Sanjay or Diana and that made Aditya feel helpless.

'Next time she calls, I will tell her that.' Sanjay paused for a bit and said, 'What have you decided about the papers? Are you going to talk to Maya? Or are you going to sign them?' He looked around the room, as if searching for words and then continued, 'Diana will kill me for saying this. But why don't you just sign the papers and end the agony?'

'I don't know. I want her to be happy. But I know I will never be able to live without her and Aryan.'

'Then don't you think you need to proactively do something about it?'

'Hmm . . .' Aditya nodded. 'I don't know how to get her to believe me.' He thought for a second and reached out for the phone lying on the table in front of him. Sanjay went to fix himself a drink. Aditya keyed in the password and brought up the dialled numbers list. He saw Maya's number and touched it. The call connected. Maya came on line.

'Yes, Sanjay.'

'Maya, it's me Aditya.'

'Oh. Yes, Aditya? Why have you called?'

'Can I come over and meet you right now?'

'All I need from you now are the divorce papers. I don't think I want to meet you, ever.'

'Maya. Please Maya,' Aditya pleaded. 'Don't you think I deserve another chance? You want to wish away fifteen years of togetherness for one mistake of mine?' Aditya heard a call waiting tone in the background. He glanced at his screen. Shreya was calling. He ignored it for the time being.

'Correction, Aditya: one known mistake.'

'There has been no other mistake, Maya. None. Trust me. I swear on Aryan.'

'Stop it, Aditya. I don't want your mistakes to weigh heavily on our son's future.'

The call waiting tone came up again. It was Shreya this time too. 'I regret everything that happened, Maya. I am terribly sorry. Believe me.'

'If that was so, would you still be in touch with that woman? You are happily tweeting and facebooking about her and her books. And you expect me to believe you, Aditya? Come on. You might think so, but I wasn't born yesterday.'

'Can I come and see you please? I will explain everything. I will leave everything and be with you and Aryan.'

Shreya was calling again. He looked at the screen before holding the phone to his ears. 'Maya, I am in a soup. I will be doomed if I don't play along. I am stuck. It's not that everything that I am doing is because I want to do it. Give me a chance to meet you and explain. I am confident that I will be able to convince you.'

'Forget it, Aditya. I am not interested in carrying on this conversation further. I have got to go,' she abruptly disconnected the line.

Aditya kept the phone on the table and walked to the other room. Sanjay was waiting for him at the bar. His Laphroaig had already been poured in his glass. He picked it up and downed it in one go.

'Wohooo. Hold on, buddy. Not so fast!' Sanjay exclaimed. 'Eat something if you are going to drink like this.' Sanjay walked towards the kitchen. 'Let me see if we have something.'

Aditya sat there thinking about his conversation with Maya. He didn't like the way it went. In fact he didn't like the way it began. It was playing on his mind. Something was not right. He couldn't figure out what it was. And it was bothering him.

Sanjay returned with two packets of chips and some cashews.

'Is Diana coming?' Aditya asked sinking into the beanbag next to the bar.

'She might. Some old friends have come over and she is spending some time with them.' He picked up the drink from the counter and handed it to Aditya. 'Here,' he said as Aditya reached out for the glass.

The second peg of Laphroaig didn't take much time to finish either. All it needed was a couple of gulps. His phone vibrated. He pulled it out and looked at the screen. It was Shreya.

'Hi, Aditya. Where are you?' she said the moment he picked up.

'At home with Sanjay. Sorry missed your calls.'

'What? Oh okay,' she said, surprised. 'Someone from Poonam Saxena's office, from *Hindustan Times*, had called in the evening. I couldn't call you earlier because you were on a flight. You had spoken to them about me I guess. They wanted to do a telephonic interview tomorrow. I haven't dealt with these media guys; wanted some *gyan*. They said that she will call me at ten tomorrow morning.'

'It will not be too complicated. She is an experienced and professional journo. You won't have any problem with her. Just be yourself. Don't try to ape anyone. It will be . . .' The shrill ring of a phone interrupted him. He looked around. Sanjay smiled at him. 'It's Diana's. I set a loud ringtone for her. Of late she has been accusing me of missing her calls too often.' He rushed to pick up the call, leaving Aditya alone talking to Shreya.

'Where were we,' Aditya said. 'Oh yes—Poonam, the *Hindustan Times*. You don't need to worry at all, Shreya. It will be fine. You will be one of the first debutant authors that they would have covered, if they end up covering you that is.'

'She is sure to ask me about you. What should I say?'

'Tell her that I am your boyfriend and that I am someone who you are madly in love with.'

'Shut up, Aditya. Seriously, tell me please.'

'Just say that it is too personal for you to answer and that if she needs any clarifications she can talk to me. That should work.' He advised Shreya on a few other things and disconnected.

He went to refill his glass. Sanjay was in the living room still talking to Diana. He looked at the clock on the wall. It was fast approaching midnight. He refilled the glass and plonked himself in front of the TV. Star sports was playing highlights from the Indo-Pak world cup pre-quarterfinals match in 1996. It was always fun to watch India vs. Pakistan matches. He recollected those days from campus when they would go to watch the matches in the stadium. They would go in a large group—Maya, Sanjay, and a few other friends of theirs. Great atmosphere, great company, great energy. He missed those days.

73

ADITYA PICKED UP Shreya on his way to work next morning. She wanted to prepare for the Poonam Saxena interview.

'If you max it, and she ends up being impressed with you, she can work wonders for you,' said Aditya. He gave her tips on how to manage tricky questions. 'Do not let your guard down at any point in time,' he told her. Just as he was driving into the office building, he added, 'One last piece of unsolicited advice. There is nothing off the record for the press. If anything has to be off the record, then keep it that way. Don't say it.'

*

Diana came looking for Aditya that afternoon. 'I wanted to talk to you yesterday. But Sanjay told me that you had conked off.'

Aditya gave her a wry smile. 'I had a drink too many,' he confessed.

'I had a long chat with Maya yesterday.'

'About?'

'You. What else?'

Aditya's interest was aroused. He sat up straight and rested his elbows on the table in front.

'She is upset. Really upset to see that you are still with Shreya helping her launch her book. She was referring to your tweets. I tried explaining to her that you are doing it more for visual impact. But she is not ready to believe it. She thinks that's a tale you are spinning for our consumption too.'

'I would have been disappointed had she not got upset. She just refuses to talk to me. I can't even speak to her and explain,' Aditya rued.

'I know it is none of my business, Aditya, but I was a bit concerned,' Diana continued. She looked nervous. The pen in her hand was nervously scribbling on the blank paper lying on Aditya's table. 'I was talking to Sanjay yesterday and . . .'

Their conversation was interrupted by Aditya's subordinate who walked in without knocking. Not wanting Diana to leave, Aditya stepped out of the room leaving Diana behind.

'Asshole . . . These guys can never do anything on their own,' he complained as he walked back five minutes later. 'Anyway, what were you saying Diana?'

'I was saying that I had mentioned this to Sanjay in the past and he didn't seem too perturbed. That's probably because he knows you for a bit too long now. But if you promise me that you won't get upset, I will tell you what is bothering me.' She was struggling to look him in the eye, probably embarassed to ask him something which she felt might offend him. The pen in her hand was constantly scribbling away on the paper on his table; a sign of her being jittery and anxious.

Aditya noticed. 'What is it, Diana? The days when I was upset with you are over. Now I know you are on my side.'

'I know we had rationalised this in the past, but the fact remains that Shreya has caused much angst—she screwed up your reputation, set you up in a manner that made you vulnerable to accusations of being a plagiariser. In essence she ruined your personal and professional life. I'm worried that in the quest to save yourself by sleeping with the enemy, are you getting deeper and deeper in the quagmire? Are you getting into an inextricable position?' Diana looked up at him, worried.

'Nothing in life can put you in an inextricable position unless you yourself want to be in such a position,' Aditya said.

'But she can harm you. If history is something to go by . . .'

'True but history also gives you a precedent to go by. History tells you what to expect. And now that I do know, I am very careful. Trust me, Diana, I know what I am doing.'

'I will never understand this,' Diana sighed. 'As far as Maya is concerned, all I can say is that she will take a helluva lot of convincing.' She got up from the chair. 'And by the way, the expense management committee inputs from your team are pending. I have got the reco from all the other teams. Can you send it by tonight?'

'Shit. I completely forgot about it,' Aditya said. 'I'll get cracking on it right away. Can you give me one more day please?' Diana looked annoyed, so he requested, 'Sorry, Diana. With all the confusion in my personal life, I completely forgot about it. Just one more day?'

'Okay, fine. One more day,' she said and left the room.

Aditya looked at all the papers lying on the table, gathered them together and moved them to a side. As he was doing that he spotted the paper Diana had scribbled on. Even the scribble was neatly done, in the form of neat patterns. Her fidgety behaviour amused him. He was about to crumple the piece of paper and throw it into the waste paper basket, when something struck him. He smoothed out the paper and looked at it again. He had seen similar scribbles somewhere else. He couldn't remember where. He tried hard to, but his memory failed him.

He went back to his laptop. As Diana had said, the expense committee inputs were due. He didn't want to delay it further.

74

Worried about the costs in the Retail Bank going up, despite them sacking 300 people, Tim had set up a cross functional expense management team under Diana. The Financial control team had sent details of all costs incurred in various departments to the respective department heads and asked for their recommendations on how to bring the overall cost down.

Aditya cursorily looked at the cost lines. The branch rentals had remained stable. They hadn't opened a new bank branch in the last one year. The salary costs had marginally gone down, but the cost of separation of 300 people had hit them badly. That apart, the only cost line which seemed high was that of miscellaneous expenses, the incidentals—the cost of tea and coffee in the branches, the cost of client entertainment, staff entertainment, telephone bills, communication, stationery, courier, etc. He forwarded the mail to Diana with a comment. 'Let's look closely at stationery, branch entertainment, communication and local conveyance. We might get some joy there.'

He called his planning officer and asked him to get access to the bills paid and give him a top-level analysis. Hardly had he kept the phone down when Shreya walked in.

'Finished the call?' Aditya smiled and asked her.

'Yaaa!' Her eyes were round in excitement. 'Poonam Saxena is a terror!'

'Haha!' Aditya laughed. 'Why, what happened?'

'The kind of questions she was asking me, my god! She is so persistent. Kept nudging and prodding, till I answered all her questions.'

'Forget all that. Is she putting you on the cover or not?'

'How can I ask her directly, Aditya? But she herself came up with an interesting proposition. I didn't know how to respond. So I told her that I would ask you and confirm.'

Aditya looked at her wondering what it could be.

'She said she is happy to do a big story if you are willing to come on board.'

'What does that mean?'

'If you are willing to be a part of the story, they will do a master-apprentice kind of a feature on the two of us. A cover story!'

'A master-apprentice story or a relationship story? I will do it, if it is the former.'

'So you will be a part of the story?'

'Of course. Anything that helps you. Don't worry. I will speak to her.'

'Really? Oh, that would be so awesome!' Shreya exclaimed. Her eyes gleamed with excitement. 'I'll be on the cover of *HT Brunch*. Wow!'

'Only thing that worries me is that if I come on it, they will give me all the weightage and it will take the focus away from you. I just want to make sure that they don't do that.'

'Thanks, Aditya.' She was still grinning from ear to ear. 'You have made my day,' Shreya said as she walked out of the room.

The moment she left, Aditya dialled Poonam's number.

'Hi, Poonam,' he said the moment the phone got picked up.

'Hey, Aditya. I have been wanting to call you,' she said, her voice clear.

'No wonder I was feeling so lucky today, Poonam.'

'Haha! You are in the news. This new chick in your life is making waves.'

'Oh that ... The party line is that I am helping her promote her new book. Wink Wink,' he laughed.

'I was speaking to her a while ago. She asked me if I would put her on the cover. Even established authors and celebrities don't ask me that question so directly.'

'She did?'

'Yes, she did. Stumped me for a minute. I didn't know what to say.'

'Rare occurance, you getting stumped,' Aditya laughed.

'Exactly. But I told her that if she gets you to be a part of the story, I will put both of you on the cover.'

'So gracious of you, Poonam.'

She laughed. 'You know how it is. Anyway, the moment I said this, she got excited and agreed. She said that she will be able to get you to agree.'

'When do you plan to bring out the issue if I do agree?'

'Our next three weeks are already scheduled—closed out. So I guess the earliest we can do is five to six weeks from now.'

Aditya looked at the desktop calendar in front of him. 'Five weeks from now should be fine. I will come on board.'

'Would you mind if I help you to make it interesting?'

'Not at all,' Poonam readily agreed. 'It will only lend authenticity to the entire story.'

The ring of his extension interrupted the conversation. 'Great. Let's do a story which no one has done before.' He hurriedly closed his conversation with Poonam and hung up.

'Yeah?' he said as he picked up.

'Can you come up to my room for ten minutes?'

'What happened?'

'Come up. I will tell you.'

'Be there in a flash,' he said and disconnected the phone.

As promised he was in Sanjay's room in five minutes. Sanjay was talking to one of his team members and asked him to wait in his cabin. Aditya walked in and sat down on the Featherlite chair. He stretched himself to the fullest and raised his hands way above his head. He was tired. He looked around the room. Sanjay was very organised. A place for everything and everything in its place — Sanjay was one of the few men who believed in the adage. The pens were in the pen-stand and not on the table, papers were neatly filed away, books were arranged systematically, held in place by the bookends which Diana had gifted him. The mail was neatly opened and envelopes stapled to the letters. Everything was so perfect.

Aditya looked around as he thought about his life. If only his life was as clean. The plagiarism issue now threatened to mess up his writing career as well. No publisher would touch him if they ever found out. He had to do something to get out of this mess that life had become.

'Hey. Sorry I kept you waiting,' Sanjay said as he walked into the room. He patted Aditya and sat down in front of him.

'What happened?'

'I wanted to show you this,' said Sanjay. From the neat pile on his table, he pulled out a small bunch of papers and gave it to him. Aditya looked at the papers and looked back at Sanjay.

'Some asshole in Kolkata has filed a case against us,' Sanjay informed him, thereby saving Aditya the trouble of going through the papers.

'Why?'

'He claims he has been wrongly laid off, for no fault of his. Though actually his performance ratings tell a different story.'

'Okay. So?'

'The court has issued summons in our names; our personal names. The Kolkata lawyer has asked for some clarifications to respond. I called you so that we can respond jointly and send it across.'

'Okay,' Aditya said, and started reading the papers.

'Sir, we are ready to cut the cake,' a junior HR officer, knocked on the open door and announced.

'Cake?' Aditya asked, looking up from the document he was reading.

'Birthday?'

'Whose?'

'Mine?'

'Yours? Crap!' Aditya exclaimed. 'Yours is not until day after tomorrow.'

'I am not in office tomorrow and am on leave the day after. So these guys are doing the cake-cutting today.'

'Wow! Then you go ahead. I am taking these papers. I'll send them back once I am done. Let me leave you in peace.' Aditya got up to leave. He looked around for one last time. 'Wonder how you read these Baldaccis and Grishams and Pattersons,' he said, commenting on the books that Sanjay had displayed in his room.

'Because I don't write books, I get time to read them. But the flip side is that because I don't write books, I don't get the fame which you guys usurp,' Sanjay joked as Aditya made a face. 'Nor do we get the adulation from women,' he cheekily added.

75

DIANA HAD PLANNED a party to bring in Sanjay's birthday. That afternoon she went to Aditya's cabin, to chat with him about the guest list.

'Going home early today?' Aditya asked after she had discussed the small invitee list with him.

'Hopefully . . . If some generous souls help.'

'Why? What is holding you back?'

'I have to submit the first cut of the cost control project today and Tim's biggest business line has not given in their submissions. Unless I close it, I won't be able to go home.'

'Work in progress, Diana,' Aditya smiled. 'It is almost done. I had sent you something yesterday, more coming in today.'

'I was planning to leave by four,' Diana said. 'Is it possible to send your stuff by then?'

'Oh shit. Hold on then,' Aditya quickly opened his mail on his laptop and scanned through them. 'Shankar should have sent it. He is normally very particular about deadlines.' There was a pause as both of them stared into the email inbox. 'Aah . . . here it is,' Aditya breathed a sigh of relief and looked at Diana. 'Sorry, Diana, let me go through it and send it to you ASAP.'

'If you don't mind, we can go through it together. It'll save me time too.'

'Be my guest.' Aditya opened the entire worksheet, which Shankar had sent him. There were twelve expense management initiatives listed on that sheet, which would help cut branch banking costs by 10 per cent. Aditya went through all of them and found some to be very immature.

'If I send these to Tim, he will have me for breakfast,' he said as he ran through the proposed cost-cutting initiatives. 'Rubbish. What crap is this? "Reduce stationery cost by controlling distribution of pens. Programme printer to print both sides to save paper . . . Use of internal chats instead of mobile phones during the day . . ." We need to refine these,' he said as he moved on to the page marked "Issues in Cost Allocation".'

On that sheet, Shankar had sent him a listing of all expenses which had been allocated to Branch Banking but actually pertained to other businesses. 'These expenses do not pertain to the branch banking business. These should not have been debited to us,' Shankar had written as one of the recommendations.

'These have to be reversed out from the branch banking expenses and debited to the correct business lines,' Aditya said to Diana.

He looked down at the list of expenses. First on the list was the rental of an office they had let go. The corporate bank had taken up their space. The rent was still being debited to Aditya's team. He had raised the issue with the property services team too but no one had done anything.

'Include this in your list. I will take it up and get it done,' Diana volunteered.

'There are thirty people listed here whose salaries are being debited to me. But they don't belong to branch banking,' Aditya said as he moved down the list.

'Expenses pertaining to the following staff, in other units, are being debited to branch banking,' Aditya read out loud as his eyes scanned the list. 'Nothing extraordinary about this . . . Happens all the time.' He moved on to the next point.

'Hold it. Go back, go back,' Diana called out.

'What happened?' Aditya asked her, scrolling back to the previous point.

'Isn't Shreya in your team?'

'Don't you know that?' a surprised Aditya asked.

'Why does her name figure in the list which, according to Shankar, is of people belonging to other units whose expenses have been debited to you?'

'Aah. That's because all MTs are on HR rolls. Maybe that's why Shankar wants to reverse out her expenses from our cost centre to HR cost centre,' said Aditya as he casually clicked on the expenses mentioned against Shreya's name which Shankar had claimed to be incorrect.

'All regular expenses,' Diana declared as she quietly scanned it.

'I sign off all her expenses,' Aditya claimed.

'I am sure,' said Diana. 'Who else will? Let's move on.'

Aditya moved the cursor to go back to the earlier page, but stopped. He didn't click. He was staring at the worksheet.

'Aditya,' Diana called out. He didn't hear her.

She touched his shoulder and called out his name again, 'Aditya.'

'There is a travel claim of 24,000 rupees for official travel and hotel stay. She never travelled on work. More importantly, I don't remember having approved any such bill for her.'

'It could be someone else's bill which they wrongly showed under Shreya's name. Ask for the reimbursement voucher from Accounts. We will get to know.'

'True,' said Aditya as he moved on. His mind was still on the voucher. After a couple of minutes, he called Shankar. 'Shreya's travel bill of 24,000 . . . Can you please show me the copy of the bill? If you don't have it, get it from Accounts.'

'I have it here, sir. I asked for copies of all the contentious bills. I'll mail it to you.'

In no time, the bills were in Aditya's Inbox. He clicked it open.

'Travel to Goa for recce of an off-site? What's going on?' he exclaimed as he scrolled down to the bottom of the voucher where the approver's signature was. The moment they saw it, Diana froze. 'It cannot be,' Diana said as Aditya turned and looked at her.

'Maybe it's a mistake.'

'No it's not.'

'Are you . . .' Aditya began but before he could finish, Diana shook her head. 'No. It can't be. I may have many imperfections, Aditya, but a bad memory is definitely not one of them.'

Aditya was perplexed. He wondered what the hell was going on. He repeated his question, 'Are you sure you didn't approve the voucher, Diana? 100 per cent sure?'

Diana looked equally baffled. 'Let's confront her,' she said.

'Hold it, Diana. Let's think this through. Confronting her will make matters worse. Let's ask Sanjay. Let's see what he recommends,' he suggested. Diana looked upset. Aditya stared at her hand—her fingers moved subconsciously, pen in her hand. She was nervously scribbling on some paper on Aditya's table. That's when it struck him. The doodles! Aditya had seen them before. Despite the chaos in his mind, this time, he clearly remembered where he had seen them.

'Have you read Wendy Doniger, Diana?' Aditya asked calmly.

'What?' The question surprised Diana. 'What does Wendy Doniger have to do with all this?'

76

THE DISCUSSION WITH Diana after the discovery of Shreya's false expense claim had got Aditya worried. He wanted to get to the bottom of this.

He looked at the phone and dialled another extension.

'Siddharth Ananth's office,' an impersonal voice sounded out.

'Put me through to Ananth please.'

'Sure, Aditya.' The secretary's tone changed to a very pleasant one, the moment she figured out that it was Aditya.

'Hey, superstar! When is your next book coming out?' Ananth came on the line. He was the corporate banking head of National Bank.

'Some time away, boss. The last one came out only a couple of months back.'

'Oh yes, I read it. The one based on your own love story—yours and Maya's—was fabulous. I loved it.'

'Thanks, Ananth.'

'Tell me. What can I do for you?'

'Taj Hotels.'

'What about them?'

'They are a large account for us, right?'

'One of the biggest.'

'I need some information from them,' Aditya said and then went on to outline what he wanted.

'Not sure if they will oblige but I will try,' Ananth said. 'Promise me that you will not make me a character in your book,' he added, laughing.

'Haha! If you are good to me I might consider this request.'

'Bastard,' Ananth laughed and cut the call.

In twenty minutes Ananth called back. 'They will take a day to get the information you wanted. Will that be okay?'

'Should be fine, Ananth. Thanks a ton,' Aditya said and disconnected the call.

The same afternoon, Aditya was in his cabin, thinking of the discussion with Diana and Ananth.

His phone rang. The name Ram Kumar flashed on his screen.

'Can you pick me up in the evening today? I don't want to land up with my hair in a mess.'

'Sure. At nine?'

'Done,' Shreya said and hung up.

The moment Aditya hung up and kept the phone on the table, it hit him like a bullet. How did he miss it? Hurriedly he went back and checked the call log on his iPhone. The night that he had called Maya to discuss the divorce papers—the calls pertaining to that night was what he wanted to see. He had not made more than a hundred calls after that night. The log was still on his iPhone.

His eyes grew wider as he checked his phone. He started

sweating. Unable to fathom what was happening, he kept the phone down on the table and leaned back on his chair and shut his eyes. *What was going on?*

After a lot of thought, he opened his eyes, reached out for his mobile phone, and dialled a number.

'I have a hypothesis,' he said on the phone. He went on to lay his entire theory threadbare.

'Can you prove it? Evidence?' The voice on the other side asked.

'Circumstantial at best,' Aditya confessed.

77

Sanjay's birthday party was a very personal affair. There were about twelve people in all—Aditya, Shreya, Diana, a couple of Diana and Sanjay's friends, Sunaina; who had accompanied Shreya, and a few others.

Sanjay was thrilled. Diana had bought a Bose music system for him; something which he had been planning to buy for a long time.

Aditya picked up Shreya and Sunaina and came in around ten. He had not discussed the details of the expense voucher with her. He had agreed with Diana that they would decide the next course of action only after speaking with Sanjay.

Shreya was wearing a dress. Flaunting a smokey eyeshadow comprising shades of black and grey, she looked gorgeous. A fair complexion darkened a bit by the bronzer, added to her sensuality. A single strand pearl necklace around her slender neck and hair parted in the centre, she looked every inch a stylish corporate executive in party mode. Sunaina in comparison was soberly dressed.

Music from the seventies was blaring from Sanjay's new sound system. Everyone was having a good time. Sanjay, who was a good singer, took to the microphone and sang along with the recorded music. The karaoke was an instant hit. Shreya hung around Aditya and enjoyed her drink, occasionally chatting up Diana and the others.

At 11.45 the doorbell rang. Diana ran to open it. When she walked back into the room, Aditya was stunned. Shreya stood up from where she was; the glass of wine almost slipped from her hand. Standing at the door, next to Diana, was Maya. She was looking her gorgeous self in blue denims with a white designer shirt, tucked in. With minimal make-up and her hair tied up in a pony, she looked beautiful. Sanjay took the lead and walked up to her. 'So nice to see you, Maya,' he said as he gave her a hug. 'You are looking lovely.'

'Happy birthday, sweetheart,' she responded. Her eyes were trained at Aditya and a little towards his left, on Shreya who couldn't really figure out what to do with her nervous fingers. She kept the glass of wine down on the table and walked to the safe confines of the restroom.

'I can see you are still going strong with that tart, Aditya,' Maya said the moment he walked up to her.

'How are you, Maya?' Aditya asked ignoring her jibe.

'Good, good,' she replied, nodding her head. 'I'm doing good. God is great. He is kind too.'

'Maya,' Aditya started to say something. 'I am . . .'

Hardly had he said anything when Maya interrupted. 'Save it, Aditya. I am here for Sanjay, not to listen to any of your crap. So don't even try to say anything.' She turned away from Aditya and walked towards Diana. She had seen Aditya sitting right next to Shreya and that had ticked her off.

'Maya, wait. I need to speak with you,' Aditya called out. She walked up to Diana and stood next to her, talking to her friends. Shreya came back just in time to see Aditya trail Maya. Apart from some momentary awkwardness she felt stung by pangs of jealousy. The possessive streak in her came to the fore. She strode up to Aditya and stood right next to him, her shoulders brushing against his.

Maya noticed her. 'Hi Shreya. Hope your toy is taking care of you.'

Shreya stood there silently. The visit to the washroom had calmed her nerves and she now looked ready to battle for her space.

'When you are done and dusted with him, just throw him out of the house. Do not pass him on to someone else. He is not worth anyone else's time,' Maya said and turned away. Finding Aditya and Shreya together, she was beginning to lose her cool.

'It is okay, darling,' Diana stepped in. 'Come. We have a minute left for midnight. Let's find Sanjay.' She pulled Maya and dragged her away from Shreya.

The clock struck twelve. A chorus of 'Happy Birthday, Sanjay' rang all around. The cake was cut and everyone celebrated. Maya quietly made her way to the bar and poured herself a large whisky. For a fleeting moment she considered the appropriateness of drinking but flinging aside all concerns for her own well-being she guzzled the whisky down. That she had a check-up scheduled with Dr Krishnan the next day didn't even occur to her at that time.

Aditya scooped out a generous helping of the cake and

plastered Sanjay's face with it. Sanjay looked like a zombie with white and brown cake all over his face. Shreya went a step ahead and plastered even more creamy cake on his head and hair.

'Are we done?' he asked once the mayhem had stopped. 'Can I go and clean up, you assholes?'

'Go, go. You look pathetic,' said Diana.

'Come with me,' Sanjay said, as he walked towards the bedroom. Once inside his room, he removed his shirt, emptied his pockets—his wallet, his phone, his car keys—on the dressing table and walked into the bathroom. Diana waited for him outside the door. Sanjay's phone rang.

'It's Gregory,' Diana called out. Gregory was in Sanjay's team.

'Pick it up. He probably wants to wish me. Tell him that I will call later,' Sanjay's voice came from inside the bathroom.

*

In the living room, Maya gulped down another peg of whisky in a hurry. This was the first time she was seeing Aditya and Shreya together after getting to know about the two of them. The facade of a bold, fearless female was being shattered by the insecurity of a middle-aged woman. She took a refill and gulped that down too. She was not a whisky drinker. At best she would drink two bottles of breezers through the evening, and here she had downed two large ones and was midway through her third.

'Maya, please stop. Don't do this to yourself,' Aditya walked up to her and pleaded.

Maya didn't respond. She picked up her glass from the bar counter and gulped the remaining whisky in one shot. There was a bottle of Laphroaig next to her. She picked it up and was about to pour herself another glass when Aditya stopped her. He held her right hand, which held the bottle, and forcibly took it from her.

Maya jerked her hand and freed herself from Aditya's grip. 'Don't you touch me,' she yelled. Her voice was loud enough for others to hear. Everyone turned towards the two of them. 'Who the hell are you to ask me not to drink? Is this your party? Did you invite me here? Did I come with you? Then who the hell are you?'

Hearing the commotion Diana came out of the room. She was talking to Gregory on the phone, while waiting for Sanjay to clean up and emerge. He was taking a while. She cut the call, dumped the phone in the back pocket of her jeans, rushed back into the room and knocked on the bathroom door. 'You need to come out quick. Maya is having a go at Aditya.'

The bathroom door opened and Sanjay came out. He hurriedly wore another pair of trousers and a shirt and rushed out of the room. By that time the battle had worsened. Maya was spiralling out of control. She had now started abusing Shreya. She called her a slut, a whore, a woman of loose moral character. She called Aditya an opportunist, a man who had scant respect for family, a person who would drop his pants at the slightest hint of a woman giving him attention. She seemed unstoppable. After her tirade, Maya picked up her bag and walked out of the house. She was in a bad state. Tears were flowing non-stop from her eyes. Aditya tried following her. She yelled at him to stay away.

Sanjay came out of his bedroom, just as Maya was exiting the house. 'Stop her,' he called out to Aditya as she closed the main door behind her. She is drunk. She will land herself in trouble.'

'Someone go and bring her back,' Diana said, a bit frantic. No one else spoke. When no one except Sanjay and Aditya seemed to be bothered, Diana dashed back into the bedroom, came out with Sanjay's car keys and ran out of the door. Sanjay followed. The two of them caught up with Maya in the lift lobby.

'Have a great life, Sanjay. You are a sweetheart. Don't be like that slimy husband of mine.' She smiled wryly at him. 'I am sorry I made a scene but I couldn't stay back with Aditya there. I have to leave.'

'That's fine, Maya,' Sanjay spoke, 'but you can't go back home in this state. You are too drunk to drive.'

'It is okay. I will manage.'

'I will drop you, Maya. It is only a twenty-minute drive at this time,' Diana volunteered.

'Don't be silly. You are three pegs down,' Sanjay interrupted her. 'I seem to be the only sober person here.' He looked at Maya and held her by the elbow. 'Come, Maya.' He took the keys from Diana and walked to his car. 'Leave your car here. You can take it tomorrow,' he told Maya.

After some persuasion, which took a little bit longer than normal, for Maya felt guilty about pulling Sanjay out from his birthday party, she got into his car. 'I should be back in forty-five minutes,' Sanjay said as he drove off.

The party didn't last for too long after that. Shreya and Sunaina left immediately. The other friends too left in the next fifteen minutes.

By the time Sanjay got back at around 1.15 am, only Diana and Aditya were left in the house.

'I was beginning to get worried,' Diana said the moment she saw him. 'I tried calling you a couple of times.'

'I think in the melee I left my phone behind or I would have called you. Bad traffic,' he volunteered.

'Aww. What a beginning to your birthday,' Diana said. She walked up to him and hugged him again. 'Happy birthday, baby.'

78

THE NEXT MORNING, Maya walked into Dr Krishnan's clinic for her first check-up post her release from the hospital.

'Alone? Where is my friend?' Dr Krishnan asked her, when he saw her walk in.

'He is not in town, Dr Krishnan,' Maya lied. Dr Krishnan did not question her further and did all the checks without any comments. He drew three syringes full of blood even as he informed Maya that most of the test results would come in by that evening.

As she got up to go, he called out after her.

'Maya,' he said, very softly. 'You are a very bad liar.'

Maya looked on silently.

'The guy who didn't move from this hospital for a single day in the three weeks that you were here, would never let you come alone for a test, even if it is a simple follow up test.' He walked up to her. 'He is a good man who made some mistakes. But he loves you more than he loves himself.'

'That's the impression he has given everyone, Dr Krishnan. Don't believe it.'

'All these stories about him and that author friend of his are in the past. It's over. He himself told me so. He regrets all his mistakes. There is more strength in forgiving than in walking away, Maya, especially when you see true remorse. Just remember that.'

Maya just nodded and left.

The results came in that evening. Everything was clear. Maya was free of Ebola.

79

THE NEXT FEW weeks were extremely hectic. Preparation for a book launch is always chaotic, more so for a debutant author. The feel of the book, the smell of the paper, the thrill of standing on the podium in front of hundreds of people and unveiling a book along with some celebrity . . . each has its own excitement. But a lot goes behind the scenes as well.

'Who should we call for launching the book?' Shreya asked Aditya.

'Hmm . . . How about Anurag Kashyap?' he proposed. The Out of the Blue event was fresh in his mind when he recommended the name.

They fixed up a meeting. Anurag, given his relationship with Aditya, immediately agreed to do the honours. Not only that, he even agreed to buy the film rights for the book and said that he would announce it at the book launch.

The moment they were out of Anurag's office and inside the safe confines of the car, Shreya let go. She shrieked with joy. 'Awesommeeeeee. Aditya, you are absolutely awesome,' she exclaimed and kissed him on his cheek. Aditya turned and looked at her.

'Won't this make a great media story? A debutant author's work being picked up for a movie even before the book gets launched,' Shreya said excitedly.

'Media will lap it up. It will help push the book.'

'How lucky I am that I know you,' she gushed. Aditya didn't respond. His eyes were trained on the road ahead as he drove towards Shreya's house.

'Care for a drink?' Shreya asked him as they neared her building.

Aditya looked at his watch. It was well past dinner time. He had an early morning meeting with his team. But then he also felt that a couple of drinks wouldn't do him too much harm. In any case he would be alone at home, Sanjay was travelling on work. He parked the car and walked up to Shreya's apartment.

He made himself comfortable on the couch. Shreya poured out a large peg of single malt and gave him the glass. 'I will be back in a jiffy,' she said as she disappeared into her room to freshen up. He got up and walked around the room, glass in hand. He stepped out into the terrace and felt the cool breeze waft past his face. It began to drizzle. They were reaching the end of the monsoons. He walked back. A few books were piled up on the table in front—spillover from a large book shelf. He looked up and saw a copy of Eleanor Catton's *The Luminaries* lying on the table. He picked it up and flipped through it. It was a big book. As he flipped through it, he saw a piece of paper stuck inside the book. He stopped and looked at it. It was a bill from Reliance TimeOut, Hill Road, Bandra. The place from where the book had been bought. The charge slip was attached to the bill. He glanced at it and kept it back. He would never read that book. It was over a thousand pages. He placed it back on the shelf and walked up to the bar. He had finished his whisky, and he needed a refill.

He switched on the TV and watched some inane discussion on a news channel, played around with his phone and responded to a few messages as he waited for Shreya to come back.

Shreya returned, freshly showered and wearing pyjamas and a T-shirt. She poured herself a glass of red wine and sat down next to him.

There was a long period of silence, when neither of them spoke. They just sat there holding their respective glasses and looking at something playing out on the television screen in front of them.

'I was so thrilled at what Anurag told us today,' Shreya finally said. She was still reminiscing about the meeting with Anurag Kashyap. Aditya just turned and looked at her, probably wondering which part of the discussion she loved. 'When he told us that he will option the film rights . . . I felt like jumping and kissing you then and there. I was so so happy.'

Aditya was silent. He smiled.

Shreya gazed at Aditya. 'Now I will become a successful author, as big as you. Won't I, Aditya?'

'Of course you will. Maybe even bigger than me.'

'I love you for saying that, Aditya,' Shreya squealed as she kept her glass down, turned and hugged Aditya. She released him from the hug and looked at him. Her face was inches away from his. She caressed his cheek feeling the evening stubble pushing its way forcibly through the smooth skin. She reached out to his lips and ran her finger along the periphery. She closed her eyes, bent down and in slow motion her lips touched his. Her lips engulfed his lower lip and sucked on them slowly. Aditya pushed her back.

'No,' he said. 'No, Shreya. Not now. Please.'

Shreya looked at him, surprised. This was not the first time Aditya had pushed her back. But this was the first time he was firm. There were no signs of temptation. It was not as if he was holding himself back. He was just not interested. 'What happened, Aditya? Is something bothering you?'

'No, Shreya. It is just that I am not in the right frame of mind. There are too many things going on right now. Aryan, my divorce, your book—everything has to come to a closure,' he said.

'It will be fine, Aditya. Don't worry. It will all sort itself out.'

80

'BIG DAY FOR Shreya Kaushik. Debut book, *The Girl from Chhattisgarh* launches today. Best of Luck @authorShreya,' screamed a pre-programmed tweet that went out from Aditya's twitter handle that morning. It got 120 retweets within the first five minutes. Shreya's book had generated a fair amount of buzz. It was the no.1 book on Amazon, spurred on by the pre-order sales. The media interest was disproportionate to what it should've been in a debutant.

The persistent beeps of Aditya's tweets and retweets woke Shreya up. She looked at them and whooped in joy. She had a packed day ahead. The *Hindustan Times* shoot was at noon. Aditya had said that he would come directly from work. She had taken the day off.

For the shoot, Aditya came dressed in a suit—pin-striped and sharp, in line with his image of a banker. The *Hindustan Times* photographer wanted them to hold hands. Shreya readily moved closer to Aditya who refused. The photographer then took a few solo shots.

When he was done with his shoot, and the photographer was busy with Shreya, Aditya called Poonam Saxena. It was a long call. When he was done, he walked up to Shreya.

'She has promised a cracker next week. Let's wait for it.' The two of them walked out of the venue. Aditya headed back to his office and Shreya went home. She had to get ready for the launch.

81

THE KEMPS CORNER Crossword wore a very festive look. In one corner there was a giant backdrop which carried the image of the book cover, and logos of Crossword and Kiwi, apart from a larger-than-life image of Shreya. When Shreya saw it, she quickly went up to the stage and took some selfies with the backdrop before people came in.

Over sixty seats were laid out in front of the podium.

The two-level Crossword store was a preferred destination for book lovers in south Mumbai. On the first level, the store even had a Moshe's café. In fact it was one of the first bookstores to have an in-store café. The glass walls of the café overlooked the larger part of the ground floor. Anyone sitting there could look directly into the space where the launch event was to happen.

Anurag Kashyap arrived at 6.30 pm sharp. He was a stickler for punctuality. Shreya was at the door to receive him. The publisher from Kiwi had come down from Delhi, especially for this event—an honour rarely bestowed upon a first-timer. Aditya was already there, backstage, checking if everything was under control.

A number of people from National Bank had turned up

for the event. The seats had started filling up. It looked like it would be a full house.

For the benefit of those who could not attend, two video cameras had been set up to cover the event. It was being streamed live.

In Mumbai, there are three things that interest journalists—movies, murder and sex. Interest quotient in books and authors is at the barest minimum. Yet, a number of journalists were present at the launch. Whether they were interested in Shreya's book or Aditya's relationship with her, remained to be seen.

Aditya walked up to Anurag who was talking to Shreya in a corner of the ground floor, right next to the bestseller rack and shook hands.

'Shall we?' he asked pointing towards the stairs and led both Shreya and Anurag to Moshe's café on the upper floor.

'I can't see a copy of your new book, Aditya,' Anurag commented as they walked up the stairs.

'Might have sold out, Anurag. I will have it checked,' Aditya responded as he walked into the café. 'We are waiting for a few more people to arrive before we start. I hope it is okay with you?' Aditya asked Anurag.

Anurag looked through the glass walls of the café, down to the Crossword shop floor. 'More people?' he exclaimed, 'How many more?' In a surprised tone, he added, 'Can the store even take in more people?' There were already 150 people in the store.

'We just need room for six. They will all be here in two minutes, sir.'

Within the promised two minutes Sanjay and Diana walked in. They were followed by Tim Xavier and then by Sunaina. When Shreya saw the person next to Sunaina, she freaked.

'Melwin!' she exclaimed. 'What are you doing here?' Suddenly she looked a bit anxious. 'Sunaina, you are still in touch with Melwin?' she asked. 'You never told me.'

'Hold on,' Aditya stepped in. He nodded to the security person standing at the entrance. The guard pushed the sliding door and watched it softly glide into its position effectively cutting off the people in the room from the rest.

'Shall we begin?' asked Aditya the moment the door shut.

'Shouldn't we be heading down? Aren't we getting late?' Shreya said. She was getting nervous.

'Not at all. We have thirty more minutes. Normally all book events start thirty minutes behind the scheduled time. You know it . . . You have been to so many of these events.'

'Of course,' she smiled nervously. Her eyes wandered down to where people were gathering. There were over two hundred people in the crowd now . . . and growing.

But something else was making her anxious.

Finally the sliding door to the café opened and in walked someone who Aditya had specially invited for the evening.

'Good evening, sir. It's great to see you. I'm so happy you could make it,' said Aditya as he extended his hand towards his guest.

82

Thirty minutes later: 7.00 pm

The emcee for the evening took over. 'Ladies and gentlemen, Crossword Bookstores welcomes you to the launch of *The Girl from Chhattisgarh*, the first book by Shreya Kaushik. For those of you who don't know Shreya, she is a management graduate from IIM Bengaluru, and a banker by profession . . .'

The emcee went on to introduce Shreya and finally invited her on stage. After that she introduced Aditya and Anurag and called them up on stage too. The two of them walked up to a thunderous applause. On stage, they unveiled the book—*The Girl from Chhattisgarh*—and held it up for everyone to see. The audience clapped till their hands hurt.

'May I now request our guest of honour Mr Anurag Kashyap to say a few words about the book,' the emcee said.

'Friends,' Anurag began, 'I have read many books. But I am not a reader who experiments. I am not one who would pick up a book by a debut author, on my own. But after being forced to read Shreya Kaushik's book, I can say with surety that I have been wrong all along. I should have had the courage to pick up debut authors. The freshness in their voice, the desire to produce a quality product, shows. After reading Ms Kaushik's work, I have become her fan. And such a big fan that I have decided to make a film on her book,' he paused for the applause to begin and grinned wide till it died down. He looked at Aditya, 'May she become a bigger author than you.' He smiled and said to the audience, 'All of you must read the book. It's highly recommended.' He turned to his left, looked at Shreya and extended his right hand, which she gladly accepted. 'Congratulations,' he said before returning to his chair.

'Thank you, Anurag sir. That, I am sure, will be one cracker of a movie,' the emcee said into the microphone. 'We will all watch the movie; first day, first show. And with that I would like to call the woman of the moment—debutant author and banker with a difference—Shreya Kaushik! Ladies and gentlemen, presenting to you, for the first time ever—Shreya Kaushik.'

It was as if the entire bookstore had erupted. The noise was deafening. Shreya walked to the front of the stage and started speaking. 'Can you hear me?' she said. 'At the back?' When she didn't get adequate response, Aditya stepped up. 'Hold it closer to your mouth,' he said, pushing up the handheld mic towards her lips. Shreya smiled at Aditya gratefully and began:

'Friends, thank you all for coming here on a working day to be a part of an event which is extremely special to me. You have no idea what this means to me. This book, my first novel is more important to me than everything else. Possibly more important than life itself,' said Shreya. While she was comfortable on stage, something seemed to be holding her back.

'This book, *The Girl from Chhattisgarh*, is inspired by a true story, the true story of a woman who was brutally raped when she was fifteen. How she gathered what was left of her life and came roaring back, is what the book is all about. It's a poignant story of a woman's struggle for her dignity, for her life and for justice,' she paused. Aditya had asked her to write down what she wanted to speak about and had made her memorise it entirely. He had also helped her improve her diction and told her where to pause for maximum effect.

'I am extremely thankful to Aditya who has stood by me through good times and bad. He has helped me at a time when he was going through trying times at a personal level. I owe the book to him. Without him, I would not have achieved anything. Thank you, Aditya. You are special.'

Tremendous applause sounded out. An irritated Maya was watching this on YouTube with morbid curiosity.

Shreya then thanked Anurag and the crowd for their support and quickly finished her concise speech with an emotional appeal to the crowd to spread the word about her book. 'When it comes to books, nothing works like word of mouth,' she gave her parting shot and walked back to her seat. Aditya could see that there were tears in her eyes.

'Moving on,' the emcee announced. I would now like to invite Mr Aditya Kapoor to say a few words.'

The ovation that Aditya got was the loudest. The flashbulbs lit up the stage, cameras started clicking furiously and the audience clapped enthusiastically.

'Friends,' he began.

Maya moved closer to her laptop screen. She pressed a few buttons, only to realise that the volume was at its maximum. Cursing herself that she had left her earphones in her car, she got up and turned off the fan and the AC to reduce the noise in the room. She could hear Aditya better now. Just as she was about to settle down, her phone rang. It was Dr Krishnan. Why was he calling her now? She didn't have any tests scheduled. She ignored it. She would call him back after the event.

'People often ask me why my books sell and the only answer I give them is that they sell because I have lovely readers like you.' The applause that followed thereafter was not new for Aditya. He was used to it, the showman that he was. 'I want you to give the same love and affection to Ms Kaushik. I have read her manuscript and I can assure you that this is the first time I have been so moved by the writing of a debutant. Mark my words, she is the future of Indian writing. And I wish her all the best. This is her first book so please give her a chance,' said Aditya.

Maya who was watching the live streaming of this event at home, squirmed. She didn't like the look of what she was seeing. Aditya was publicly praising Shreya, and it hurt her. She wondered if she should watch any further but decided to persist.

'I say this because after forty years and multiple books, I make mistakes even now,' Aditya paused, 'and one of those mistakes has cost me fifteen years of my life.' He turned towards Shreya and then looked at the audience. Sanjay was sitting in the front row expressionless.

At home, Maya's phone rang again. She looked at it, Dr Krishnan was calling. Maya was not in a mood to talk to anyone. She turned the phone to silent mode and went back to watching the live streaming. There were three messages from Dr Krishnan. She swiped the screen and read them, all in a matter of seconds. Dr Krishnan had asked her to call him back urgently. She ignored his pleas. Nothing was more important than hearing what Aditya had to say right now, even if what Dr Krishnan had to say had to do with Ebola.

'There comes a point in time when the direction life takes is decided by the choices you make. And I made some wrong choices. As an author, one is expected to be humble, to have his feet firmly on the ground. Being an author carries a certain element of glamour, particularly for people who don't belong to this profession. That glamour, if it comes your way, can blind you. A successful author and a balanced human being, needs to sift through life's experiences and figure out the difference between glamour, vanity and truth.

'I was vain. When I got attention, I became weak. I couldn't resist. Middle age made me a lot more susceptible to vanity and I succumbed. I would like to confess today that Ms Kaushik and I were in a relationship. A relationship which was not one of convenience, as *Bombay Times* put it, but was genuine. She got attracted to my stature as an author and I was attracted to her youth, ambition and obvious beauty. Perhaps in me, she saw everything that she aspired to be. And somewhere, unknowingly, both of us made choices which were wrong. As my wife Maya says, adultery is not a mistake, it is a choice. I made a choice. Do I regret making the choice?' he paused. 'I definitely regret the consequences of that choice on my family. That was not something either Shreya or I had bargained for. How naive I was to assume that the adulterous relationship would last for ever, on my terms,' Aditya ruminated.

There was pin-drop silence in the room. The applause had stopped. People were more interested in listening than clapping. Shreya looked at the nailpaint on her toes and didn't move a muscle. Sanjay kept fidgeting in his chair.

'If my wife Maya is watching this live streaming, I would like to publicly apologise to her, for all that I have done. My relationship with Ms Kaushik never ever impaired my love for Maya. But this is difficult to prove; for the underlying assumption is that you fall into a relationship only when you fall out of another. This is not true. I miss Maya and Aryan even more than I have ever done. I love them even more than I have ever done.'

Normally in long speeches at book launches, people get fidgety and start moving around and talking to each other. In this case, nothing of that sort happened. Mobile phones came out and people started recording Aditya's speech.

'Maya, please forgive me. Let us go back to our lives. I need you and Aryan. Nothing is the same without you.' A tear flowed out of the corner of his right eye. His right hand holding the mic instinctively went up and he wiped the tear away with his shoulder.

★

Maya was watching this, sitting at home. She had tears in her eyes. The divorce notice had been sent out in frustration. She hadn't expected this when she sat down to watch the launch.

Suddenly a mail popped up on Maya's screen. Fed up of trying to reach her, Dr Krishnan had sent her a mail. The subject line was, 'You need to see this ASAP'. Maya's laptop was configured in such a manner that new mails always came up on the screen and had to be wished away. Maya clicked on the mail and quickly read it. Her mind was still on what Aditya was saying at the launch but Dr Krishnan's mail left her shell-shocked. She clicked on the link in the mail which led her to a video. She watched the short video. When she was done watching it, she just couldn't stay put. She picked up the phone and with shivering hands, dialled the driver's number.

*

'I am sorry, Shreya,' Aditya continued, 'I have usurped your launch. But it is important that I clarify an issue on which you and I have generated a lot of gossip. We won't get an occasion better than this and it is important that you embark on this new journey, on a clean slate.'

Shreya just nodded her head. She was in tears. But she had no choice. She couldn't have said anything else.

'When I began speaking, I spoke about mistakes in my personal and professional lives. It has just been brought to my notice that some passages in my latest book, bear an uncanny resemblance to lines from a few contemporary books. Six such passages have been identified. This is completely unacceptable. The book passes through multiple hands at the time of editing and publishing. Who, at what stage of editing, inserted those lines—intentionally or erroneously remains to be seen. However as a responsible author and a reputed publisher, it is our duty to make sure that creative licence does not mean infringing on anybody else's rights.

'Hence my publishers Kiwi and I have, as of today, pulled back all copies of my book from the market. These will be pulped and the book will be edited, rechecked and then brought back into the market. However given that a large number of copies of the book have already been sold, my publisher and I have decided that the royalty that I make on it, will be paid, not to me, but to any organisation that works on Ebola care. Kiwi will work on identifying these agencies and pay the royalty amount to them directly. My wife went through hell in those three weeks that she was in isolation as an Ebola patient. I don't want anybody else to go through that pain.

'My publishers have been kind enough to agree that their share of profits arising out of this book will also be contributed to this cause. This is our own way of repenting for not having done our complete due diligence. I would like to apologise to my readers for this oversight and assure you that this is inadvertent and we will more than make up for it. On realising this oversight, we have made sure that everything in Shreya's book is perfect and there are no such gaffes. It is pure unadulterated reading pleasure; I guarantee you that. I wish Shreya all the very best not only in her writing career, but in her life too,' he said. He looked at Shreya and raised his hands above his head and clapped. The audience responded by following suit.

Aditya continued, 'Life is binary in many ways. There is no way that we can move away from each other slowly and painlessly. It has to be a complete exit. Towards that end, I have this evening submitted my resignation to my bank. I am going to make an honest attempt to make it work with my family. I also want to focus on fulfilling my wife's dream of bringing education to the poor and will dedicate myself to that cause. May you fulfil your dream of becoming a rock star author, Shreya. My wishes are always with you. God bless,' Aditya completed his speech and handed over the mic to the emcee. He stepped down from the podium and walked towards the exit. He didn't even stop to say goodbye to anyone.

Everyone in the audience stood up as Aditya walked on. There was a look of admiration on everyone's face; awe and respect for the rock star author who had his feet firmly on the ground. Everyone in the audience clapped. The clapping continued for a while, even after Aditya left the store.

The sudden change of events stunned everyone in the Kemps Corner store. Nobody knew what had transpired in the café before all of them came down to the venue of the launch.

83

Half an hour back: 6.30 pm

'I think we should head down. We are getting late,' Shreya said. She was getting nervous.

'Not at all. We have thirty more minutes. Normally all book events start thirty minutes behind the scheduled time. You know it . . . You have been to so many of these events.'

'Of course,' she smiled. Her eyes wandered down to where people were gathering. There were over two hundred people in the crowd now . . . and growing.

But something else was making her anxious.

Finally the sliding door to the café opened and in walked someone who Aditya had specially invited for the evening.

'Good evening, sir. It's great to see you. I'm so happy you could make it,' said Aditya as he extended his hand towards the guest.

'Well, you are one of the few guys I can profess to be a true fan of. How could I have not come after getting your personal invitation?'

'Thank you, sir,' said Aditya. He turned towards the rest in the room and called out, 'Tim, meet Commissioner Ramesh Karia from Mumbai Police.'

'Aah. Yes of course. Who doesn't know him?' Tim walked up to him to shake his hand.

Ramesh Karia looked at Shreya. From the big backdrop on the ground floor he could make out that she was the one whose book was being launched. 'Feeling good?' he asked her.

'Of course she will be. What a big day for her!' Sanjay responded and smiled, looking at Diana. Sunaina and Melwin were standing in one corner. Shreya consciously avoided looking in their direction. Ramesh Karia went ahead and sat down on one of the many empty chairs and ordered his coffee.

When everyone had settled down Aditya looked at Shreya. 'Good crowd today. Newcomers would die for this kind of an attendance at their book events. Looks like the *Bombay Times* article has done us a world of good. It has given you instant recognition. Without spending a paisa, you have become a sought-after celebrity. Must say you have a brilliant mind,' Aditya said.

'Me?' Shreya looked surprised at this statement. She looked around the room, embarrassed. 'We have been through this Aditya. I told you, I didn't speak to *Bombay Times*,' she said. 'Why are we even discussing this today?'

'You were the only one who benefited,' Aditya coolly shrugged his shoulders and said.

'That's how it turned out to be,' she said as she understood the implication of the accusation. 'That doesn't mean that I did it. Why would I do anything that impacts our relationship negatively?'

'Well, why wouldn't you?'

Seeing a stunned look on Shreya's face, Sanjay got up from where he was sitting and walked up to Aditya. He kept his hand on Aditya's shoulder. Shaking his head, he said, 'Cool down, buddy. These things can be discussed later.' He looked around the café and added, 'Probably after the event is over.'

Encouraged by Sanjay's intervention Shreya responded, 'I love you, Aditya. Nothing else matters to me. I can't imagine doing anything that will harm you.'

'Well, you did,' Aditya insisted.

'Never.'

'The sentences that were inserted in my book ... I'm sure you gave me that sheet accusing me of plagiarism, because you felt that it would do me good, right Shreya?'

'I didn't do that, Aditya,' Shreya said and immediately covered her mouth. She had just said something she was not supposed to.

'I never doubted that. I knew it was not you,' Aditya said, a complacent look on his face.

Aditya turned to Tim, who was getting restless. He was not able to comprehend what was going on. 'Tim, I just want you to remember that this was a consensual relationship, one where no coercion was employed. I'm saying this to ensure that tomorrow if a harassment charge is brought against me, then it can be defended by you. And all of you,' he said, looking around the room.

Shreya was shocked. 'Aditya, what is going on? What are you trying to prove? Are you setting me up here?'

'Playing it safe, baby. Just to make sure that once I am done with my commitment, no one screws around.'

Shreya was shocked at his demeanour but Aditya seemed unaffected. He walked up to Ramesh Karia and whispered something in his ear before returning to Shreya.

'The day the *Bombay Times* article came out, which further rocked my relationship with Maya, I knew that it couldn't have been you. But when Melwin called me that evening, my faith in you took a beating,' he said pointing to the guy standing with Sunaina.

'What does Melwin have to do with all this?' Shreya asked angrily.

'Aah . . .' Aditya started off, 'well nothing.' He looked at the others and said, 'Meet Melwin. He will pass out from IIM Bengaluru this year. He was in fact Shreya and Sunaina's batchmate. Not only was he in a serious relationship with Sunaina, he was also the batch topper. At the end of the first year, it became clear that the batch gold medalist would be either Shreya or Melwin. They were way ahead of the rest. For Shreya the only person standing between her and her ambition was Melwin. What complicated the issue was Sunaina's relationship with him.

'The super possessive streak in Shreya came into play. Sunaina being in someone else's life meant she was going away from her. Shreya hated that. And so she fixed Melwin. During their summer internship, she got close to him, seduced him and then threatened him with consequences. The poor fellow was so scared that he went away from campus, away from Sunaina for a year. He came back only after she had completed her MBA and left the institute. Sunaina didn't know the true story and believed that he had deserted her. Thankfully the administration at IIM-B saw reason in the excuse he gave them and agreed to give him a one-year deferral and allowed him to come back. It would have been even more tragic had Melwin had to compromise his career and future,' Aditya disclosed.

'But why would Melwin, of all people, call you?' Sanjay asked him casually.

'Because the way Shreya seduced Melwin on a drunken evening was exactly the way she did it with me. The way mentioned in *Bombay Times*: recording a misleading conversation which, to anyone hearing it, suggested a lot but ended in nothing.'

'Don't believe Melwin, Sunaina. He is lying,' Shreya pleaded.

'I want to believe that he is lying. But . . .' Sunaina paused. She was choking, struggling to get words out of her mouth. 'I even believed you till Melwin spoke to me. If it was only Melwin's fault and you had no role to play in it, you would have told me about the entire incident. You chose to remain silent, despite knowing how much I pined for Melwin after he left midway. The fact that you did so is reason enough for me to believe that Melwin was not at fault but set up by you. On the day of the *Bombay Times* news-break, Melwin finally gathered courage and called me. I put him on to Aditya,' she said.

Shreya looked on, stunned. She didn't know what to say.

'When he played out the recording of the conversation, it shocked me. And Aditya too. Well you can argue that what he said to me doesn't prove anything, Shreya, except for the fact that you are an obsessive, extremely possessive, psycho woman, who will go to any extreme to get her way,' Sunaina spat out angrily.

'What are we doing here, Aditya? Can't we discuss these personal issues later? We need to head down. The crowd is getting restless,' Anurag stepped in.

'I need ten more minutes, Anurag. Please bear with me.' Aditya looked at Sunaina and requested, 'Sunaina, can you please tell the organisers to make a holding announcement that the event will start in 10 minutes.' Sunaina exited the café and walked down.

'Manipulations have been immortalised in literature. Macbethian manipulations are not all that uncommon. Something we see almost every day. A few days back, when I was discussing ways to get the initial sales push for your book and discussed corporate sales as an option, Shreya, you asked me to speak to HR because you didn't enjoy a close rapport with Sanjay,' Aditya continued.

Shreya stayed silent.

'You were not comfortable enough to ask him to order 200 copies of your book for corporate gifting, but you were comfortable enough to send him the manuscript of my yet-to-be-published book,' Aditya announced.

'Utter nonsense,' Sanjay protested. 'She didn't send me anything.' He stood up from his chair, looking furious.

'Hold on, Sanjay. Relax. I am not saying it's your fault,' Aditya looked at Shreya, before he looked at Sanjay and Diana again and whispered, 'yet.'

Sanjay sat down. Diana's hand moved on top of his and held it firmly. She looked nervous and fidgety.

'So,' Aditya continued, 'you sent the manuscript I sent you, to Sanjay.' Sanjay started to get up again, but Diana restrained him. 'The same manuscript, which I sent you in confidence, even before Maya had seen it. A manuscript, an edited version of which you sent back to me with the lines which had been copied from other popular international books,' Aditya stated the facts calmly though his eyes burned with rage.

'Why are you putting the responsibility for your plagiarising ways on me? I have nothing to do with it,' Shreya said. She looked out through the glass walls at the crowd down below. She wanted to walk out of the conversation, but couldn't. She had a book launch to do. Walking out would jeopardise the event. She was trapped between Aditya's allegations and her ambitions.

Aditya ignored her response. 'Kolkata: the day my problems started. I was having dinner with Sunaina. She was reading Wendy Doniger's book, *On Hinduism*—a controversial book which had been withdrawn by its publishers. She told me that she had borrowed it from you Shreya,' he charged.

'What's wrong with that?'

'No, no,' Aditya shook his head. 'There's nothing wrong. Absolutely nothing.' He looked around the room. 'This copy of the book had some crazy doodles on the first few pages. Some weird, crazy, eye-catching doodles; not very forgettable,' he said.

'So? How is it even relevant?' Shreya asked.

'It didn't strike me till a few days ago, till I saw a paper which Diana had left behind on my desk at work. The doodles that she had drawn on that paper resembled the doodles that I had seen on the book. Similar, not exact, but same family—clearly they had been drawn by the same person. I asked Diana if she had read Wendy Doniger. And she said she hadn't. But . . .'

Everyone looked at him with anticipation, wondering what he was going to reveal next.

'. . . But, she had tried. And when she was unable to read through it, she gifted that book to Sanjay.' He looked at Sanjay who was staring at Diana and Aditya alternately.

'Cut the crap, Aditya. What if it was Sanjay's book? How does it matter?' Shreya was beginning to turn aggressive.

'It matters because I have known Sanjay for as long as I have known Maya; over fifteen years. He is a black hole as far as books are concerned. He never lends his books to anyone. He has over 8000 books lying all over his house—on shelves, packed in cartons, some even warehoused. So much so that when you walk into his house you may feel like you've walked into a bookstore. He buys, buys and buys books, but has never as much as lent it out to friends to even flip through. Ever. Maya has tried borrowing from him. I tried a few days back and failed. On campus he had a reputation for being possessive about his books. In fact if you read the comment about him in *iimpressions*, this is what it says:

'The deceptively serious looking self-proclaimed fitness freak,
Would struggle through jogging, gym and ten hours of sleep.
After crunching all available novels in a sleepless night,

He would awake sleeping wing mates and give gratuitous advice.
His room gave you the feel of an old bookstore,
You will be hit instantly with a sense of vellichor.
Books are his solace, books are his zone,
Never lending them to others, for that he is known.
In the first year, romance took his life by storm,
But his lady turned him down before too long.
"Let's be friends" ahh the cliched curse,
He was left at the water tank, with a broken heart to nurse.
He was an HR genius from day one, for he understood
hierarchy and rank.
Everyone agrees, that for Sanjay, there is glory in store,
He'll make us proud, he is an achiever to the core.

'He has been like this for ever. Try touching the books that he has in his cabin and you would know. It is such a strong trait of his that the fact that he did lend books to you is reason enough for antennae to be raised,' Aditya proclaimed.

'She was desperate to read it, so I did give it to her. I don't see a problem in that,' Sanjay said. He was unhassled. He assumed that it was Shreya who needed defending. Aditya was happy that Sanjay had agreed that he had lent the book to Shreya. If he hadn't then Aditya had another ace up his sleeve. The charge slip that he found inside *The Luminaries* was in the name of Sanjay. The bookshop Reliance TimeOut, from where the book had been bought, had closed down two years ago, much before Shreya came to Mumbai. He had the charge slip in his pocket, ready to produce, just in case Sanjay refused to acknowledge the fact that he lent books to Shreya.

'You are right. There's nothing wrong with that,' Aditya concurred. 'Just that she sent the manuscript to you, which she shouldn't have. And you lent her a book which you never do. Both may seem trivial but, to me, both are red flags. Exceptional behaviour; yet it doesn't prove anything.'

'Bullshit,' Sanjay exclaimed.

Aditya paused, let Sanjay calm down for just a second, and continued, 'Had it stopped there, it would have been fine. I would have thought that it was coincidence. But then the manuscript comes back to me with a number of edits, which I, like an idiot, accept because I am smitten by Shreya. And then I am told, much later at the most inappropriate of times that those lines are plagiarised; that too from international bestsellers, which I have never read,' he said with a laugh.

'For a minute let's assume that Shreya did clandestinely insert those lines in the manuscript. She would only insert lines from books she has read, otherwise it will be almost impossible to force-fit arbitrary lines from one book into the another. It has to look good and read good. No?' Aditya went on. Seeing the blank look on everyone's face, particularly Anurag Kashyap and Ramesh Karia's, he went on to tell everyone about the lines which had been deceitfully plagiarised into his book.

'Fair assumption,' Anurag spoke up this time. 'For anyone who has not read a book to pick up lines from that book and insert them into another manuscript is a bit difficult, if not impossible. Not to mention time-consuming. I have seen this happening in film scripts too and your assumption is correct.'

'Yes. And look at the books from which the lines have been inserted in my manuscript—Dan Brown, John Grisham, Baldacci, Ken Follett—all thrillers, in line with the fact that my books are thrillers too. A perfect fit.' He picked up a glass of water from the table and gulped it down.

'But,' he took another gulp and continued. 'But the problem is,' he said looking at Shreya, 'she doesn't read thrillers.' Everyone looked at Shreya who had no expression on her face. 'The only thrillers she has ever read are my books.' He paused for effect and then said, 'Or so she claims.'

'I can vouch for that,' Sunaina spoke up. 'I know what she reads.'

'And now look at this,' he said, as he opened his phone and brought up a picture on his screen. He turned it towards everyone else. Everyone either moved closer or squinted their eyes to look at what Aditya was showing them.

'This is the picture of Sanjay's table a few days back. If you notice there are twenty-six books here. All the six books from which lines have been plagiarised into my book are also here.'

'Are you seriously out of your mind, Aditya?' Sanjay yelled at the top of his voice. 'Like really? This is what it has come to?' He shook his head furiously. 'Why are you dragging me into your personal issues? You are the one who screwed up your personal life, you are the one who messed with your career, you are the one who didn't think twice before engaging in an affair with Shreya. Now how dare you put the blame on me?'

'Well I would not have, had you stayed away. All the

books that you copied lines from are thrillers. And you read every single thriller that comes in the market. Fourteen of the twenty-six books displayed here are thrillers,' Aditya said, his voice emphatic. He turned towards Tim. 'I am sure they are still there in his room. You can quickly check that out.'

'Yes, I like to read thrillers. So do many others. It is not difficult to find these six books in anybody's personal collection. Your insinuations are baseless and insulting,' Sanjay yelled. 'It just shows that you have lost your balls and you no longer value our friendship. You are sick. Go see a doc,' Sanjay lashed out.

'Really?' Aditya asked him sarcastically. 'Well, you know what, Sanjay? The fact that you got the manuscript from Shreya . . .' he was immediately interrupted by Sanjay, who said, 'I didn't.' Aditya ignored him and went on, 'The fact that you read thrillers and the fact that all the six books from where the lines were copied are on your table right now, doesn't prove anything. I agree. I would still have given you the benefit of the doubt had Maya not called me, Sanjay. Had it not been for numbers!'

'Numbers?' Tim mumbled, confused.

'Yes, Tim. Numbers,' Aditya said and looked around. In the room were ten people—Aditya, Shreya, Sunaina, Melwin, Sanjay, Diana, Tim, Anurag, Vaishali and Rakesh Karia.

'How many of you have iPhones?' Aditya looked around the room. 'Six,' he counted.

'Sanjay,' he called out. 'Can I look at your phone?'

'Why do you need it?' Sanjay asked aggressively.

'It is locked, isn't it? Then why are you scared?' Aditya said. Sanjay handed the phone over to him; it was locked. There was no way Aditya was going to get into it without unlocking the phone using the passcode.

Aditya held the phone in his hand. 'Nice picture,' he commented on the wallpaper and placed the phone down on the table. All eyes were on the phone. 'Normally most people have dates as passcodes, right?' Everyone nodded. 'Normally,' he reiterated. 'Not always.'

'It is either your birthday, anniversary, the day you met your love for the first time, the day you got your first job, or other such significant dates in your life. Correct?' Aditya continued. No one disagreed.

'Now, let me guess Sanjay's passcode using this logic,' said Aditya. Sanjay had an arrogant smile on his face: the 'fuck only cares' kind of smile. Aditya took a piece of paper and quickly noted down Sanjay's birthday, Diana's birthday, various anniversaries and even dates on which Sanjay had shifted jobs. There were twenty-eight possible codes he wrote down. Sanjay looked at the list and waved his hand nonchalantly.

'I am good with numbers,' Aditya boasted as he keyed in the first number. The phone didn't come up. He keyed in the second. Same result.

Third

Fourth . . .

One by one he keyed in eight codes from the list in front of him. He was about to key in the ninth when Sanjay panicked.

'Hold it, dude,' he yelled. 'The iPhone is programmed to erase itself after ten wrong passcode attempts. So, stop this crap.'

'Do not worry,' Aditya said very casually as he walked way from him and keyed the first three digits. Sanjay was in a state of seizure. He had lots of data on his phone and didn't want his phone to get erased. 'Chill, bro,' Aditya reassured. 'If it doesn't come up now, I will give it to you and you can unlock it using the right code.'

He looked around the room, moved his finger to the iPhone screen and pressed the fourth digit.

The keypad disappeared and the phone came on immediately. The passcode was correct. Sanjay looked at him shocked.

'So my logic was correct,' Aditya looked around with a wide grin. 'But there is a problem. The code I keyed in is not a date which should normally have had any relevance to Sanjay.' He looked at Ramesh Karia. 'It's not a date on this list,' he said, as he held it up for people to see.

Sanjay looked stricken.

'2309,' he paused. 'That is the code I keyed in. And if I know Sanjay I cannot think of any relevance that the date 2309 might hold for him. Maybe he can tell us. What say, Sanjay?' he asked.

Sanjay was too shocked to speak. 'I don't think I need to tell you anything about it. My passcode is my prerogative,' Sanjay hissed. He extended his hand to collect the phone back, frown intact.

'Oh yes. It is, it is. I have got to be a fool to even ask you.

I am sorry, Sanjay. Unfortunately I got swayed because my passcode is also the same,' Aditya revealed.

'What?' Shreya asked. She had a strange look on her face.

'Yes, darling. 2309 is my passcode too. The day Sanjay told me that Maya was upset at our pictures from Royal China making it to the papers, I called her. Fortunately or unfortunately, I had mistakenly picked up Sanjay's phone, thinking it was mine and called Maya using that,' he said. He looked at the others in the room and said, 'We have the same phone. iPhone5.' He pulled out his phone and placed it on the table. 'Maya, when she picked up the phone, addressed me as Sanjay before she realised it was me. It didn't strike me even then,' Aditya said.

After a quick glance to gauge if he was making sense and if what he was saying was sinking in, he continued, 'While I was talking to Maya, Shreya called a few times. I thought she was calling me. But she was actually calling Sanjay. That too at 11.30 at night. No one calls the head of HR at that hour unless there is something very important and urgent. A few days later when I was mulling over what happened, it just struck me that I had used Sanjay's phone to call Maya. And our passcodes are the same. That's why, when I picked up his iPhone assuming it was mine, the passcode worked.'

'How come both of you have the same passcode?' Ramesh Karia stepped into the discussion and asked Aditya.

'You need to ask him. I can explain mine. It's 2309. 23rd September is Maya's birthday. I think his is 23rd September because of the same reason. I know he was fond of her right from our college days. He had even proposed to her,' Aditya said, stressing on the last sentence.

'That was before she started seeing you,' Sanjay countered.

'Yes. It was before she started going out with me. And when he had proposed,' he paused and looked at Sanjay, '. . . under the water tank, she had politely declined. They stayed good friends. But I didn't imagine that he would be so fond of her as to keep her date of birth as his passcode; to mess up her life by attempting to sabotage her husband's career and passion. Well done, Sanjay,' Aditya said bitterly. He was beginning to get upset and it was showing. Diana looked at Sanjay, in anger.

'Is this true, Sanjay?' she asked him. 'It comes as no surprise that you kept postponing our wedding date. Looks like you were hoping that you would be able to separate the two of them and then cast your dice.'

'No, Diana. He is lying. It is not true at all. 2309 was just an arbitrary number which came to my mind.'

'Why was Shreya calling you at midnight?' she probed further.

'I have no clue. I didn't speak to her.'

'You are such a liar Sanjay. Wonder how I got myself entangled with you,' Diana said. She stood up from where she was sitting and went and stood right next to Aditya.

'Can you explain this?' Diana pulled out a copy of a 24000-rupee voucher and placed it on the table.

'How would I know?' Sanjay exclaimed. 'It is signed by you.'

'Yes it is, but I never signed it. I think you know that, Sanjay,' she said, staring at him in anger.

'It has been sent for payment processing from your office. Your office records prove that. Can you explain how Diana's signature appeared there?' Aditya queried.

'And what were you doing in Goa with Shreya?' Diana was furious.

'Me?' Sanjay asked. He had a sincere look on his face. 'Why do you even ask? I didn't go there with her.'

'Let it be, Sanjay. Don't bother pretending. We have a copy of the hotel bills and confirmation from the hotel. They are a big corporate client for the bank. So it was easy to pull strings and get information,' Aditya lied.

'The room is in her name. Isn't that what you said?' Sanjay asked him.

'Yes. That's what I said. The room was in her name but it was paid for using your credit card. I don't know whether you were there with her in the same hotel,' he paused. 'In the same room,' he added forcefully. 'Or whether she had access to your card and paid using that, I can't say. If I wanted to, I could have dug deeper and found out. But I didn't want to raise any more muck on it, Sanjay,' Aditya declared.

'If it is true, you could lose your job on multiple counts,' Tim stepped in. 'For forging Diana Moses' signature, for wilfully billing wrong expenses to the organisation and passing off a personal holiday as an official trip.'

Sanjay had no answer.

'This is turning out to be a potboiler. Even better than the book,' Anurag stepped into the conversation. 'But Aditya, how did you figure out that it was his phone and not yours that you had called from that day?'

'I was an idiot to not have figured it out the day all this happened. I only figured it out much later—the day Diana and I realised that there was something wrong with Shreya's Goa voucher. After my discussion with Diana ended, I was brooding over the entire issue when Shreya called me. Her name flashed on my screen as Ram Kumar which is how it's stored on my phone.

'That's when it came to me in a flash. The night I was speaking to Maya from Sanjay's phone, Shreya had called. I recalled that she had called thrice and her name had flashed as Shreya. It never struck me at that time that had it been my phone, her name would never have flashed as Shreya. Once I figured it out, I checked my entire call list. There was no call made to Maya that night from my phone. It was not difficult to put two and two together. It was not my phone, period. I had called Maya from Sanjay's phone. It couldn't have been any other way.'

'I don't know what you are talking about. Seems like a truckload of bullshit to me,' Sanjay yelled. He looked at Shreya. 'Count me out,' he screamed. 'I am out of here.' He got up from his seat.

'Leaving already? But the real story is yet to come,' Aditya said. Sanjay started panicking. He looked at Diana and held her hand and pulled her. 'Come,' he said. 'Let's go. This guy here has gone nuts.'

'Hold on,' a voice thundered through the café. Everyone turned towards the source. 'No one leaves the room till I say so,' Ramesh Karia's baritone resonated in the room. When the Commissioner of Police says something you have no option but to listen. Sanjay's shoulders began to droop.

'On your birthday, when you went to drop Maya and accidentally left your phone behind,' Diana started. 'Remember . . .?'

Sanjay just stared at her. She was beginning to cry. The feeling when you know that your love has failed you can be crippling. That's exactly what Diana was going through.

'There was nothing accidental about it. The phone was there with me, in my pocket. I didn't give it to you intentionally. We wanted to, and were able to, see everything on your phone,' she continued. 'Your messages, your mails, your facebook posts and chats, everything. Those messages are on your phone right now. We challenge you to prove us wrong. The mail trail to Shreya with the plagiarised lines is there in your mail box. You didn't even tell her that you copied those lines. You just told her to use the edits supposedly made by you to impress Aditya. And that morning when Aditya called off his relationship with Shreya and she came running to you to complain, you sent the plagiarised lines to her. Your exact message to her was, 'Keep it. Use it under extreme circumstances.'

'Your mail trail with the *Bombay Times* journalist, giving pictures of Shreya in the hospital with Aditya and the audio file which Maya presumably air-dropped to your iPhone for safekeeping just before she was taken to the hospital, are also there. The Dropbox link you sent the journalist is still active. Do you want me to show you that, Sanjay?' Diana was in tears.

Aditya had a shattered look on his face. He had lost his family, he had walked away from the one he loved and now his friend of fifteen years had turned out to be a traitor.

'There is no way you can now say you didn't do it, Sanjay. The question is: why did you do this?' he asked.

'Aditya,' it was Tim who spoke. 'It is a bit difficult for me to comprehend what's going on, but the fact is that you are not coming out clean in this entire episode. Yes, Sanjay may have fudged bills, may have tried to fix you for he had a soft corner for your wife and hated your success, but yet, your tryst with Shreya is something which cannot be just written off as a rendezvous between consenting adults.'

Aditya knew this was coming. Tim had been quite caustic about his relationship with Shreya. 'Undoubtedly, Tim. Save this for later today. We will talk about it, after the event,' Aditya killed the discussion. 'I will surely give you an answer; I am not avoiding it,' he reassured him.

Tim nodded and turned to Sanjay and asked him, 'Any explanations here, Sanjay? I am definitely going to relay this conversation to the CEO. It is for him to decide your future in the company.'

'These guys are lying, Tim. They are setting me up.'

'Oh really?' Diana spoke up. 'Really, Sanjay, I never knew that you were such a venomous character. You tried to set up your own friend and pushed him down the path of adultery.'

'No, Diana.' Aditya turned towards her. 'I don't think you can push anyone towards adultery. It's a state of mind one gets into. It was my own vanity. And to be fair, I pushed Sanjay into hiring her. Once she was hired, he sensed an opportunity to disgrace me. Maybe not immediately, but somewhere along the way, he did. The mutual interest that

Shreya and I showed in each other just helped him smell blood and go for the kill. He was never the perpetrator of the adulterous relationship. He just fanned the fire and took advantage of it to drive a wedge between Maya and me by doing the *Bombay Times* article and further disgraced me by accusing me of plagiarism.'

'You are just making me the convenient reason for your sins. You did what you had to, and now that you are facing the heat, you are conveniently passing the blame. Grow up!' Sanjay was furious.

Aditya chuckled, more out of desperation and pain than humour. 'Sanjay,' he started off. 'You are a friend, an old friend. Relationships that thrive for two decades are not written off in a hurry. If I have not called the cops to accuse you of compromising my writing and of fraud in your professional life it's because . . .'

'Oh?' Sanjay cut in. He had an expression of ridicule on his face as he glanced at Ramesh Karia, before looking at Aditya.

'Mr Karia is not here as Commissioner of Police. He is here as a patron. And he will not do anything on this, till either me or you or anyone else complains formally. So relax.'

Sanjay looked the other way with a wry smile on his face.

'If I have not called in the cops it is only because I value those years,' Aditya continued. 'I don't need to prove anything to you. And I don't need you to own up. You know what you did. All I can say is that as of today, you have lost your dearest friend in me, your ardent supporter in Maya and the love of your life, Diana. You have lost almost everything you had. What more am I going to gain by getting you to confess? Unlike the courts of law, in matters of relationships, we all don't look for evidence. We look for honesty. And that's where you have failed miserably. All along I thought Shreya was using me, without realising that you were using her. Manipulating her from behind the scenes . . .

'And Shreya,' he said, turning to face her. 'I am sorry. But I really loved you. You are old enough to judge what is right and what is wrong. But you made the choice of working with Sanjay against me. Maybe you did what you did without realising its impact or maybe you did realise it. In any case, I didn't lie when I said I loved you. I just said loving you was inappropriate. You never loved me. The day I got to know that you went to Goa with Sanjay for the weekend break during your induction in Lonavla, despite the fact that we were in the thick of our relationship, I realised that.'

'I was upset with you. You were planning the entire awards show without me,' Shreya said, desperately.

'And that justifies what you did? How lame!' Aditya cried out. 'My doubts were confirmed the day I saw that Sanjay had paid for the trip with his card,' he said. 'Now, I am sure our relationship was a mistake. I put my family at risk for you. It was not worth it. Actually nothing is worth putting one's family at risk. I liked the time I spent with you. Thank you for those memories. I committed to you that I will make you a star—you are already a star. You cannot blame me for not keeping my promise. From after this event you are on your own.'

'Come. Let's go,' he said to everyone in the room, and walked out of the café.

As he was striding out, Vaishali walked alongside. 'Aditya, I know you well. It could not be the commitment made to Shreya. It has to be something more. What was it that made you wait for this day? You could have confronted everyone earlier.'

'I am not a fool, Vaishali . I could have confronted these guys the day Diana and I figured out that something was wrong. Melwin only proved to me what I already knew. I chose today because it is a big day for Shreya. She won't mess it up at any cost. Any other day, she would have walked out and maybe even dragged me into a legal suit. Sexual harassment cases are not easy to deal with. People pass judgements even before they investigate. But today, the odds are in my favour. The media is here, the readers are here, no one can contest my revelation. I have a winner all the way.

'Any other day, had they gone to town on the plagiarism issue, I would have looked like a cheat. Anything I offered to say in my defence would have sounded like a reactive explanation. Today it will sound like a genuine mistake which I am correcting. I will emerge the hero in this. Today I have hit them the hardest. Both of them will spend their life under the realisation that I knew what they were doing, all along. Whenever they relive this incident in their life, they will always live under the ignominy of having come out as losers. Isn't that a bigger punishment?

'As far as my side of the story is concerned, Poonam

Saxena is coming out with an exclusive issue on me and my books this Sunday in HT Brunch. I gave them the story as an exclusive. As we speak, it's going into print. Shreya set out to write a bestseller. If I was convinced that what happened over the last two months was only her mistake, my approach would have been different. But I was equally responsible. It was my mistake as well. If we allow others to take advantage of us, we lose the right to cry when they do. I allowed Shreya to take advantage of me. And that made me vulnerable. Sanjay all along wanted to show me down. Jealousy at a personal and professional level can be dangerous. Sanjay exploited this vulnerability. The problem was me, Vaishali. Me. Why blame others?' Aditya concluded.

He looked back. Everyone was walking down behind them: everyone except Sanjay. He waited for just that extra second before he ran back to the coffee shop. Sanjay was sitting there, staring into thin air. Aditya's entry interrupted his reverie.

'Not coming down?' Aditya asked him

'How does it matter to you? Just get the fuck out of here.'

'Well the call is yours, Sanjay. I just felt it will look a bit weird if you sit here alone. There are a number of people from National Bank in the crowd. But as I said, the call is yours,' he said and turned and walked away from Sanjay towards the main door of the café.

'So you fucked me over, today as well,' Sanjay's desolate voice rang out. Aditya turned back.

'Sorry. Me?' He looked shocked. 'I thought that line was supposed to be mine.'

'You must be very happy to see me like this, isn't it Aditya?' Sanjay whispered. 'Once a loser, always a loser.'

Aditya looked surprised. 'So everything I said. My hypothesis was true.'

'You have screwed me at every stage in your life, Aditya, every stage. You even snatched my first love away from me,' ranted Sanjay.

'She was never with you, Sanjay. Maya's association with you was always as a friend. She even clarified that to you that night when you proposed to her below the water tank.' After a pause he added, 'Years ago.'

Sanjay ignored him and continued, 'And when Diana and I tried to explore a relationship, you messed up her reputation and her career. Not only that, you also made sure that our relationship would not work out. She will never come back to me now.' He had his head in his hands. 'Helping you get a job in National Bank was a mistake. Life away from you was so peaceful. I had gotten over Maya, forgotten all that happened on campus ... and then you came roaring back. Letting you guys back into my life was a big mistake. You have taken away everything that I had. Shreya, too, used me to get to you. The moment you came into her life, she dropped me like a hot potato. The Goa trip was where she finally called it off. The moment you started indulging her, she walked away from me. At every stage you have messed with my life, Aditya. You think that after bringing me to this state, you will live in peace? You will rot in hell, Aditya, you will rot in hell. I curse you today, you will rot in hell.' Sanjay stormed out of the room, down to the Crossword store.

Aditya smiled a wry smile: a smile which hid the emotional turbulence he was going through, on having lost someone close.

The emcee's voice suddenly rang loud and clear. 'Ladies and gentlemen, and now for the big event that all of you have been waiting for. Please welcome on stage . . .' The voice was drowned in the applause that followed.

Aditya strode down to the venue. It was showtime.

84

MAYA WAS WATCHING the event on live streaming. She had tears in her eyes when Aditya publicly apologised for his relationship with Shreya. Maya realised that he meant every word of what he said. Owning up to a mistake in front of everyone is not easy and only a person with good intent and high levels of regret can do it. But then, something was holding her back. She had been wronged and a cheating spouse can leave a trail of trauma and devastation for the cheated one. It was because of this that Maya was unwilling to forget and forgive. That was when Dr Krishnan's email popped up on her screen and she clicked on it.

'I might lose my job for this,' Dr Krishnan had written in the mail. 'But I am convinced there is no alternative. I am watching the live streaming. Ever since you came to the hospital for a check-up, Maya, I have been wondering how it is that the best couple that I have ever met, fell apart—a couple that lives and breathes together, a couple that even Ebola couldn't separate, a couple that till a few months back was a model couple. I couldn't bear to see them fall apart.

While you were in hospital, Aditya did confide in me. In fact it was after that, that he requested to be allowed into your room, a day before all of us expected you to die. Your chances of survival were almost zero. Aditya wanted to see you in your room, alone. Breaking protocol, I allowed him. I could have lost my job for doing that. It was a risk I took. Today while seeing Aditya speak, I remembered that confession. The confession made in front of a dying Maya. The isolation ward is under CCTV surveillance. I had specifically got the security tapes containing Aditya's visit to your room, sent to me, because had anyone else seen it, I would have got into trouble. Aditya's speech today reminded me of that. And that's the reason I am sending this to you. The guy genuinely loves you. I have seen it in his eyes, Maya. I can't ask you to get together with Aditya again, but all I can do is request you to see this short video once. After that, take whatever call you feel is appropriate.

Please respect my intent and do not share this video with anyone. I will find it hard to explain. And by the way, the day you came for the check-up, Aditya called me to confirm if everything was normal. Don't know why, but just thought that you should know he cares.

Maya clicked on the video link. In no time, it started playing. She saw herself on the screen, lying in one corner of the room, sick and immobile. And then the door to her room opened and someone walked in. When she looked closely, she realised it was Aditya. She heard everything Aditya had said that day, and by the time the video went back on loop, she had tears in her eyes.

When she saw Aditya fall on his knees and beg her to come back, she felt desperate. She loved him. It was clear that he really wanted her back. All along, her feeling of rejection coupled with disbelief over the fact that Aditya, who could do nothing wrong, had hurt her so terribly, had held her back. But now the public apology and more importantly the video moved her. When Aditya had confessed to her in the ward, he could have had no ulterior motive to tell her that he would come back to her, for she had been near death. He was not even sure that Maya could hear everything that he was saying. Yet he had said what he said. He had promised her that he would call off everything and be with her and Aryan. He had pleaded with her to come back to him, for both him and their son. Dr Krishnan's words rang in her ears. 'There is more strength in forgiveness than in walking away.'

She made a choice.

She tried calling Aditya but couldn't get through. Hurriedly she dialled the driver and asked him to take the car out. She got into the car and rushed to Crossword Kemps Corner. The rain had stopped. The heavy drizzle earlier had had its impact and kept most of the crowd away from the roads. The driver was able to zip across. Trying to hold back her tears, Maya watched the live streaming all along the way. She didn't want the driver to see her sobbing.

When Aditya ended his speech and walked out, she was still half a kilometre away from Crossword. She was stuck at the signal. She calculated that it would take her six minutes more if she walked. It might take less than that if the traffic cleared, but that seemed less likely. She kicked off her sandals and stepped out of the car. Barefoot, Maya walked;

walked at a pace she had never walked before. The earphones connected to her phone kept her in sync with what was going on at Crossword. In five minutes, she reached the Kemps Corner flyover which was right alongside the road where the store was. She could see a crowd outside the store. And then she saw him: surrounded by television cameras, media, and fans. She slowed down. He was not going anywhere. She walked slowly and within a minute she was standing right outside the store. Not too far from where Aditya was. She stood there silently, patiently waiting for him to get away from the crowd surrounding him.

He had erred. But he had displayed the courage to accept his error of judgment in front of the whole world. He wouldn't be doing that if he didn't care for her and Aryan. She had forgiven him. She wanted him back—back in her life for good.

Aditya looked up, as if something had alerted him to her presence. He saw her. He pushed aside the microphone thrust in his face by a television channel and walked towards her. She stood rooted, tears in her eyes.

The water in his eyes breached the banks as he walked up to Maya. Hugging her, he stood there silently. Thunder and lighting lit up the skies. The dark clouds opened up, their resistance on the wane. It began to pour. Everyone around rushed for cover, everyone except Aditya and Maya. They stood rooted, in each other's arms, probably hoping for the rain to wash out any remnants of the hangover of the past. When a penitent Aditya tightened his hug and said, 'I am sorry, Maya. Please give me one more chance,' Maya had no choice. Tears started flowing incessantly from her eyes. Her arms tightened their clasp around Aditya. The intensity of water pouring from the skies paled in comparison to the water that had crashed the banks of Maya's eyes.

'Let's go home,' she said.

EPILOGUE

MAYA AND ADITYA got back together. Aditya left his job with National Bank and joined his wife in her quest to make education available for all. They now run a school and have focused their efforts on educating students from the economically deprived strata of society.

After pulling back the book from the market because of plagiarised lines, it took Aditya a fortnight to put the sanitised version of the book back in stores. The controversy spurred by the Aditya-friendly cover story in Brunch fuelled repeat sales of the book. True to his word, Aditya donated every rupee earned from the book towards Ebola care. Kiwi too did the same. In return Aditya offered his next book to Kiwi for an extremely low advance. Kiwi was only too happy to oblige. Aditya is writing his next book and is content spending his time with Aryan and Maya. He continues to be India's top-selling author by a margin and is now enjoying his new-found freedom from a boring banking job. Maya was extremely happy that Aditya was back. So was Aryan. Life for them got back on track.

Sanjay resigned from National Bank. He was smart enough to understand that had he not quit he would have been sacked. His tryst with Shreya, his fraudulent expense billing and the way he manipulated Aditya, didn't go down well with the management. Tim was furious and made sure that the CEO got to know about the conversation at Moshe's. That didn't leave Sanjay with much of a choice. He tried for reconciliation with Aditya, but it was too late. Aditya had moved on and not for a moment did he look back and try to reconcile with Sanjay. He had betrayed his trust and tried to break up his family and Aditya had decided to make sure that their paths never crossed again.

Diana pulled the plug on her relationship with Sanjay. His clandestine affair with Shreya, his pining for Maya and his manipulations to get his way, created an irreparable rift between the two of them. The day she walked out of Crossword Kemps Corner after the book launch was the last she ever saw of him. Career for her has taken a positive turn. After Aditya left, she became the head of Branch Banking for National Bank and has been doing a fabulous job. The CEO loves her commitment so much that she is now spoken of as the next head of Retail for National Bank. She is still in touch with Maya and Aditya.

Sunaina got married to Melwin and settled down in Mumbai. She works for *Times of India*, the newspaper that carried the story on Shreya and Aditya. She has consciously stayed away from the paid media, and is trying her luck at becoming a serious focused journalist of substance.

Spurred by the controversy of her dalliance with Aditya, Shreya's book went on to become a big hit—the biggest sales clocked by a debut author in a long long time. It was sad that the fact that the book was actually written fabulously was overshadowed by the noise surrounding it. Shreya became an instant celebrity, a superstar. After the book launch, the media hounded her. She got projected as a homewrecker. At work too, she didn't get the respect that she felt she deserved. Sanjay's exit reflected poorly on her. Tim knew about the issues between Aditya, her and Sanjay. Over a period of time, the porous walls of the organisation came into play and people started talking about her past. All this in general and specifically Aditya walking away from her in the manner that he did, impacted her negatively. She lost interest in writing. Whenever people would ask her about her next book, she would avoid answering the question. If pushed to a corner, she would say, 'The story finds the writer. When a great story will find me, my next book will take shape.' It was only she who knew that she would never ever be able to write another story. Her debut novel, *The Girl from Chhattisgarh*, would remain the only bestseller she wrote.